DAVENPORT PUB LIBR (IOS)

REQUEST ID 150947705

AUTHOR Mayhue, Melissa
TITLE Take a chance

DUE DATE 08/13/2015

BORROWER OKM
LENDER IOS

Take a Chance

Chance Colorado Series - Book One

Melissa Mayhue

Published by Melissa Mayhue
Copyright © 2013 Melissa Mayhue
Last Updated - 11/2013
Cover art by Inspire Creative Services
Edited by Editing 720
All rights reserved.

Print Edition ISBNs:
ISBN-10:0989827216
ISBN-13:978-0-9898272-1-8

Ebook Edition ISBNs:
ISBN-10: 0989827208
ISBN-13: 978-0-9898272-0-1

DEDICATION

For all the wonderful, generous authors who've walked
this path before me.

And, most especially, for all the supportive readers waiting
for the next book.

ACKNOWLEDGMENTS

No book is ever written in a vacuum and the Chance, Colorado Series is no exception.

Special thanks go out to my wonderful friend, <u>Elaine Levine</u>. Without her encouragement and assistance, this book might never have seen the light of day. This talented author took time out from her own writing to mentor me through the process of publishing this story and for that, I will always be grateful. You can see her books at http://ElaineLevine.com

Other Books by Melissa Mayhue:

~Chance, Colorado Series~

1 - Take a Chance (2013)
2 - Second Chance at Love (Coming in Summer 2014)

~ Warriors Series ~

1 - Warrior's Redemption (2012)
2 - Warrior's Last Gift (2012)
3 - Warrior Reborn (2012)
4 - Warrior Untamed (2013)

~ Daughters of the Glen Series ~

1 - Thirty Nights with a Highland Husband (2007)
2 - Highland Guardian (2007)
3 - Soul of a Highlander (2008)
4 - A Highlander of Her Own (2009)
5 - A Highlander's Destiny (2010)
6 - A Highlander's Homecoming (2010)
7 - Healing the Highlander (2011)
8 - Highlander's Curse (2011)

PROLOGUE

As prom nights go, this one had turned out to be one of the worst ever.

"So what have you got to say for yourself, Allie? Is Lacey telling me the truth? Have you really been dating me just so you'd have a chance to see Logan when he comes home from college?"

Allison Flynn's hands balled into fists at her sides, clenched every bit as tightly as the growing knot in her stomach. Humiliation at having been exposed warred with hurt and disbelief that her best friend could have betrayed her confidence this way.

But lying to Ryan O'Connor was no way to make herself feel better. She wouldn't do that to him. He'd been too good a friend to her.

"Yes," she forced herself to say, the heat of embarrassment threatening to set her face aflame.

"I can't believe you," he whispered, shaking his head

as he stared at her. "What kind of girl dates a guy just to get close to his brother?"

A desperate girl who fancies herself in love.

"What did you think you'd accomplish? Everybody in town knows Logan's already asked Shayla Jenkins to marry him after he graduates from college."

A strange tingle swept through Allie's body, as if all her blood had rushed to her head and just as quickly rushed away, leaving her world wobbling around her.

Not everybody knew Logan was planning to marry. She hadn't known. Not even her best friend, Lacey, had known, or she would have told Allie. And since Lacey was Shayla's sister, if anybody should have known, it was her.

Unless... Unless Lacey *had* known and that was why she'd betrayed Allie's secret.

"And using me like this? If nothing else, I thought we were friends. This is low, Allie," Ryan continued. "Slinking-on-your-belly-in-the-mud kind of low."

What if Lacey had known and that was why she told Ryan about Allie's attraction to his older brother? What if she'd told because her strongest loyalty was to her older sister instead of to her best friend? Allie's grandmother always did claim blood was thicker than water.

"I'm sorry," Allie managed through quivering lips when Ryan stopped talking. "We are friends, Ryan. I never meant to hurt you. I was wrong to have..." She stumbled to a stop, numbed by the pain in Ryan's expression. "I don't know what else to say to make it better. Just... I'm so sorry."

"Yeah, you really are," Ryan answered, pulling his keys out of his pocket. "Sorry, that is. Come on, let's go. I'm taking you home. I don't want to be here anymore."

He didn't say the words aloud that he didn't want to be with her anymore, but he might as well have. She felt their stinging rebuke to the center of her being.

The silent car ride home was the longest of Allie's life. Ryan said nothing to her, not even when she stepped out of the car.

"I'm really sorry," she tried once more, leaning down to look in the window, but he didn't spare her a glance as he gunned the motor.

Watching the dust flung up by his tires as he drove away, Allie knew that no matter how awful she felt right now, things were only going to get worse from here on out. By Monday afternoon, everyone at school would know what she'd done. By Tuesday morning, everyone in town would know what a scheming sneak she was. Worst of all, Logan would know.

How could she ever have trusted Lacey Jenkins with the most secret desires of her heart?

She'd lost her best friend tonight, and that betrayal hurt, but she could only place part of the blame on Lacey. Through her own deceitful stupidity she'd lost Ryan's friendship and the respect of everyone she'd ever known.

All because she thought she was in love with someone who barely knew she even existed.

"Love," she huffed, chewing the word and spitting it out.

What did she know about love, anyway? Nothing but what she'd read in those books with happy endings and, considering the way she felt right now, there was no happy ending in her future. In fact, if this was what love felt like, it was sheer misery and she wanted no part of it ever again.

With a deep breath, she squared her shoulders and

headed up the walk toward her house, praying that her parents had already gone to bed. They'd hear about this soon enough but please, oh please, not tonight.

By tomorrow she'd be stronger. By tomorrow she'd be able to lift her head and look beyond all this to focus on her future.

A future that she now knew couldn't possibly include Logan O'Connor.

She let out a shaky breath and pulled open the old screen door.

None of this mattered. Everything would be okay. She wouldn't allow this awful night to be a total loss. It hurt like hell, but she'd learned a valuable lesson. Never again would she trust anyone with her deepest feelings. Never again would she sacrifice her integrity for any man.

The humiliation she would suffer when everyone learned what an idiot she was would be a burden, but it would only last for the next three months. Thank God she'd applied to out-of-state schools in spite of her dad's objections. Come August, she was out of here.

She wasn't going to be like the women in this town. She wouldn't spend her life dependent on some man for her happiness like her mom and so many of the others she knew. She'd strike out on her own and take a chance to build the life she wanted for herself.

And once she had Chance, Colorado in her rearview mirror, she was never, ever coming back.

CHAPTER ONE

Allie Flynn held her cell phone at arm's length and inhaled a deep, slow breath, giving herself a few necessary seconds to regain her composure. With all the stress in her life right now, the last thing in the world she wanted was an argument with her grandmother.

Putting the phone back up next to her ear, she forced herself to continue much more calmly than she felt. "All I'm saying is, she should be here. Matt needs her. We almost lost my brother, Mama Odie. Her only son. Matt almost died. Doesn't she understand that?"

Not only had her mother come up with an excuse not to travel to Germany when Matt had been transported there after the roadside attack in Afghanistan, now she wouldn't even come as far as San Antonio, where he'd been sent to complete his recuperation.

"What's wrong with her? What kind of a mother acts this way?"

"Oh, for piss' sake, Allie. You don't have a clue about what's going on with your mother." Irritation colored Odetta Flynn's normal, no-nonsense tone. "You should count yourself lucky to have a mother as good as Susie. If anything, she's always been way too easy on you and your brother both. But I won't let you fault the woman for not sitting at her son's bedside in San Antonio when she's laying flat on her back in the hospital over in Grand Junction."

"What?" Allie's voice rang with an edge of hysteria that she couldn't begin to control. "When did this happen? Is she okay? Why didn't you guys call me?"

"Because she didn't want you to know, that's why. Told me you had too much going on right now and she was worried about you being all stressed out," her grandmother huffed. "But I'm damned if I'm going to stand here and listen to you bad-mouth your mom like that. She's been sick since well before what happened to Matt. If you'd been around her at all, you'd have known that. It just finally got completely out of hand day before yesterday. If it hadn't been for Grainger barking his fool head off, who knows how long she might have laid out there in the back field before we found her."

This couldn't be happening. Allie leaned against the big metal door frame, seeking the support her legs suddenly didn't want to provide anymore, while her stomach curled into a fist-sized knot of fear. Beginning with her father's death two years ago, her whole world had begun a slow spin out of control. Matt had nearly died and now her mother was in the hospital. It felt as if everything she'd ever cared for was being destroyed, piece by piece.

"What happened?" she asked when she was able to speak again. "Is she going to be okay?"

"We don't know." A long pause on Mama Odie's end of the line was followed by a frustrated sigh. "They're testing for all sorts of things, baby. You know your mom's been depressed since your dad's accident and all that... that garbage that came out because of it. But this is different. It's gotten to the point that she's just been so damned exhausted she could barely drag herself out of bed every day. And when she did manage that, half the time she was too dizzy to walk without holding on to something. We've tried to keep an eye on her, but she needs somebody over there at the house with her." Another pause. "A good daughter would move home and look after her mother."

Oh, Lord. Had her grandmother actually stooped to playing the infamous Flynn guilt card? It wouldn't work on her. Not this time. Allie refused to be manipulated like that.

"I can't come back home, Mama Odie. I've built a life out here. I have a good job and a serious boyfriend. I can't move back to Chance."

She wouldn't. Eight years ago, when she'd escaped that little wide spot in the road, she'd sworn she'd never go back again and she'd meant it. The world was too big to spend her whole life in Chance, Colorado, where everybody in town knew everything about her.

Her job in Waco was perfect. Or it would be, just as soon as the economy improved enough that the owners could pull their little bookstore out of its death spiral.

And even if the store did close, she still had Drake. He hadn't popped the question or anything yet, but that didn't matter. What they had was stronger than any formal bond. He told her so all the time. And though it had taken nearly two years, she'd finally let him inside her defenses. Part of the way inside, at least. Full trust was something she wasn't sure she could ever give any man.

A disapproving snort sounded on the other end of the line, drawing her attention back to the conversation.

"Blood is thicker than water, and don't you go forgetting that, young lady."

Her grandmother didn't understand. Didn't want to understand. Odetta had spent her whole life in their little hometown, so she couldn't possibly be expected to accept Allie's need to be anywhere in the world except Chance.

Still, Allie knew her grandmother meant well.

"Once Matt is all settled in here at the hospital, I'll see if I can get some time off from the store. Maybe I can come and stay for a week or so."

With each word of her offer, the knot in Allie's stomach twisted tighter. She hadn't been home for eight years. Even when her dad had died, she'd made the excuse that she couldn't get away from work long enough to do more than attend his burial ceremony at Fort Logan in Denver.

"A week or so," her grandmother scoffed. "You need to get your head on straight, Allison Elise. You better get your priorities in order before it's too late. What you have out there—a job, some man—they don't mean jack squat in the long run. Push come to shove, it's only your family that will be there for you. And now's the time you need to be there for your family."

8

Allie couldn't have this discussion right now. Not standing here with the smell of alcohol swabs and disinfectant pounding at her senses. She couldn't even think straight, let alone deliver a convincing argument to her grandmother about what she needed for her own future.

"I have to go, Mama Odie. Promise you'll call me the minute you hear anything about Mom, okay? I mean it. The very minute."

"Okay, Allie, I will. But you think hard about what I said. Now, you go tell Matt that his Mama Odie is keeping a dialog ongoing with the man upstairs that he should heal real fast and come home to us where he belongs."

"I will. Love you."

Silence pulsed into her ear as she held the phone close to her cheek for a few seconds longer before shutting it down and slipping it into the pocket of her jeans. With a glance down the long, empty hallway, she headed out through the big glass doors and breathed in the fresh morning air.

The nurse would be back any time now to take her up to Matt's room, but Allie needed a second to sort out her tangled emotions before she spoke to her brother. Guilt was eating her alive, but how could she possibly pull up roots and go back to Chance? She couldn't.

Here in Texas, she was her own woman. In Chance, she'd simply be that pathetic Flynn girl who'd had the hopeless crush on her older brother's best friend. She wasn't sure her ego could stand that. Besides, she had too many good things in her life to simply turn her back and walk away.

Drake.

Once more she wished he'd been able to get away from work to come with her today. A quick call to hear his voice and she'd no doubt feel more centered and strong enough to face all of these challenges head-on.

Three rings and the call went to voice mail, so she ended it and waited a full minute before trying again. Odd that he wasn't answering. He should be in the office by now, because he'd said he had a heavy schedule and couldn't get off work today. That was why he couldn't come with her.

Only one ring this time before the line came to life.

"Hello, hello!" a familiar female voice sang into her ear as Drake's voice boomed in the background.

"Goddammit, Cara. I told you not to answer my cell. Hand it over right now."

Cara? As in her neighbor, Cara? The one who always had some excuse to show up at her front door to ask for Drake's help whenever he was over? It was always something with that woman——her car wouldn't start or a door was stuck or she had a box she couldn't lift. *That* Cara?

"Hey, lover." Drake sounded breathless, like he'd been running. "I didn't expect to hear from you this morning. I thought you were going to be tied up with your brother all day."

Tied up with her brother and too busy to check on him? Apparently, that was exactly what he'd thought.

"And I thought you had to work. What's going on there, Drake?"

A surreal stillness settled over her as she waited for his answer. She should have expected something exactly like this. She'd been a fool to think he wouldn't betray her the first chance he got. She'd been a fool to think he was somehow a better man than her dad had been. They couldn't help it — not even the best of them. One day, something snapped, and they turned into this.

Time felt as if it slowed, magnifying all the sounds coming through the phone in her hand. Giggling in the background. A squealed "Where'd you hide my panties this time?" A nervous chuckle from Drake.

"It's not as bad as you're imagining, lover. Really, it isn't."

It didn't take too much imagination to figure out exactly what was going on.

"No? Then how bad is it... *lover*?"

"It's not what you think. I just came over to help Cara with a leaky faucet. That's all."

"A leaky faucet," Allie repeated, her voice echoing coldly in her own ears. "What part of the repair required hiding Cara's underwear?"

"Listen to me, Al. I can explain everything. It was an accident. One thing led to another and it just sort of happened. I swear to God, it was only this one time. And only because you were gone and I was lonely. It'll never happen again, I promise. I'll come over when you get home and we'll talk through this whole thing. We'll get everything straightened out."

No, they wouldn't.

She wasn't that stupid. What was happening there was exactly what it had sounded like. He'd confirmed it for her. She'd seen the signs for the last few months and had chosen to ignore them. But now, the time to ignore had come to an end. Betrayal of her trust was something she couldn't forgive.

"I don't think so, Drake. There's nothing to straighten out. I don't want to talk to you. Not about this or anything else. We're done. Don't bother coming over again."

"But lover…"

"Seriously. Don't bother."

Allie ended the call and turned off her phone in case Drake tried to call her back. She waited for some sort of fury or pain to set in, but they didn't come. She didn't even feel surprise over Drake's cheating. It was as if her emotions had gone into total hibernation.

She felt completely numb. A numbness that permeated her whole being, accompanied by something strangely like resignation.

She'd been wrong. Drake was no different from any other man. No different from her own father had been. He'd cheated on her just like her father had cheated on her mom. The only difference was that he'd started earlier and she'd found out now, before their relationship went any further. Unlike her mom, who put twenty years and two kids into a relationship without knowing what her husband was capable of doing behind her back. If his car hadn't gone off the side of the mountain with his mistress sitting next to him, she might never have known.

It was better this way. Better to have his cheating ways out in the open before her heart had a chance to grow any more invested in him. In them.

Allie smoothed her hair away from her face with a shaking hand and pushed back through the glass doors in time to see the nurse hurrying down the hall in her direction. Pasting a smile on her face that she didn't feel, she waited to be taken to see her wounded brother.

The world seemed determined to tell her something this week. Her job was likely to end in the next few months and her boyfriend was... well, he wasn't much of a boyfriend, after all. So maybe she didn't have as many reasons to stay in Waco as she'd thought.

Maybe it was time to get her priorities straight like her grandmother had advised. Maybe the time had come to consider going home.

* * *

Odetta Flynn stirred her coffee, staring out the kitchen window, her mind working feverishly. If she couldn't even persuade her own grandchildren to return to Chance, what prospects for survival did her hometown have?

"Well?" Harley Flynn filled his cup from the coffeemaker and crossed to where his wife stood. "Any luck with that stubborn granddaughter of yours?"

"Mine? That girl is pure hardheaded Flynn."

"I'm the hardheaded one?" Her husband of fifty-three years chuckled and leaned over to give her a quick kiss on the cheek. "You still make me laugh, Odie, you know it? That's why I've kept you around for so long."

"Who's kept who around?" Odetta replied, gifting Harley with a smile. "Don't you worry about our Allie. She'll do the right thing. I could hear it in her voice."

"In that case, maybe she is pure Flynn," Harley said with a wink. "I know I can never resist your wheedling."

"Hardly!" Odetta snorted, shaking her head. "Her stubborn streak comes from you, for a fact. But that practical bit, she got that from me."

"Fair enough," Harley answered, finishing up the last of his coffee. "If you're right about her coming home, you'd best be working on a way to convince her to stay once she gets here."

As if Odetta hadn't already spent her share of sleepless nights worrying over exactly that challenge.

"I think I have that one figured out. With a little help from our girls, we should manage it just fine." She rubbed her palm down her husband's arm, ending with a pat to his hand. "As I told you last night, Papa, saving Chance is going to take more than just bringing Allie home. It's past time we do whatever we can. We've sat back and waited for far too long for the rest of the town to wake up and do something."

"And now it's your special mission, is it?" Harley grinned and turned away, stopping to set his empty cup on the end of the counter. "Well, more power to you, woman. If you and Dot can't revive Chance, then it's a task beyond anyone's doing. As for me, I'm headed into town. You need me to bring you anything?"

"No, thanks," she answered absently, her mind already brooding over the problem at hand.

Unless someone did something—and soon—Chance was in danger of becoming one of those pitiful ghost towns that were no more than a footnote in some dusty old book. Though many of the old mining towns in the Colorado mountains struggled to stay alive as time passed, the real culprit in Chance's demise could be pinpointed to a single year and a single man. It was the year that Daniel Reilly had used his millions to make sure the big highway detoured around Chance to cross through his family's property, all but dumping tourists in the lap of their ski resort.

Probably the only halfway smart business decision that useless wastrel had ever made, other than choosing Helen Maxwell as his bride. And even then, he'd only done it out of spite and revenge, not because he was smart enough to see the monetary advantage to the Last Chance Ski Resort.

"Lazy son of a bitch," Odetta muttered. "May he rest in peace."

She and her best friend, Dorothy O'Connor, had wrestled with the problem of what to do about their dying town for over a year now. Dot, to her credit, had seen some success in keeping her family in Chance. But after a generation-long exodus of their young people, simply keeping family here wasn't enough. They needed to find a way to make Chance more attractive to outsiders.

As much as she hated to acknowledge what she needed to do, Odetta accepted that the time had come for more drastic action. She had no choice left but to take off the kid gloves and call in some long overdue favors.

She set down her cup and reached for the telephone, quickly punching in the numbers she hadn't forgotten, not even after all these years.

"Helen Reilly," she said into the receiver. "Just tell her it's Odetta Flynn. She'll take the call."

CHAPTER TWO

Allie had never asked to be one of those superwomen who had it all. Deep down she suspected those women were a myth anyway, living only in the pages of the books she loved so much. She'd never asked for the perfect job, the perfect man, the perfect two-point-five children *and* the perfectly clean little house surrounded by a white picket fence. She was practical enough to accept that such a bounty of perfection was way beyond her reach.

But, honestly… shouldn't a girl have the right to expect to end up with at least one out of four?

"Apparently not," she muttered under her breath. "Not this girl, anyway."

"Oh, this is primo." Matt Flynn kept his eyes closed as he spoke, his head resting against the passenger-side window. "First I have to listen to that crazy cat of yours howling nonstop across three states and now you're talking to yourself. Out loud. I suppose next you'll be answering yourself. This road trip with you is just getting better and better by the mile."

"Chester isn't howling." Allie spared a quick look over her shoulder toward the puffed-up ball of fur her brother had disparaged before fixing her gaze back on the winding road ahead. "He's only trying to communicate with us."

To be fair, the cat had been *communicating* since they'd pulled away from Allie's empty apartment yesterday before sunrise. She should have tried harder to find someone in Waco to adopt him, but Chester wasn't the type of cat people warmed to easily. He came equipped with sharp claws and a seriously bad attitude. Most of the time, she wasn't sure that she even liked him.

Not that liking him was necessary. She'd found him a year ago—a pitiful, starving kitten wandering downtown and, when no one claimed him, she'd made her decision. Fate had dropped him in her path so he was her responsibility. And responsibility was something Allie took very seriously.

"Only communicating with us, huh?" Matt shook his head, but kept his eyes closed. "You're starting to sound as crazy as that cat of yours."

Allie didn't bother to respond. Matt's assessment wasn't that far off the mark. She felt as if she were indeed perched on the edge of Crazy Canyon right now, with one foot already dangling off the wrong side. Over the last several months, everything she'd found comfort in had been snatched away and her plans for her life had been turned completely upside down.

When she'd left her hometown of Chance, Colorado

17

eight years ago, she'd sworn never to set foot in that gossip-filled little backwater again. But life had a way of taking your dreams and even your best-laid plans and crushing them to dust.

Her life did, anyway. And now, here she was, barreling toward Chance at sixty miles an hour as if she had good sense.

Which, obviously, she didn't, or she wouldn't be headed back there, no matter what the reason.

Beside her, Matt shifted in his seat, a movement that brought with it an involuntary grunt of pain. His face paled and his lips clamped in that same determined grimace he'd worn ever since she'd first visited him at the military hospital in San Antonio.

"Want to stop and stretch your legs for a bit? There's a little town up ahead where we can pull off."

"I'm okay. We're only a couple of hours from home. I can make it."

Matt's words denied his need, but the pain etched in the lines of his face told another story. He needed to keep those muscles moving. She'd been sitting there when his doctor had told him so before he'd left the hospital.

Damn that stubborn Flynn pride of his for getting in the way of common sense again. She of all people should know. She suffered from the same problem too often not to recognize it when she saw it in her brother.

He might not be willing to admit what he viewed as a weakness, but that didn't mean she couldn't do what was necessary.

"Maybe the way you drive it's only a couple of hours. But since I'm not up for any speeding tickets on this trip, it's going to take us a little longer than that to get home.

I'm stopping off."

She headed down the next exit, toward a little town called Scarlet Springs. It turned out to be one of those classic old Colorado mining towns, its main street lined with eclectic buildings. Not so very different from Chance, really.

Though she'd filled up her tank before they'd left Boulder, she turned off into the Pump-N-Go gas station, pulling her old car up close to the first pump.

"What?" Matt opened his eyes and sat up, immediately alert. "Why are you stopping?"

"I told you," she answered with as much patience as she could muster. "Why don't you go inside and grab something for us to drink. I'll do the honors out here."

Matt stared at her for a moment before getting out of the car. His weary expression as he untangled his wooden cane from the handle of the cat's cage served as all the proof she needed that her excuse to get him up and walking was completely transparent.

Whatever. He might be her big brother, but if he wasn't going to do for himself what he needed to, it was up to her to see it done. Those damaged leg muscles weren't going to get any relief with him all cramped up in the front seat of her little car.

She went through the motions, not surprised when it took less than five dollars to fill her tank. She really hadn't needed gas. But, since Matt hadn't yet returned, she had accomplished what she'd wanted. He was up and moving around.

Inside the building she spotted him immediately, hunched over the racks of junk food, hunting his favorites. If he were hungry, maybe she could keep him out of the car even longer.

The clerk smiled a welcome as she approached the counter with her cans of soda.

"Afternoon, ma'am. How can I help you?"

Without being aware of exactly when it had happened, somewhere in the last couple of years she'd managed to transform from a *miss* to a *ma'am*. Considering that she felt like the most ancient twenty-five-year-old on the face of the planet today, the greeting fit.

"Is there a restaurant you can recommend somewhere nearby? Maybe within walking distance?"

"Everything in Scarlet Springs is pretty much within walking distance." The young man behind the counter grinned. "Your best bet is Caribou Joe's. You can't miss it if you head down that way. Looks like a log cabin. And if you're hanging out until later tonight, they always have some sort of live entertainment. I know that's where I'll be after I get off work."

"We're not here to hang out," Matt growled, suddenly standing at her side. "Just passing through, Romeo, so you can save the charm." He dumped an armful of cellophane packages on the counter and turned from the clerk to her. "Jerky bonanza," he explained, with the first real smile she'd seen in days.

"I guess this means you don't want to stop for a sit-down lunch?" she asked, handing over her much-used credit card to the red-faced clerk.

"That's right," Matt confirmed as he ripped into one of the bags. "All I want is to get home in time to get rested up for tomorrow."

As if his words had reminded him of what awaited them when they reached their destination, his smile faded and he headed back outside, leaning heavily on his cane.

The clerk refused to make eye contact as he handed back her card.

"Sorry about my brother," she muttered, her own cheeks feeling much warmer than they had been when she'd walked into the store. It hardly seemed enough to make up for Matt's comment, but it was the best she had to offer.

By the time Allie joined him in the car, Matt had his earphones in place and his tunes cranked up so loud she could hear a tinny thread of sound pulsing from his side of the car. Though his eyes were closed, the steady movement of his jaw as he chewed the jerky assured her he wasn't sleeping. He simply didn't want to talk.

Not that she could blame him. Having to face everyone they'd ever known in Chance tomorrow morning at the dedication of the new community center was a daunting enough prospect for her. It had to be a hundred times worse for Matt. Add that worry to the frustrations he'd wrestled today when they'd visited Fort Logan military cemetery in Denver, and it was little wonder he was seeking escape. He had a lot on his mind.

Back on the highway, Allie's thoughts drifted over the path that had led her brother to this moment.

Matt, Danny Collins and Logan O'Connor had been known as the Three Amigos since they'd become best friends in first grade. They'd done everything together, including going off to Boulder after they graduated from high school to attend college. But two years later, when Matt's money ran out, Danny decided they should all drop out of school and join the Army. Only Logan remained behind to finish his education while Matt and Danny headed off to war.

And now Danny was dead.

Had Matt hopped out of that truck a step ahead of Danny to assist those wounded soldiers, they might be naming the community center after him tomorrow.

Just thinking about the possibility made Allie's stomach roll.

She tightened her grip on the steering wheel to stop herself from reaching over to touch her brother's arm to reassure herself that he indeed sat in the front seat of her little car, safe and whole.

They'd come so close to losing him.

These last few months had taught her how important her family was to her. Much more important than losing her job or a boyfriend who couldn't be trusted the second she turned her back. Family was even more important than being forced to face down her own personal demons in order to move back to Chance to look after her mother.

It didn't matter that she'd have to see *him* again. It didn't matter that he would be married now, after eight long years, and likely have a houseful of kids. It didn't even matter that every time they saw each other she'd have to live with his knowing that she'd tricked his younger brother into dating her for the sole purpose of getting close to him.

None of that mattered because she was totally and completely over Logan O'Connor. She was over all men. None of them could be trusted as far as she could throw them.

A quick glance from the road to her passenger brought a smile to her face. Her brother might be the one exception to that rule. She admired him more than anybody she'd ever known.

Matt had endured five long months of hospitals, multiple operations, and what had to have been an unimaginable degree of pain. In spite of it all, he was here beside her, headed back to Chance to face the loss of his friend, Danny. Matt had survived and was doing what he had to do.

Just like Matt, she was doing what she had to do.

Her family was her biggest responsibility and she was determined to see to their welfare, both Matt's and her mother's.

Allie rolled her shoulders and leaned forward to squint at the sign ahead. After three hours of driving with no conversation save Chester's constant complaints, the big green sign overhead announced her turnoff in a quarter of a mile. She followed the arrows, leaving the highway behind to pick up a small mountain road. Several more minutes and the little town of Chance lay stretched out before her, looking as if time had passed it by.

In a way, it had. This was it. She was back home again as if she'd never left.

Time to check her dreams at the door and put on her game face.

CHAPTER THREE

Of all the stupid things Allie had ever decided to do, wearing these heels today had to rank right up near the top of the list. If she could manage to make the long trudge across the rutted, rocky parking lot without breaking an ankle, she'd consider herself a lucky woman. Ending up on her butt in a field certainly wasn't the impression she'd hoped to make after not having seen these people for so many years.

Allie grabbed on to the car door to stabilize herself before following behind her mother and brother as they made their way toward the gathering of people on the front lawn of the new community center.

The second time she stumbled on a dirt clod, Matt fastened a hand on her elbow.

Perfect. Both Matt and her mother were forced to use a cane to steady their steps, but who was the one stumbling into town and needing help? Her, of course.

24

The one who was supposed to be there to help them.

At least she could console herself that she was being escorted by the most handsome man in Chance. Her brother, always attractive, cut quite a figure in his uniform.

"Hey!" a cheery voice called from behind them. "Wait up, you guys!"

Allie turned toward the sound and spotted her cousin Desi hurrying in their direction, her arm raised in greeting.

Though Desi's twin followed several steps behind, there was no mistaking one for the other. The only similarities between Desi and Dulcie were their features and their size. Beyond that, they had always been as different as was humanly possible for identical twins.

Since before high school, Desi had been the more eclectic of the two, and today was no exception. From the bright purple braids twined through her long brown curls, right down to the black and white high-top sneakers peeking out from under her long gypsy skirt, Desi sported a look all her own.

Seeing her never failed to bring a smile to Allie's face.

"It's been too long," Allie said, holding her arms out to capture her cousin for a hug.

"It sure has," Desi agreed, returning the hug before linking her arm through Allie's. "You look great. But what the heck was in your head to convince you to wear shoes like that? Ten feet from the car and I'd be curled up on the ground, writhing in absolute agony."

"But they look awesome," Dulcie added as she joined them, leaning in to kiss Allie on the cheek. "I'm so glad you finally decided to move back home. We've all been so worried about Aunt Susie."

Allie allowed Desi to lead her forward, keeping her

25

eyes focused ahead of her, refusing to acknowledge Dulcie's comment. That was the thing about her family. Always had been. Even one of her favorites like Dulcie. Right in the middle of the most mundane conversation, the Flynns could always manage to serve up a load of guilt, whether they meant to or not.

"Well, would you look at that," Desi murmured. "Who is *that* hunk of gorgeous?"

Dulcie shrugged. "Probably somebody from up at the resort. You see who he's with, don't you? I heard she's been hanging out at the bar up there pretty regular."

"He is flat out drool-worthy." Desi tugged on Allie's arm. "You think you could move any faster in those darn shoes?"

"You are *not* going to tell me that you're in a hurry because of him?" Dulcie stopped in front of them, blocking their path, hands on her hips. "Honest to God, Desdemona Flynn! What's wrong with you? I swear, girl, you have the worst taste in men ever."

"I have excellent taste in men," Desi said with a grin. "It just leans more toward the bad-boy end of the scale. Anyway, just because he's hanging with a skank doesn't make him all bad."

Dulcie shrugged. "Fine. You can think whatever you want. But I have to think that any guy hanging with Shayla Jenkins is only after one thing."

Shayla Jenkins?

Allie stumbled to a stop and peered around her cousin to scan the growing crowd just ahead of them. The guy Desi ogled was out there somewhere with Shayla Jenkins? How was that even possible? And how was Shayla still a Jenkins?

"Maybe you should just kick those things off," Desi suggested, tugging at Allie's arm once again. "We could move a whole lot faster."

"No, I'm fine," Allie answered, her thoughts a million miles from her feet. "You said that guy is with Shayla? But what happened to Shayla and Logan? When I left town, they were all but a done deal."

"Oh, sweetie… you *have* been gone a long time, haven't you?" Dulcie patted her arm as they started walking again. "That whole relationship blew up a year or two after you moved away. In fact, I remember *the* ugliest scene down at the Dairy Dipper one afternoon that summer—"

"Logan made a scene?" That seemed so unlike the quiet young man she remembered.

"Oh, no, not Logan. It was his grandma! Right after Logan and Shayla broke up. Dot has always been such a pistol anyway, and that day she was parked at the Dairy Dipper when Shayla walked up, all wiggling her butt like she always does. Well, let me tell you, Dot O'Connor jumped out of her pickup and went after Shayla, who took off running, squealing like she thought she was done for." Dulcie could hardly get the story out for giggling. "And Dot was so mad, if she could've caught up with that girl, it very well might have been the end of her!"

"I remember that," Desi added with a smile. "Had the whole town talking for weeks. Then again, it doesn't take too much to set tongues wagging in Chance. That much hasn't changed a bit since you left. And it's Shayla Jenkins-Gold now. Hyphenated, mind you. Now hush up, you two. We're going to just casually saunter on over there like normal people and see if we can find out who Mr.

Gorgeous is."

"You go ahead and saunter," Allie said, pulling her arm from Desi's grasp. "I need to go check on Mom and Matt. I'll catch up with you guys later."

Though she did want to check on how her mother was holding up, what she really needed was a moment to absorb what she'd heard. After all these years of assuming nothing ever changed in Chance, it was as if the ground had tilted under her feet. Something had indeed changed. Something she'd never expected.

Not that it made a difference to her one way or another, she reminded herself. Those old feelings she'd had for Logan were a thing of the past. Besides, she'd just spent the last few months swearing off men entirely.

"Absolutely, you'll catch up with us later," Dulcie agreed. "We already planned to stop by your house after all this hoopla is over. Desi and I have something we want to talk to you about."

With a wave, Allie hurried forward to assist her mother in finding a seat among the quickly filling folding chairs.

"Here," her mother said, scooting into a row with several open spots. "I'll leave the two on the end for Mama Odie and Papa Flynn."

"You better grab a seat, too," Matt urged, scanning the crowd. "I'd say they didn't plan on nearly enough chairs for the number that's showing up."

From the looks of the people streaming in their direction, her brother was right.

"I'll stand for a bit," Allie answered. "I just want to make sure all the people who really need seats get them." Several of those people headed their direction had to be at least as old as her grandparents and standing would be a real hardship for them.

"People who really need seats?" Matt dropped his gaze pointedly to her feet. "Your call, Allie. But you wouldn't catch me standing through this whole thing if I were wearing those."

She was about to make a crack about how much she'd like to see him wearing high heels when an expression she couldn't identify flitted across his face as he stared over her shoulder. She turned to follow his gaze and spotted their grandparents headed in their direction, their grandfather wearing the full dress uniform he'd had packed away since World War II.

"God, I love that old man," Matt muttered under his breath.

Allie had to agree. They had indeed been blessed with the best grandparents ever. Odd as a three-dollar bill, there was no denying that, but both of them were the very definition of a loving family.

"Allison, Matthew," Papa Flynn greeted each of them as he waited for Mama Odie to hug both her grandchildren.

"Papa Flynn," Matt countered, with a respectful dip of his head. "Thank you for wearing your uniform to honor Danny today. It would have meant a lot to him."

"Didn't just wear it for Danny," the old man replied gruffly. "To my way of thinking, you're a hero, too, boy."

Allie backed away, her eyes filling with tears as her grandfather slowly lifted his hand in salute to her brother. Matt's silent return of the salute sent her tears brimming over the edge, and she tried to discreetly wipe her cheeks before anyone noticed.

Next to her, Mama Odie reached up to give Allie's hand a squeeze, her own eyes blinking more rapidly than usual and suspiciously shiny.

"Though there's joy in dedicating this building to honor Danny, we knew it wouldn't be an easy day," Mama Odie said. "Seems like just yesterday the three of you boys were climbing through my poor fruit trees, carrying on like wild little monkeys. Danny and Matty and Logan, all skinned knees and mischievous grins. We'd never see one of you without the others trailing right behind—usually on your way to raid my cookie jar, if I remember correctly."

"Only because you were the best cook in town," Matt said, dropping a kiss on the top of his grandmother's head.

"Pure flattery," Mama Odie said dismissively, but a smile twitched at the corners of her mouth. "It's all changed so much over the years. Though, as your grandfather says, the three of you are all heroes in your own ways. You and Danny off to fight a war and Logan coming back home to take over as a firefighter. We've always been proud of you all."

"Speak of the devil," Susie said quietly, her eyes fastened on the walk behind Allie. "There's Logan now. I wonder how he's holding up through all this."

Allie's head snapped around at her mother's mention of his name. She couldn't have stopped herself from reacting, even if she'd had the presence of mind to try.

Second most handsome man in Chance, she corrected her earlier appraisal of her brother. Second. Because, big as day, *the* most handsome man in town was headed directly toward them, his intense gaze focused on their little group.

Logan O'Connor.

Her first love. The man against whom she'd compared all others for years. Compared them and found every single one of them wanting. The man who'd never even realized she existed beyond being his best friend's annoying little sister.

Logically, she'd known she was likely to see him here today. But it was pure, crazy emotion, not logic, that sent shock waves zinging down her spine at the sight of him striding confidently toward them. The same crazy emotion that had pushed her to wear her best dress and these uncomfortable high heels.

It was beyond ridiculous of her to react this way, her heart pounding in her chest like she'd been running uphill. He was nothing more to her than her brother's best friend. Nothing more than a memory out of a long-gone childhood. Sure, he'd been her first crush, but she wasn't that same impressionable teenager anymore. She was over him. For a fact, after Drake's betrayal, she was over all men. Chester was the only male in her life now and, considering the scratch he'd left on her hand this morning when she'd tried to pet him, most days, even he was one too many males for her taste.

Logan drew closer, his deep voice rumbling in his chest as he spoke her brother's name and extended his hand in greeting.

The sharp, enticing aroma of soap and aftershave wafted from where he stood, tickling her nose and flooding her with memories of all the times she'd watched him and Matt together over the years. Her knees trembled as she breathed him in and she reached out to wrap her fingers on the back of the chair next to her, just to steady

31

herself.

She wasn't supposed to feel like this. Not after all these years. Not about him.

Seeing him in person, standing just a few feet away from him, focused everything into sharp clarity. The dawning realization hit her like a punch to the stomach.

No wonder walking away from Drake hadn't devastated her. In spite of having lied to herself for the past eight years, one thing was crystal clear in this moment. She might as well be seventeen again. All the feelings she'd denied were still there, bubbling just below the surface.

It would appear she wasn't as over her crush on Logan O'Connor as she'd thought she was.

As much as Logan dreaded the next hour, he was here now and there was nothing to be done but to face the music.

Literally.

Over the drone of his pickup's engine, he could hear the haunting strains of stringed instruments. He reached down, turned off the engine, and twirled the keys around his finger as he stared through the windshield at the gathering crowd. Sure enough, a small cluster of elegantly clad musicians sat near a long buffet table cranking out the Celtic music his sister liked so much.

It would seem that Danny's grandmother had spared no expense in dedicating the community center to her grandson's memory. What a shame she hadn't arranged for a cover band to play AC/DC. Now *that* would have made Danny happy.

Logan opened the door and stepped out into the dirt parking lot, a constant stream of self-encouragement running through his head like background music.

Put one foot in front of the other. Just do it. Time to man up. Time to face the music.

With a sigh, he brushed away all the clutter in his mind. It was time to accept that there weren't enough clichés on the planet to turn this moment into anything other than the painful ordeal he'd dreaded since he first heard the news. Today he'd be forced to accept that one friend was gone forever. And the other? The other might as well be gone, too. After Logan had deserted his best friends, he could hardly expect to encounter anything but contempt from the man he'd have to face today.

Making his way across the parking lot, memories of his friends buzzed around his head like angry bees around a hive. All their lives had turned out so very different from what they'd imagined as they were growing up together.

Danny was gone, leaving them with nothing more than their memories of him and his name emblazoned in gold on a big sign in front of the new community center.

Matt, who'd been at Danny's side as he'd breathed his last, and who had very nearly met his own end in that ambush, waited somewhere out there in that crowd.

As for Logan, while his best friends had fought for their lives in a foreign land, he'd been safe at home, plodding along with his mundane life as if everything was business as usual.

Maybe if he'd left school and joined the Army with Matt and Danny, things would have turned out differently. Maybe if he'd valued his best friends over the woman who turned out not to value him at all, his whole life would have been set on a different path. Maybe he could have made a difference. Maybe Danny would be alive today.

33

Too many *maybes* haunted him with their siren call of second guesses.

While his friends had chosen to fight for their country, he'd stayed behind for the woman and now he had to live with the consequences of his poor choice.

"Logan!"

He looked up to find his younger sister hurrying in his direction, her brow wrinkled in a perfect imitation of their mother. He was in for either a monumental lecture or a big dose of worried sister, neither of which he was in any mood to deal with right now.

"Hey, Katie-Kat." He flashed his best smile in hopes of heading her off. "You're doing that frown thing again. You're going to end up with permanent wrinkles before you're even legal."

"Twenty is legal enough, mister, and you can just quit trying to distract me. I know you too well for that little trick to have any effect on me. Besides, you're a fine one to talk. From your expression a minute ago, I'd say that frown thing must run in the family. You okay with all this?" She fluttered a hand behind her toward the crowded lawn.

Even his baby sister could see right through him.

"Hell yeah, I'm okay with it. I'm good. Danny's memory deserves all this and more."

Katie arched her eyebrow skeptically and Logan had a pretty good idea of what their grandmother must have looked like fifty-odd years ago.

Katie crossed her arms and tipped her head almost imperceptibly to the left. "Matt's here. He's standing with his family over on the other side of all the chairs. Wearing that uniform, he's looking pretty hot for a guy leaning on a cane."

"Good. I'm glad he's here." Logan filled his lungs with a deep breath as he looked across to the place his sister indicated. If only he could get his roiling stomach on board with his words. "I was hoping to see him here today. Hoping for a chance to talk to him."

The moment he'd dreaded since first hearing the news of Danny's death had finally arrived.

He forced his feet to move, one after the other, toward the spot where his friend's family had gathered. Directly ahead of him, Matt leaned heavily on the cane Katie had mentioned. As Logan drew closer, Matt glanced toward him, his eyes shining with an emotion Logan couldn't read.

Too late to turn back now.

"Matt," he greeted, extending his hand, silently praying his old friend wouldn't reject him for the disloyal coward he was, right here in front of the whole town.

Matt grasped his hand and pulled him forward, clasping him in a tight hug.

"I hoped you'd be here." Matt spoke in that quiet way he'd always had, as if he spoke only for the benefit of the recipient of his words. "Do you think we might find some time to catch up before I have to go back?"

This was so much more than Logan had expected. More than he'd ever dared to hope for. Could it be possible that Matt didn't resent him as much as he resented himself?

"Absolutely, we can. You free tonight? We could catch up over burgers and beers at the Main Street."

"At the café?" A puzzled expression swept over Matt's face but vanished in the blink of an eye. "Done. My social calendar is pretty empty these days. See you there at six?"

"At six, then," Logan agreed, turning to nod his farewells to Matt's mother and grandparents. "Mr. Flynn, ladies."

Then *she* caught his eye.

"You remember Allie, right?" Matt nodded toward his sister, a smile crinkling his face. "Not that you could very well forget someone as obnoxious as she used to be."

Logan remembered Allie all right. Just not as she stood before him now. She'd been a pudgy little girl with a head full of curls and thick glasses sliding down her nose, always trying to follow Matt everywhere he went.

Somewhere along the line, she'd ditched the glasses and all that pudge had grown into curves. And those curves had definitely shifted to all the right spots.

"You turned out pretty good," he heard himself say, as if his inner thoughts had detoured straight out of his mouth without bothering to make the full transit through his brain.

"Thanks," she mumbled, her gaze flickering up to catch his for a second before darting down toward her feet, even as her cheeks mottled a lovely shade of red.

It had been a while since anyone had blushed for him, though maybe he was misreading her reaction. Still, he found that he liked it.

"Looks like they're ready to start," Matt's grandmother noted, tugging at her husband's hand. "Sit down with me, Papa."

"I'd better be getting to my seat, too," Logan said, backing away, unable to tear his gaze from Allie. "See you tonight, Matt."

He forced himself, finally, to turn around and walk away, back to the area where members of his family had gathered.

Taking the seat his sister had saved for him, Logan ran a hand over the back of his neck, attempting to unscramble his thoughts.

Today was supposed to be about Danny, and his focus needed to be up front where Danny's grandmother tapped a fingernail against the microphone in preparation for her speech.

Still, in spite of his best efforts, he found his attention straying across the sea of chairs time and again, back to the petite blonde standing next to Matt.

What the hell was wrong with him? He was a twenty-seven-year-old man, for the love of God, not some fifteen-year-old horndog. And yet, here he was, completely unable to stop himself from staring at her. Maybe his buddy Tanner was right about needing to get back into the dating game in a serious way before he morphed into some kind of weird old man.

After his breakup with Shayla, he'd promised himself that he was never getting involved with another woman. He still felt that way. A casual evening with a female acquaintance when he hit Grand Junction or Denver was fine, but never here in Chance. Dating a woman in his hometown would be too much like getting involved in a relationship, and, as he'd learned the hard way, relationships were for fools.

"Is that Allison Flynn standing over there next to Matt?" Katie leaned around him to get a better look. "I'd heard that she was coming back to Chance to look after her mom, but I didn't realize she was back yet."

It would appear that his sister had a much better source of information for what was happening in town than he did.

"I wonder if Ryan knows she's back," Katie mused. "They used to date, you know. Most of their senior year in high school, as I remember it."

Logan hadn't known. And now that he did, he wasn't exactly comfortable with the idea.

Around him, people applauded politely as Danny's grandmother began to speak about the wild and witty young man her grandson had been. And though Logan tried to pay attention, his gaze continually wandered back to the spot where Allie stood.

So she'd dated his younger brother. Funny that Ryan had never mentioned her. Or maybe he had and Logan simply hadn't been listening.

Another glance in her direction and Logan's decision was made. He needed to make some time to have a chat with Ryan when his brother came home.

CHAPTER FOUR

She was never getting out of this chair again. Never standing on her own two miserable feet again. Not ever.

Allie stretched out in the recliner, wiggling her poor, tortured toes. If it didn't hurt so bad to stand, she'd go fill the tub with the hottest water she could bear and soak her feet.

"Pass," she murmured, closing her eyes and settling deeper into the soft old chair. This felt too good to interrupt for anything else.

Her mother and brother had both gone to their rooms to rest after the exertion of attending the dedication at the community center, so the living room was all hers. With fresh air wafting in through the open windows and only the sound of Grainger's snoring to punctuate the silence, it was beyond peaceful here. Home was comforting in a way she'd forgotten home could be. Lulled by the rhythmic noises coming from the old dog curled up on the end of the sofa, Allie felt herself drifting into that wonderfully nebulous state between waking and sleep.

It was there, in that not-quite-real world, where her imagination bloomed unchecked, that he always came to her. The only difference today was that the Logan O'Connor who invaded her half-dream was an older, updated version of the teenager she'd fantasized about for so long. Logan 2.0.

In her mind's eye, he strode toward her, his dark eyes fixed on her as if she were his only reason for being here. A smile slowly lit his face as he approached, and her body reacted to his acknowledgment of her with a shiver of anticipation.

In the space of a heartbeat he stood next to her, his gaze holding hers as his head dipped toward her. She could hear her own heart pounding, echoing in her ears, as loudly as if someone knocked on a nearby door. She closed her eyes and leaned up into him, waiting for that magical instant when his lips would caress hers.

"Allie," he breathed, in a jarring, feminine voice that sounded nothing like his own.

The perfect moment of fantasy shuddered, shimmered, and slipped away like a wisp of smoke.

"Allie? You in there?" The raised voice was accompanied by more of the knocking she'd heard before.

Well, damn.

Allie scrubbed the heels of her hands against her eyes as she pushed down the recliner's footrest and stood. Next to her, Grainger lifted his head as if that were the best he could manage.

"Some great guard dog you are," she muttered, making her way toward the front door. "Chester could do a better job of scaring people off than you do."

Her cousins, Dulcie and Desi, waited on the front porch.

"There you are!" Dulcie said. "We were beginning to worry when no one answered but we saw your car out front."

"*We* weren't worried," Desi corrected, following her sister into the living room. "Dulcie was. She's as bad as an old woman. Always has been."

That much was true. Dulcie had always been the most cautious, the most levelheaded of the three of them.

"Why don't we head back to the kitchen?" Allie said. "I've got some tea in the fridge."

They could visit out there without any worry about waking up her mother or Matt.

Her guests slid into chairs around the big wooden table in the corner of the kitchen while Allie gathered glasses and the pitcher of iced tea.

"So," she began, filling each of the glasses before sitting down herself. "What is it you wanted to talk to me about?"

The two women exchanged a look over their teas and then Dulcie leaned forward, arms outstretched on the table, her hands clasped around her glass.

"Mama Odie says you've come home to stay. Is that true?"

"I guess it is," Allie answered, consciously holding back the sigh her answer brought with it.

Though moving back to Chance certainly hadn't been her original plan, now that she was here, now that she'd seen her mother's condition for herself, there didn't seem to be any viable option but to stay. Besides, she had nothing waiting for her anywhere else.

"Have you thought about work yet? About what you might want to do now that you're back?" Desi asked. "There isn't much in the way of jobs around here. Unless you're thinking to try for something up at the resort."

Allie shared a look with her cousins. Work at the resort? Not likely. The Last Chance Ski Resort was the closest thing to a major employer in the area. Except for the fact that the Reillys, who owned it, seemed determined to hire from outside the valley. Though their two families, along with the O'Connors, had originally founded the valley together, something had happened a few generations back and they'd mostly gone their separate ways. The Reillys especially seemed determined to distance themselves from their roots in Chance. Rumor had it that their money had even played a major role in getting the big highway detoured around Chance, an event that had nearly been the deathblow to the fading little town.

Even if that weren't the case, the resort was the last place Allie would want to spend her days. It held too many uncomfortable memories.

"I honestly don't know yet," Allie answered at last, pulling herself back from her musings. "I haven't exactly thought that far ahead."

"Well." Desi tapped her dark purple nails against the glass she held. "Think about it for a minute. If you could do absolutely anything in the world you wanted, what would you pick?"

Anything she wanted? Unbidden, Logan's face floated through her thoughts. What was wrong with her? All she had to do was see the guy up close and eight years of convincing herself he didn't mean anything to her had slipped away, as if they were no more than a matter of days.

Sipping her tea, she stalled for a bit as she forced his image from her mind and tried to think of an answer to her cousin's question.

"After six years of working in a bookstore, sales is about the only thing I'm qualified to do. But, the way I remember it, most of the shops here in Chance are staffed by the people who own them, so I'm not holding out a lot of hope for a sales job here."

A queasy heaviness settled over her at the prospect of job hunting. It was why she'd avoided making any plans. She just prayed she could find something to earn a living in Chance. Her savings were minimal and her credit card hovered near its limit, so a regular paycheck was a necessity. But traveling any distance to find that paycheck would defeat the purpose of coming back here to keep an eye on her mother.

Desi stopped her tapping and leaned forward. "I didn't say anything about what you're *qualified* to do, now did I? I asked you what you *wanted* to do. Those aren't at all the same sort of—"

"Let's cut to the chase," Dulcie interrupted in her always practical way. "A little over a year ago, Desi and I cleaned out Papa Flynn's old building on Main Street and started our own business, a coffee shop. The Hand of Chance Coffee Emporium."

Now there was a gargantuan task if Allie had ever heard of one. Papa Flynn had been collecting his treasures for over sixty years, and for as far back as she could remember, that old building had been stuffed to the gills with all manner of junk.

"I wish I'd been here to see that endeavor. It must have taken quite the effort to open your coffee shop."

"I wish you'd been here to help." Desi grinned and sat back in her chair. "In spite of what my sister says, the Hand is hardly what anyone could call just a coffee shop. We do coffee, all right. Some of the best you'll find in the state, as a matter of fact. But Dulcie bakes her wonderful breads and sweets and I have a space to craft and sell my jewelry. Both of us are living our dreams in that old building. We were hoping you'd consider joining us."

Join them? What on earth could she possibly do in a bakery-slash-jewelry store? It was all Allie could manage not to laugh out loud at the suggestion. If it weren't for frozen food and microwaves, she would have starved to death a long time ago. And as for creativity, sticking flowers in a vase without breaking their stems was a major accomplishment for her.

"That's really sweet of you to offer. But I can't cook worth a darn and there's not a creative bone in my body, so I don't see me being much of an employee for you."

"There's nothing sweet about it," Desi said. "We already have a cook. And a jeweler. We're looking for something else entirely. Another leg for our business stool, so to speak. That's why we asked what you really *want* to do."

A silence hovered over the table while two identical pairs of eyes bored into Allie.

A stool leg? Allie was at a loss as to what her cousins wanted from her. "I guess I could be a waitress, if that's what you need, but I wouldn't call it my dream job."

"Oh, for crying out loud," Dulcie huffed, pushing up from the table to pace around the kitchen. "Books, you doofus-butt. You've always loved your freakin' books. Didn't you just say you'd been working in a bookstore for the past six years?"

Allie nodded, still confused by what her cousins were suggesting. "Of course I love books. But where would books fit into your shop?"

"In the back, actually," Desi said, grinning. "It would take some hard work, but we've been talking about it for a while. We just don't have the expertise. Or the time."

"The building's big, Allie. Surely you remember that." Dulcie sat back down, her eyes shining with excitement. "We hauled all Papa Flynn's junk upstairs and cleared out the whole lower level for the Hand of Chance. Even with the kitchen and seating and the jewelry side, there's still a lot of empty space. From day one we've thought it would be perfect to have a new-and-used bookstore in the back to encourage people to come in and linger. Maybe even set aside part of it to lend out books, since we don't have a library in Chance. What do you say? You think you could run your own bookstore? Are you up for it?"

Her own bookstore would be a dream come true. Especially if it involved being able to get books in the hands of people who wouldn't otherwise be reading. But the twins didn't realize what a massive undertaking they were proposing. Or maybe what they didn't realize was that she was penniless.

"Yes, of course, what you're describing would be awesome. Totally awesome. And I'd love to be a part of something like that. I'm really honored that you'd consider me for it." Allie clasped her hands together on the table. "But there's no way I can start a business of my own. Let's not even get into how many bookstores are failing now. The initial costs for something like that would be enormous. I'd need shelves and seats and, geez, tons of books. The thing is, I can't afford to buy any of that stuff. I'm basically broke."

"You wouldn't need to." Dulcie glanced at her sister, waiting for a nod from Desi before continuing. "At least not in the beginning. As far as furniture goes, you could find everything you need upstairs in Papa Flynn's stuff if you're willing to use antiques. I know we hauled some old bookcases up there. You'll just have to dig your way through everything to find what you'd like to use."

Maybe the twins were right. Maybe she could... but no. Reason reared its ugly head and dragged her back to reality.

"I don't see how I could possibly make something like that work. I'd need to order books to sell. Or, at the very least, buy used ones somewhere. The way things are right now, I'd be lucky to afford one book for my own reading."

"You don't have to make it work by yourself. *We* make this work together. Mama Odie and Papa Flynn helped us to start out. The building still belongs to them, but as one of their grandkids, you're as welcome to use it as we are. The Hand has done really well for us. We could lend you the money to order some books." Desi grinned and sipped from her glass of tea. "You could pay us back after you get things up and running and you're making a profit. Having people sitting around, reading books, they're bound to want a coffee. And once they smell the food, we make even more money. It's a win-win-win partnership."

"As far as setting up a lending library, that should be easy enough," Dulcie said. "I bet you could get people around town to donate books they have stuck away in bookcases or closets. I know there are some boxes of old books in Papa Flynn's stuff." Dulcie reached across the table and laid her hand over Allie's. "Won't you at least come over and look around the shop before you say no? See for yourself the potential of what we're suggesting. It would be so cool to have the three of us be together again, like old times."

Working with her cousins was a definite selling point. Even with a two-year age difference between them, they'd been her best friends and confidantes all through their childhood.

"Okay. I'll think about it." After all the trouble her cousins had gone to in dreaming up this plan for her, to do otherwise would be rude. "I have to drop Matt off at the café around six, so maybe, if things work out, I'll try to stop by after that."

"Good." Dulcie stood up, a grin covering her face. "We need to get going. Because of the dedication, we shut everything down for the morning, but we have to get over there and get opened now. We'll look forward to seeing you sometime after six."

"I just know you'll be on board once you see the place. It has a vibe all its own." Desi threw her arms around Allie for a hug, but pulled back, her brow wrinkled, her eyes fixed on the doorway to the room beyond. "Who's that?"

Allie turned, seeing no one until Chester's loud yowl drew her gaze downward.

"Oh. That's my cat, Chester." She leaned over and

47

stretched out a hand only to have the cat completely ignore her as he hurried past her to rub against Desi's leg. "Maybe it's more accurate to say that he's the cat who lives with me rather than calling him *my cat*."

Desi squatted down and Chester climbed onto her knees, rubbing his head against her and purring loudly.

"Hey, Henry," she murmured, her focus entirely on the animal.

"Chester," Allie corrected. "That's so weird. I've never seen him take to anyone like that. Certainly not to me. Half the time, I'm not even sure he likes me."

"He's a perfect match, isn't he?" Dulcie asked, smiling down at her sister, who now sat on the floor, the cat happily ensconced in her lap.

"I can't believe it," Desi said happily, snuggling the big cat. "It feels just like him. If I didn't know better..."

"Desi had a cat who was a dead ringer for that one. His name was Henry. He disappeared a couple of years ago and she's mourned him ever since," Dulcie explained.

"I've missed him," Desi corrected. "Not mourned. Missed. He was my best buddy and a regular bundle of love, just like this big guy."

The cat's purr sounded like a motor.

Allie had never seen Chester act the way he behaved with Desi. And she would never have described the cat as a bundle of love. All in all, her choice was clear.

"He really seems happy with you, Desi. Is there any chance you'd be willing to take him?"

Her cousin's head popped up from where she was nuzzling the black-and-white ball of fur. "You can't be serious. Are you?"

Allie nodded. "Totally serious. He's never been that

happy with me. Not even when I first found him as a starving kitten. And he definitely doesn't like it here with Grainger. They hate each other with a passion. Maybe he was meant to be with you. If you'll wait just a minute, I'll go get all his food and stuff to send with you."

"You know what this is, don't you?" Desi stood, the cat cuddled to her shoulder. "It's the hand of chance at work here. It's like fate has brought Henry back to me. You can't imagine how happy you've made me, Allie. This is like the best day ever. Best. Day. Ever."

After gathering the cat's things, Allie watched as her cousins drove away, Chester—no, *Henry* now, still happier than she'd ever seen him.

The whole visit had been so out-of-the-blue weird. Maybe fate had meant that cat to end up with Desi. And maybe fate intended her to end up with her cousins, too.

In spite of her doubts, she wasn't ruling anything out yet. Not until she'd had a look at the coffee shop, just like she'd said she would.

After all, if there was even the tiniest chance she could end up as happy as Henry and Desi had looked when they left, she had no choice but to go for it.

CHAPTER FIVE

"Are you sure you're okay with me just dropping you off like this? I can stay and wait, if you want. I don't mind. I have a book in the car."

Allie waited for her brother's reply, her stomach churning with a mixture of emotions. She wanted to wait for him. Wanted an excuse to be here when Logan showed up. Wanted them to ask her to join them for the evening.

Of course, seeing Logan carried with it the risk of her becoming a tongue-tied fool again, just as she had been this morning at the dedication when he'd spoken to her. All things considered, staying here was not a wise thing for her to do. At least not until she managed to sort through all these ridiculous unresolved feelings she seemed to be carrying around.

Matt smiled as he got out of the car, leaning down to look in the window after he shut the door. "When do you not have a book with you?"

"Never, if I can help it." Allie returned the smile. "So? You want me to wait?"

As if anticipating his positive answer, she turned off the engine and removed the key, flinching at the high whining noise the car had begun to make in the last few days. Money or no money, she was going to have to take her old baby in for a checkup one day soon.

"Don't be a goof, Allie. We're back in Chance now, remember? It's only a mile or so back to the house. Even like this"—Matt lifted his cane and shook it at her—"I could walk home easy enough if I had to."

"But you won't, right? You'll call me when you're finished so I can come get you. Right?"

"Right," Matt agreed. "I'll call. Now quit mother-henning me and go home."

"Okay," she agreed, but her resolve wavered again when she saw Matt standing there all by himself, leaning on that damn cane, staring off into the distance, looking so... alone. "Maybe I should at least wait here with you until he shows up? Just in case."

Only to make sure Matt wasn't stranded. Definitely not as an excuse to see Logan again.

"Just in case what? You think I'm in danger of getting stood up by my best friend?"

"No," she denied.

Probably not. Then again, whether or not Matt wanted to admit it, it had been a long time since he and Logan had been best friends.

"You're a piss-poor liar, little sister. Always have been." He shook his head and began his slow walk toward the entrance of the café. "See there? He's pulling in now. You can quit your worrying. All that protective sisterly

51

angst is for nothing."

He had nailed that bit about her feeling angst. Only it wasn't angst of the sisterly kind that was playing tug-of-war with her emotions.

"More like angst of the stupid kind," she muttered, putting the key back in the ignition.

Disappointment warred with practicality as she watched the two men greet one another, both of their faces breaking into grins. For a moment there, they looked like little boys again.

It really was for the best this way.

With a sigh of resignation, she turned the key and pressed down on the gas pedal.

Nothing happened.

No whine, no sputter, no clicking. Nothing.

"Come on, baby girl," she encouraged. "We can do this. Don't you die on me yet."

She just needed the car to hold on until she could get a job and a couple of paychecks under her belt.

Allie wiped her sweaty palm on her knee and reached for the ignition again. For a second time, she turned the key.

And for a second time, only silence greeted her effort.

"Oh, for piss' sake," she breathed, her grandmother's favorite curse popping out as she rested her forehead against the steering wheel.

Okay. She could deal with this. It was nothing more than a minor glitch in the big picture. Nothing she couldn't find a way around. She could walk to Mama Odie's and borrow her grandparents' pickup to come get Matt when he called. No big deal. She'd figure out some way to get the car towed later.

Lost in planning what to do next, she didn't notice the movement beside her car. A knock on the glass next to her almost sent her jumping out of her seat.

"Need some help?"

Allie's breath caught somewhere between her lungs and her throat as her eyes connected with Logan's melted-chocolate gaze. She couldn't have turned away even if she'd wanted to. And she definitely didn't want to.

Logan waited for her response, a slow, sexy grin lifting one corner of his mouth.

How could one look, one small half-excuse for a smile make her feel so... much?

Exactly like when she'd seen him earlier today, heat rose up her neck to her cheeks until she felt as if she must be radiating waves like the high desert on a summer day.

"It won't start," she managed to mumble at last, her tongue too thick for her mouth.

"Let me take a look. Pop the hood for me," he said, already walking toward the front of her car.

Her mind a blank, Allie fumbled for the release, more than grateful when her fingers finally closed over it. Only when the metal covering rose, blocking Logan from her view, was she able to breathe like a normal human being again.

To think only minutes ago she'd wanted them to ask her to join them for dinner. What a mistake that would have been. She'd likely have choked her fool self on the first bite she took sitting at a table with that man.

A couple of *clunks* and a *bang* later, the hood slammed down. Logan walked back toward her door, wiping his hands down the side of his jeans.

"Give it a try now."

Ignoring her shaking hands, Allie reached for the key and turned it in the ignition as she pressed on the gas pedal.

The car roared to life as if it had never had a problem.

Relief pushed away the more uncomfortable emotions battering at her, and she did her best to smile up at him. "What kept it from starting?"

Logan shrugged, his fingers absently stroking over his stubbled cheek. "I'm going to say you need to get this car in to Hugo at the garage. We've pretty much reached the limit of my auto-mechanical abilities here tonight."

Again he flashed the grin that all but stopped her heart, and she briefly considered whether it would be appropriate to give him a small token of her gratitude for fixing her car. A kiss, perhaps? That was exactly what would have happened in one of her fantasies.

But this wasn't a fantasy. This was the real thing with the real Logan leaning against the open window of her car, watching her, waiting for her to say something. Anything.

Under his scrutiny, her face heated another several degrees, something she would have sworn was impossible before now. She quickly discarded the entire thread of her prior thoughts and settled on a simple acknowledgment of what he'd done for her.

"Thank you. I really appreciate your help."

"No problem." He backed away from the car, his eyes still fixed on her. "And don't worry about picking up Matt. I'll bring him home when we're done here tonight."

"You don't have to do—"

"But I want to," he interrupted, turning to step up on

the sidewalk and join Matt. "Don't wait up for us!"

Allie watched them walk toward the entrance, Logan obviously slowing his stride to match Matt's. When they disappeared inside, she backed out of the parking space and headed toward home.

Only a few blocks down Main Street, she spotted The Hand of Chance Coffee Emporium. Even if she hadn't remembered which old, dilapidated building on the corner belonged to her grandparents, she wouldn't have been able to mistake the twins' shop. A big sign hung over the front of the building, sporting their logo, a woman's hand, next to the name of their business.

Since the *OPEN* sign in the window was still lit, she decided to stop and have a look, just as she'd promised. With Logan's offer to see that Matt got home safely, her whole evening had just opened up.

With nothing better to do than remember how Logan's black T-shirt had stretched over those broad shoulders as if it were painted on, an evening going through dusty furniture and knickknacks might be exactly the distraction she needed.

* * *

If Logan were here for any other reason tonight, he might be tempted to do something outrageously impulsive.

Hell, who was he kidding? He was tempted as it was; he just wasn't going to act on that temptation.

Logan stepped back from the car and away from the most intriguing woman he'd encountered in years. Another backward step and his heel banged against the curb, forcing him to break the visual connection he had with

Allie.

She piqued his interest in a way no one had for a long time and his mind brimmed with questions. Chief among them: Was there a significant someone waiting back in Texas for her to return to, or had she come back home to Chance to stay?

He pushed away that line of thought to face his old friend. Gaining information about Allie was not the reason he'd come here tonight. His curiosity would have to wait.

Physically turning away from Allie, he stepped onto the sidewalk beside Matt to confront his real reason for being here. If he could find a way, he was determined to put at least one of his demons to rest tonight.

"How did you get it going?" Matt asked, slowly moving forward, his wooden cane thumping against the concrete walk.

Logan considered trying to dazzle his old friend with bullshit but settled instead for the truth.

"I have no earthly idea. I wiggled some wires and banged a rock on the engine. I asked her to try to start it again because I was out of all my usual tricks of the trade. She needs to have someone who knows what they're doing have a look at that thing, though. I doubt my rock magic will last for long."

Matt chuckled, offering a smile to the girl who greeted them from behind the counter when they entered. Even leaning on a cane, Matt Flynn was still the one who caught all the women's attention. He nodded at the waitress who seated them, a woman at least as old as his mother, and her cheeks turned pink.

"How do you do that?"

"Do what?" Matt asked innocently.

"Some things never change." Logan shook his head in disbelief. As it had always been, Matt seemed to have no idea of his effect on the fairer sex.

"Speaking of things changing, you had me thinking you must have taken up auto repair since I'd seen you last," Matt said as they slid into their booth. "You looked pretty slick with the way you handled Allie's car."

"Not me. I was just lucky. You know I've never been the car guy," Logan responded, biting back the words that felt natural to say next.

From the time they were old enough to dig through a toolbox, Danny had been their car guy. Logan and Matt locked gazes for an instant and Logan knew his friend shared the thought that neither wanted to voice aloud.

A ripe silence settled over them as they studied their menus. Matt broke it first.

"I made Allie stop at Fort Logan on our way up here yesterday. Danny's not buried there." Although Matt's eyes remained fixed on the menu he held, his grip tightened until his fingers shook. "I'd like to know who decided against laying him to rest where he belongs. I'd like to know, because I can't imagine anyone who ever took the time to talk to Danny even for a few minutes wouldn't have known that was what he wanted."

Logan nodded slowly, pausing to choose his words carefully. The Reillys' decision to bury Danny up on Chance Mountain had surprised everyone at the time. But in a convoluted sort of way, he understood their choice. In that same way, he believed Danny would understand, too.

"It was his family's call to make. They had to do what was best for them."

"What about what was best for Danny?" Matt closed

his menu and laid it purposefully on the table in front of him, brushing his fingers across the shiny plastic before clasping his hands together in front of him. "I guess they won, then, didn't they? In spite of everything that was important to Danny, when all was said and done, no matter what he'd always wanted, his family had their way."

Their waitress returned with two beers, her smile directed at Matt as she took his order first. Logan held his thoughts until she'd left.

"I don't think it had anything to do with winning or losing. Talk around town said that Danny's mom is having a real hard time coping with what happened to him. In the end, I guess she wanted him up on the mountain with her, not down in Denver."

It had been the conversation he'd had with his own mother that had helped him to accept that.

"Danny earned his place of honor in the national cemetery. It was what he wanted. It was the last thing he said to me before…" Matt paused, his lips drawn together in a tight line as if he was fighting for some inner control. "It was what he wanted," he repeated at last.

"Well, it's done now," Logan reasoned. Danny's family made the choice that was best for them, and that was that.

"I let him down," Matt said quietly. "He expected me to make sure it happened the way he wanted, but I failed him. I should have been here for him."

A perfect opening if ever Logan had heard one.

"Like I should have been there for both of you when the shit went down?"

If he'd gone with his friends when they'd enlisted, *if* he'd been at their sides when they'd rolled up on that firefight, maybe things would have turned out differently. Maybe Danny would be here with them right now. It was one of the big *if's* that haunted Logan's life.

"What did you say?" Matt looked up at him like a man surfacing from a deep dive. "You think you should have been with us? There in Afghanistan, you mean? No way, man. That was the last place on the planet for you to be. Two of us in that hellhole was two too many."

Matt drained his glass and held it up to attract their server's attention. When their refills arrived, he lifted the full glass and clinked it against Logan's.

"This one's for Danny," Matt said, a finality in his voice that seemed to indicate he'd brought the conversation to a close.

"For Danny," Logan agreed.

The moment they'd shared earlier had passed. It no longer felt as if Logan could pursue his friend's true feelings about him remaining behind while they'd gone off to risk everything for their country. In spite of his best intentions, his demons would have to remain unappeased tonight.

Their food arrived and Logan bit into his burger, waiting for Matt to lead the conversation. He considered asking about Allie, but any questions he could think of all seemed designed to encourage Matt to ask why he'd want to know. And since even *he* wasn't completely sure why he wanted to know more about Matt's sister, he steered clear of that discussion, determined to avoid any mention of her. Instead, their conversation turned to resurrecting old memories of school days and comparing employment ambitions for the future.

The evening slipped away, and by the time they paid

their check and headed out, it was as if they'd almost recaptured the familiar rhythm of their old relationship.

Maybe he'd been wrong. Maybe he could retire a demon or two after all.

"Hey, isn't that Allie's car?" Matt twisted in his seat as they passed The Hand of Chance Coffee Emporium. "I'm sure it is. I wonder if that beat-up POS of hers stopped on her again?"

That would be Logan's guess, considering the vehicle sat all alone in the empty lot next to the darkened shop.

"I guess we'll find out soon enough," he answered, turning down the road toward the old house where Matt's family lived.

Logic told him he really didn't need to go inside when he dropped Matt off. Even if Allie's car had broken down, there was nothing he could do for her tonight. Her best option was to have Hugo tow it to the garage tomorrow.

But it wasn't logic that urged him to turn off the engine and follow Matt into the house.

Susie Flynn sat in her recliner, eyes closed, bathed in the soft, flickering glow emanating from the television.

"Hey, Mom," Matt greeted, dropping a kiss on the top of her head. "Where's Allie?"

"Still over at the Hand, I guess. The twins stopped by on their way home to check on me and let me know that they left her going through Papa Flynn's stuff up on the second floor." Susie shifted in her seat, seeming to notice they had a guest. "Welcome, Logan. Make yourself comfortable. I think there's pop in the fridge."

"Thanks, Susie." Logan automatically reached to pull his cap off his head, remembering only at the last second he wasn't wearing one tonight.

"What's she doing that for?" Matt asked.

Susie fluttered a hand, her eyes fixed on the television screen. "The girls are trying to talk her into setting up a bookstore or some such thing. I guess she's hunting through the old furniture Papa Flynn has stored up there. You don't need to worry about her. The girls said she should be along shortly."

If Allie was considering her cousins' offer seriously enough to wander around in that junkyard of her grandfather's this late at night, surely that must mean she was planning to stay here in Chance. And planning to stay must mean there was no special attachment waiting in Texas, where he'd heard she'd been living.

In spite of his expectations, his questions were getting answered after all.

"How long ago was that, Mom? What time was it when the twins stopped by?"

"How long?" Susie lifted a hand to her forehead and rubbed it over her eyes. "I'm not sure, Matty. I'm sorry. I might have drifted off to sleep after they left. But you don't need to worry. Your sister has been taking care of herself for a long time. Besides, you need to remember that you're back in Chance now, not in some big city."

"Yeah, that may be true, but it's after midnight, Mom, and I am worried." Matt walked over to the window and twitched the drapes back to stare outside. "I'm not all that comfortable with her still being over there by herself. The place looked completely dark when we drove by."

Offering to help seemed the only sensible thing to do.

"I can stop in to check on her. I go right by there on

my way home, so it won't be any trouble."

It had been a long time since chance had dropped such a perfect opportunity in his lap.

CHAPTER SIX

Allie climbed the squeaky stairs, the old key Dulcie had given her clutched tightly in her fist.

"Enjoy!" Dulcie's voice floated up the stairs after her. "Hope you find a trove of buried treasure."

Treasure. Right. Allie's biggest hope was that she didn't encounter mice or an inordinate number of spiders. If she hadn't been so consumed with whether she'd get to see Logan again, she might have remembered to bring some plastic gloves.

At the top of the stairs, she turned to her left and opened the first door she came to, inching her way inside. As her cousin had promised, a lamp stood next to the doorway and she flipped the switch.

Light settled over the cluttered room, but hardly made a difference in beating back the shadows that clung stubbornly to the far corners. Odd shapes danced in those shadows, created by furniture and stacks of boxes and plastic bins.

Allie vaguely remembered the downstairs looking very much like this the one time she'd peeked inside as a child. A creepy, scary-movie feeling had filled her chest and she'd avoided the old building after that, in spite of her grandfather's invitations to join him.

That same feeling tightened her breathing now.

"I'm not a child now." She spoke aloud into the silence to reassure herself.

Besides, it was only dust filling her lungs, not some Hollywood-type premonition of monsters and knife-wielding murderers wearing goalie masks.

She lifted the antique floor lamp and carried it with her as far into the room as its cord would allow.

"Wow."

For as long as she could remember, her grandfather had haunted estate sales, auctions and generally any place he could haggle for a bargain. If he didn't have the entire second floor of this building to store it all in, he'd make a perfect candidate for a study on hoarding.

Though the original facade of the building made it appear misleadingly small from the outside, it was, as her cousins had reminded her, really large.

Chairs of every description occupied the room, along with a variety of tables, all neatly stacked. If the other rooms held even half as much as this one, her cousins had been correct. She'd have no problem furnishing an area to serve as a bookstore and lending library.

A huge old bookcase stood against one wall, peeking out from behind two tall stacks of classic cardboard storage boxes. From here it appeared she'd found an excellent piece to use in setting up a bookstore downstairs, though she'd need to move the stacks to get a better look.

She stuffed the key she still held into the pocket of her jeans. Dulcie had told her she'd need it to lock up after herself if she stayed up here very long, since they'd be leaving soon. Allie had taken it, though, in truth, she doubted she'd need it. She didn't plan to be here long tonight. In the bright daylight with the windows wide open, it would be much easier to explore this area. And much less creepy.

Still, it wouldn't take long to move the boxes and quickly inspect the bookcase to make sure all its shelves were intact.

The boxes turned out to be extraordinarily heavy for their size. A closer examination revealed the word *BOOKS* scrawled on the side of each one.

Her breath caught again as she lifted the first lid, but this time neither dust nor fear was involved.

Hardbacks stacked two layers deep filled the box.

W. Somerset Maugham, James Joyce, Harper Lee, Mark Twain, William Faulkner and John Steinbeck.

This find was too good to be true. If she actually did set up a lending area, these books would provide a great head start.

She lifted another lid and found paperbacks in this box. Romance, science fiction, mystery. The third box held more hardbacks, and she still had four more boxes to look through.

Obviously she'd been too quick to scoff. Papa Flynn had indeed accumulated a wonderful trove of treasure.

"We're leaving now!" Her cousin Desi's voice echoed up the stairs. "You want us to lock you in?"

"No!" The idea of being locked in this place all by

herself was much creepier than simply wandering around up here in the dark. "I'll be down in just a few minutes."

How long could it take to unstack these boxes and check the bookcase? Five minutes. Ten tops.

Dragging all the boxes to the center of the room where the light was best took considerably longer than she'd anticipated. Once she had them all down and within reach, she knelt in the middle of her newly found treasures and lifted their lids, one by one, pulling out books and sorting them into stacks.

Gone With the Wind, Wuthering Heights, Jane Eyre and...

"Oh my," she breathed, carefully running her hand over the cover of one of her all-time favorites, *Pride and Prejudice*.

It had been years since she'd last read Elizabeth and Darcy's story. On her lap, the book almost seemed to fall open by itself, and her fingers flipped the pages as if controlled by someone from afar. Her eyes flickered over the words, slowly at first, then more quickly as the story took on a life of its own.

Allie was over a third of the way through the book before she surfaced back to reality. Some sliver of noise had broken through her barriers and into the magical world in which she'd immersed herself. Some noise that snagged her attention and caused her to lower the book. Head tipped to the side, she listened. It had been a noise like...

Damn. She was normally so observant. This sort of thing only happened when she lost herself in a story. Her brain had definitely registered something out of the ordinary, but she wasn't sure exactly what it might have been.

How long had she been up here, anyway? Her cramped muscles told her it had to have been quite some time. With the draperies pulled over the windows, she had no way of judging if any light was left outside. Maybe the twins had come back to check on her. She started to call out to them to let them know where she was but caution—and that familiar trickle of dread—held her tongue.

What if it wasn't the twins?

Again she listened, holding her breath to eliminate any outside noise. That might have worked if her heart hadn't been pounding so loudly in her ears that it drowned out everything else.

There! Another sound. A squeaking noise she recognized.

The stairs.

"Shit," she whispered, clutching the book to her chest, where her heart thumped a quickening tattoo against her ribs.

It could be anyone! She'd told her cousin to leave the door unlocked, and from the looks of how far she'd read into the book, that must have been hours ago.

She fought the panic pressing against her lungs and forced herself up to her knees in spite of her left foot having gone to sleep where she'd sat on it. It was ridiculous giving in to a silly childhood fear this way. Of course she'd hear squeaks up here. The building was well over a hundred years old. If she'd been paying attention instead of being lost in her reading, she'd probably have heard all sorts of groans and creaks. She only heard it now because her foot had lost all feeling and was already pulling her out of the book.

Yeah. That was it. That had to be it.

Another squeak sounded, closer than before, followed by a thud that could be nothing other than a foot on the stairs. A big foot.

Her panic returned, so well reinforced this time that her throat closed off and the expletive she wanted to shout had no hope of passing her lips.

When a large figure filled the doorway, she drew back her arm and launched the only weapon she had at hand—her precious hardback book.

* * *

The coffee shop was dark when Logan pulled up, but he could swear he saw light flickering behind the window coverings on the second floor. He knocked on the door once and waited.

No response.

Allie's car was still parked in the lot, so she had to be here. Either that or her car had died on her again and she'd walked home.

Only she wasn't at home, so he refused to even consider that possibility. She had to be inside.

The second time he pounded on the door, he also wiggled the handle. The knob turned easily in his hand and, with only a little forward pressure, the door swung wide open.

The whole shop was bathed in the black that comes only on an almost moonless night, and Logan's senses sharpened. He pulled the high-powered little flashlight he always carried from his pocket and switched it on.

He didn't like this. Not one damn bit.

"Allie?"

He waited for a full minute in the silence that followed his call before heading to the back of the building, where he knew he'd find the stairs to the upper level. The twins had told Susie that they'd left Allie going through the storage items up there.

Midway up the stairs he paused, listening for any sound of activity.

"Allie?" he tried again, a little louder this time.

He'd been up here about six months ago conducting a fire inspection. Thanks to Harley Flynn's lifelong passion for "collecting," the second floor was a hoarder's fantasy. Even as neatly as the twins had tried to arrange things, the old man's obsession had ensured that the place was loaded to the gills.

Remembering how it had looked on his last visit, Logan quickened his step. Anything could have happened up there. Allie might have fallen and hurt herself. She could even be trapped.

The thought of her wedged under a pile of toppled antique furniture sent him pounding up the remaining stairs toward the light spilling out through the open door.

He'd no more than stepped into the doorway before a missile flew directly toward his head. He ducked, deflecting the heavy projectile with a quickly lifted forearm.

"What the hell?" he grunted.

Crouching or shifting behind the doorframe would have been the smart thing to do, but Logan thought of neither. He barged into the room, ready to deal with whatever had attacked him.

"Logan?"

Allie knelt in the center of the room, surrounded by stacks of boxes and books piled higher than the top of her head. Her voice sounded small and breathless, and her wide, rounded eyes confirmed the surprise he'd heard there.

"What are you doing here?" she asked. "You scared me half to death!"

He could understand that easily enough. This place, with its looming shadows, was creepy as hell at night.

"I yelled your name a couple of times. You didn't answer. Your family was worried when you didn't come home." At least, her brother was worried.

"I didn't hear you." She pushed up to stand, teetering on one foot while she dusted off her hands on her jeans before making eye contact with him again. "I got into the books and sort of lost track of time. And then I heard some noises and..." Her words trailed off and she shrugged one shoulder.

"So that's why you launched the aerial attack?"

Shaking her head, she defensively crossed her arms in front of her. "I told you. It's kind of weird up here in the dark and, I'll admit it, I freaked a little. You don't look any worse for it though."

"Yeah? Well, you and..." Logan leaned down to pick up the object that she'd thrown in his direction, pausing to glance at the cover. "You and Jane Austen almost took my arm off."

For the first time since he'd entered the room, the beginning of a smile curved her lips, an expression that lit her face. "Then I guess we can both be thankful that Jane and I were off our game tonight, because I was aiming for your head. Well,"——her eyes darted away toward the floor again—"not actually *your* head. The head of whatever creature was coming after me."

Her eyes flickered back up toward him, and he returned her grin as he gradually made his way through the furniture and boxes to the spot where she stood.

"Your mom says you're thinking of opening a bookstore downstairs."

"And a lending library." Her expression turned wistful. "If I can get my hands on enough books. I think there's plenty of furniture up here to set up shop. I just need to haul it downstairs."

The idea of her surrounded by books seemed to fit. Now that he thought of it, he seemed to remember her, as a kid, dragging a book around with her more often than not.

"Have you thought of asking for donations for the lending library? I know my mom and Katie have boxes of books stacked out in the barn. I bet they'd be willing to help."

"That was something the girls—" She started forward but stopped, her face wrinkling as if she were in pain when she put her weight on both feet.

"Are you hurt?" He cleared the distance remaining between them by vaulting over the boxes blocking his path.

"No." She chuckled, accepting the hand he offered as she teetered on one foot. "I sat on my foot too long and cut off the blood flow. Now it's at that icky, tingly stage."

Not quite what his imagination had conjured when he'd started up the stairs tonight. Instead of finding her trapped and injured, he'd found her alone and frightened. Almost as bad.

"Listen. I'm off duty tomorrow. I'll come by your place to pick you up and we can come up here together to figure out what you need to take downstairs. I make a pretty decent moving man."

Allie stared into the dark shadows, shaking her head. "You don't need to do that. It's kind of a lot to ask."

"No, I don't *need* to," he said—though in an odd way, he felt as if it was exactly what he needed to do. "But I want to."

She looked up again, her expression hard for him to read. "Okay, then. If you're sure."

"I'm sure. I'm also sure that what we need to do now is get you out of here."

He swept an arm behind her legs and lifted her off her feet, ignoring her startled little squeak just as he tried to ignore her arms slipping into place around his neck.

"I can walk out of here on my own," she said quietly, her warm breath feathering over his cheek.

"I'm sure you can," he agreed. "But it's already almost one in the morning, and with the way you're limping, I'd have to clear all those boxes for you to be able to get out of here. This is much faster."

He wouldn't add that holding her like this was a lot more enjoyable than stacking boxes could ever be.

She seemed as if she might argue the point that it would only require waiting a few minutes for her to fully recover, but she didn't. What that might mean he didn't know and didn't care. All that mattered was that they were on their way out and she was in his arms.

"Flip that switch for me." He motioned his head toward the floor lamp they stood beside.

"Off?" Her voice squeaked with the question, as if

she couldn't believe she'd heard him correctly. "You want me to turn it off?"

"We can't very well leave it on all night, unattended. It's an old lamp and this is an old building." The last thing he wanted to be responsible for was starting a fire he'd get called back to put out before the night was over. "Burning this place down would look bad on my record. Firefighters don't get promotions for starting fires."

She smiled at him then, as if the little joke helped relax her, and she grasped the switch. Instantly the inky black that had been held at bay by the old lamp engulfed them. Her free arm fastened around his neck and a shiver ran through her body.

"There's a flashlight in my shirt pocket," he offered, not wanting to risk falling over something while carrying her.

Her fingers stroked along his chest as she hunted for the pocket opening before sliding down the soft fabric to retrieve the light. In the dark, the movement felt somehow more intimate than he had expected, and his heart raced with an increased blood flow.

"There's a button on the end," he said softly, his lips close to her ear.

She fumbled with the light, her breath coming in short, quick little puffs. Heat radiated from her skin, warming him. After what seemed like an eternity, the bright beam shot down toward the ground to guide his feet, and he made his way from the room.

The big grandfather clock struck one as he stepped off the last stair and Allie jerked, clamping both her arms around his neck, pressing her cheek close to his shoulder. He could live with that. In fact, one of the best new ideas he could think of was to take that old clock on all his dates.

Only this wasn't a date, he reminded himself. This was his best friend's little sister.

"I'm... My foot is..." She seemed to search for words, her breath catching before she started again. "I can walk by myself now."

"I guess you can at that," he agreed, reluctantly lowering her legs to the floor, but keeping his arm around her back as if his brain had forgotten to tell his muscles he was supposed to let go.

Her face tipped up toward his, barely visible in the sliver of moonlight reflecting through the big windows up front. Her breathing matched his own ragged pace and her heart thudded against his chest.

Or was that his heart?

As if some strange spell possessed him, he felt himself unable to move, his face hovering above hers. And then, as if drawn by a force outside his control, he dipped his head toward hers, every fiber of his being straining toward the kiss he was about to take.

She lifted her left hand to his cheek, her fingers soft and trembling against his skin. Her right hand followed, still clutching the ultrabright little light, shining the beam directly into his eyes.

With the jolt of light, his senses cleared, returning from wherever they'd been held captive. Hers too, apparently.

"Jiminy Christmas," she muttered, backing away from him until she bumped into one of the small café tables, sending the condiment bottles clattering against one another.

Logan cleared his throat and slipped the flashlight from her hand, shining a path ahead of them. "We need to make sure your car starts so we can get you on your way home," he said.

She muttered something that sounded vaguely like agreement as she followed behind him. At the entrance, she stopped and pulled a key from her pocket, her fingers trembling in the beam of light as she locked the door behind them.

Her car started on the first try.

"Whatever you did earlier must have done the trick," she said.

"Yeah, well, you still better get it in for a checkup."

"Right," she said, putting the car into gear. "See you tomorrow, I guess. If you're sure."

"I'm sure. See you tomorrow," he echoed, watching as she drove away, remembering only after it was too late that they hadn't specified a time for him to show up at her house.

Not surprising, really. How could he be expected to think of something so mundane after what had felt like his world quaking a nine on the Richter scale?

Shaking his head, Logan climbed into his pickup and started the engine.

Whatever time he planned to arrive at her house, one thing was clear. He was in for a long night waiting.

CHAPTER SEVEN

Nine in the morning! Allie could hardly believe the clock on her dresser. She couldn't remember the last time she'd slept so late.

It shouldn't be such a surprise, though, when she considered that it had to have been well after four before she was finally able to get to sleep. An evening alone with Logan O'Connor had proven to be a powerful stimulant.

"On multiple levels," she muttered, kicking off her covers and stretching her arms above her head.

The man was like chocolate to a compulsive dieter.

Even in the bright light of day, she could still feel his touch if she closed her eyes and concentrated hard enough. It was almost as real as the embarrassment she felt at her own reaction to him.

Her eyes popped open at that thought and she sat up, swinging her legs over the edge of the bed to rest her feet on the cool wooden floorboards.

He must think her an absolute idiot. She had certainly done her best last night to prove that she was one.

Over the years, she'd imagined being in Logan's arms countless times. She'd dreamed up hundreds of scenarios. That particular fantasy was the way she'd put herself to sleep at night. In those moments after her head hit the pillow, it had been images of him that had filled her thoughts and transported her into her dreams, like little stories she'd act out in her imagination.

In each of those imaginary encounters, they'd meshed wonderfully. They'd bantered so seductively, behaved so comfortably, it was almost as if those moments had really existed.

So when the time had actually presented itself, when fate had thrown them together and hoisted her into his embrace, what had she done?

She'd panicked like some silly schoolgirl.

No clever banter for this gal. No sir, not her. The best she could manage was some incoherent stuttering, a massive case of blushing and then, oh, best of all, then she'd topped everything off by nearly blinding the guy when she'd thought he was going to kiss her.

She groaned and scrubbed her hands over her face.

"As if," she muttered.

And how desperate was that? Assuming he was going to kiss her just because it always worked out that way in her little imaginary scenarios.

Another groan and she made her way to the bathroom to stare at herself in the mirror. Mascara she hadn't bothered to wash off before falling into bed ringed her eyes in raccoon-like fashion and her hair was a tangled mess of curls.

Yeah. Like Logan O'Connor would ever have any interest in trying to kiss that.

She turned on the shower and headed back into her bedroom to lay out her clothes for the day. It should be a busy one. She needed to get back over to the coffee shop to determine which pieces of furniture she'd need to drag downstairs and...

The jeans slid from her hand as she froze in the middle of the room.

Logan had said he was coming to pick her up this morning.

Damn.

As if acknowledging that memory had set the world in motion, Matt chose that moment to knock on her bedroom door

"You up and at 'em, Allie? You got company."

And double damn.

"Be right out," she called, bending down to retrieve the jeans before hurrying back to the bathroom.

He'd come, just like he'd said he would. Maybe this meant he wanted to see her again. Maybe he wanted to spend time with her as much as she'd wanted to spend time with him.

No time for a shower this morning. A quick scrub would have to do. She ran a brush through her hair and twisted her curls up into a ponytail before she grabbed for a washcloth. At least she could make the raccoon look go away, even if she didn't have time for more makeup.

Faster than she could ever remember, she was dressed and headed down the hallway. Matt and Logan waited in the living room, near the front door.

"About time." Matt stood barefoot and bare-chested, sipping from a steaming cup, his eyes tracking from her to Logan and back again. "I'd offer to come along but I doubt I'd be much help as a furniture mover."

"No problem," Logan said. "Katie's waiting out in the truck. You remember my sister, right? She might be small, but she's a powerhouse when it comes to getting things done."

He'd brought his sister along? So much for the fantasy of him wanting to spend time alone with her. Likely as not, he'd forced Katie to come to protect him in case Allie got all weird again.

"Coffee?" Allie made the offer as she turned toward the kitchen. Whether her guest wanted some or not, she certainly needed caffeine. Almost as much as she needed a minute or two to disguise her disappointment.

"Not when I'm headed to the Hand." Logan grinned in a way that made him look ten years younger. "No offense. It's just that coffee doesn't get any better than what Dulcie brews. You might want to reconsider that yourself."

"Good point."

It did seem rather silly to be bringing her own coffee, considering where she'd be in just a few minutes.

To her surprise, it wasn't the aroma of coffee that captured her interest when they opened the door to The Hand of Chance Coffee Emporium and walked inside. It was whatever her cousin was baking this morning.

"What is that heavenly smell?" she asked, following her nose to the counter in the back.

Dulcie's face lit up as if she'd just received the world's best compliment.

"This week's special. Caramel apple bread. Want a piece? It's fresh out of the oven. I'll toast some for you and bring it over."

Did she ever want some! She wanted it every bit as much as the coffee Dulcie was pouring as she spoke, and coffee was like Allie's lifeblood first thing in the morning.

She nodded gratefully and joined Katie and Logan at a table to wait for her toasted slice of heaven.

"Oh. My. God." Katie closed her eyes and licked the fork she held after her first bite. "This is practically orgasmic."

After her own first bite, Allie knew it had been well worth the wait. "Absolutely orgasmic," she agreed.

Even if she hadn't skipped dinner last night, this was still one of the best things she'd ever tasted.

"And you would know about that how?" Logan asked, setting his cup down to frown at his sister before turning his glare in Allie's direction.

"You know you don't really want an answer to that question." Katie wiggled her eyebrows at her brother and grinned before she stuck another bite in her mouth. "I would come here every morning if I lived in town," she said after she swallowed.

"And then you would be as wide as you are tall," Logan grumbled, pushing back his chair to stand up. "And I wouldn't have to worry about you tempting men anymore. Maybe you should have a second helping. I'm going up to start hunting for shelves that might work. I'll see you both up there."

Allie watched him head for the stairs, thinking, not for the first time, that some men were just born to wear jeans and tight T-shirts.

"He's grumpy enough today, isn't he?"

Katie's comment snapped Allie's attention back to the table.

"Oh, yeah? I didn't really notice." Allie tried for a nonchalant response, fixing her gaze on the last bites in front of her. If she was lucky, maybe Katie hadn't realized she'd been staring at Logan's backside as he'd walked away.

Katie nodded, finishing off the last of her bread and washing it down with coffee. "I don't think he wanted me to tag along this morning, but oh well. That's what little sisters are for, right? Besides, I wanted to see what was going on in town." She grinned and stood up, pinching her fingers together. "I'm going to wash off this sticky caramel sauce and then I'll meet you guys upstairs. Behave yourselves until I get there!"

It would appear that Katie hadn't missed a thing.

Allie's face flamed as she gathered up their plates and carried them back to the counter, forcing herself to concentrate on the task at hand rather than the man upstairs.

"Thanks for doing that," Dulcie said as she took the stack from Allie. "Do you think you'll start moving things down today?"

"I don't know yet." But it wouldn't surprise her. Contrary to what she'd expected when she made the decision to come back to Chance, circumstances in her life felt like they were moving at the speed of light.

* * *

Damn, but that woman rattled him.

Logan carried another box of books out into the hallway, placing it on top of the stack he'd already started.

Allie only needed to turn those big, blue eyes in his direction and he had trouble thinking of what to say next because his brain morphed into a confused mush. How else could he explain what had happened downstairs?

"Lack of sleep," he muttered, tipping the big bookcase on its end to drag it out into the hallway.

Four nights on call at the firehouse and three off with no vacation breaks must finally be getting to him. That had to be it. He could come up with no other reasons for his temper to flare over some silly girl-talk between Allie and his sister.

An anxious twitch rumbled through his chest and he jerked the heavy bookcase into place.

As ridiculous as it sounded, the idea of Allie with another man — any man — set his jaw tight enough to crack nuts.

He'd already tried to convince himself it was only because Allie was his best friend's sister and he viewed her in the same light as his own little sister. It was as good a working theory as any.

"Wow. You really got a lot done up here. I'm impressed."

She stood at the top of the stairs, one hand on the banister and the other on her hip. Blood raced through his veins, pounding at his eardrums in response to her compliment.

So much for his working theory. That reaction alone was enough to prove he felt anything but brotherly when it came to Allie. He was back to square one, where he could only assume he was responding in this unusual way because he was too tired to control his reactions.

Her expression changed, her nose wrinkling as she looked from the stacks in the hallway to the stairs and back again.

"You think we're going to be able to manhandle that heavy furniture down these stairs?"

She had a point. He could certainly carry his end of the effort, but neither she nor Katie would be very useful.

"How about we stage everything you want to take downstairs out here in the hall and then I'll grab someone to help carry the heavy stuff down this evening after the girls close up shop? Sound like a plan?" He felt sure his partner at the firehouse wouldn't mind lending a hand.

Relief lit Allie's face as she nodded her agreement.

"Tanner?" Katie's head popped out behind Allie on the stairs. "If you're asking him to come help then I'm definitely coming back to watch tonight. That man has some serious muscle definition going on."

His sister only giggled when he pasted his best big-brother glare on his face. Allie appeared to be hiding her own smile as she ducked into the next room to begin her search for more usable furniture.

"You could probably get Cody to help, too," Katie offered as she followed Allie into the second room.

It was a good suggestion. As local marshal, their older brother saw it as one of his missions to help people and businesses in the community any way he could. This should certainly qualify.

"So if that's all, that's not going to be nearly enough." Katie turned as Logan entered the room. "Don't you agree, Logan?"

Rather than answer, he held up his hands as if to

defend himself from an onslaught. The way his morning was going, there was no way he was going to agree to anything without knowing what the two women were talking about.

"You're safe. Even I agree with her," Allie said on a sigh. "The books I found last night aren't anywhere near enough to start a decent lending library, let alone to set up a used-book sales section."

"You should advertise. Post a notice or something."

His sister just might be on to something.

"Katie makes a good point. Bobcat is an old friend of your grandfather's. I bet he'd be willing to run an ad for what you're trying to do. Maybe even let you ask for donations in his paper." He should have thought of that himself without Katie's suggestion.

A smile crinkled the corners of Allie's eyes as she pushed a loose strand of curls back from her face, leaving a smudge of dust on her cheek. "I remember Bobcat Baker. He still runs the newspaper here?"

"Still running the paper, all on his own. Puts a new issue out every other Monday," Logan confirmed. "You should go call him right now. He might have space to put you in the next issue."

"Maybe what you should do is call your grandfather. Let him ask Bobcat," Katie suggested. "You know how those old guys are sometimes."

"Great idea." Allie headed for the stairs, stopping only long enough to grab a box to carry down with her. "I'll go call Papa Flynn right now."

Logan let his gaze follow her progress, resisting the urge to chase after her and take the box from her hands.

"When are you going to pull yourself out of that

overdeveloped, self-imposed load of misery you wallow in?"

He jerked when his sister spoke standing right next to him. He hadn't even noticed her move across the room in his direction.

"I don't know what you're talking about."

Katie snorted her disbelief. "Like hell you don't. Don't you think it's about time you stopped living like a monk?"

"I don't live like a monk," he denied, knowing as soon as the words were out of his mouth that he should have kept quiet.

"Oh, really? Well, I can't remember the last time you brought a woman to the house to meet the family. Oh, wait!" Katie did that wide-eyed fake-innocent thing he hated so much. "I *can* remember. It was five freakin' years ago."

"Just because I don't bring anyone home doesn't mean I don't see anyone." Bringing a woman home to introduce to his family would indicate a relationship, and that wasn't going to happen. He didn't do relationships. Not anymore.

"Obviously you like Allie. You should just ask her out already and get it over with."

He shook his head, doing his best to display total disinterest in whatever else Katie said.

He *obviously* liked her?

That would never do. If he couldn't control himself any better than that around Allie, his safest course of action just might be spending less time around her.

Either that or reconsider everything he'd decided up to this point in life.

CHAPTER EIGHT

"If Harley himself hadn't called me up, I wouldn't be sitting here right now talking to you. I hope you know that."

Allie wrapped herself in a calm facade as the old man across from her leaned forward, examining her as if she were some strange exhibit in a biology class. It took everything she had not to squirm under his inspection.

No wonder he'd always been such a good reporter.

Robert "Bobcat" Baker sat back in his overstuffed chair and picked up the pipe lying by his computer keyboard. He puffed away, reminding Allie of a cartoon train she'd seen on the television as she'd walked through the living room this morning.

"I appreciate very much your making time to see me."

"I should hope so," he said. "I seem to remember you as an altogether different girl, trailing around after

Harley. You wore glasses back in those days. Big, square brown ones, as I recall. Why aren't you wearing something like that now?"

They'd been thick as Coke bottles, too, but Bobcat hadn't used that description. Maybe he'd wanted to spare her feelings.

"I had laser eye surgery a few years ago."

The process had depleted her meager savings account but, after a couple of unsuccessful tries at wearing contacts, she'd considered the expenditure well worth the price.

The old man sitting across from her tapped the bowl of his pipe against his desk and continued his inspection. "You used to be a real roly poly little thing, too, as I recall it. What happened with that?"

So much for sparing her feelings.

"I guess I grew up, Mr. Baker." She could feel her carefully neutral mask beginning to slip as her face heated. She needed to move things away from the past and confront her future plans. "Right now I'm hoping we can come to terms on an ad of some sort in your paper to help me collect books to start a lending library at The Hand of Chance Coffee Emporium."

"Mr. Baker?" He smiled around the pipe clamped between his teeth. "That was my daddy. I'm just plain ol' Bobcat. Why don't you tell me why you think this plan of yours is such a good idea for our little town."

"Because we don't have a public library in Chance and people love to read."

"Not enough people," he muttered. "So what's in it for you, girl? You can't make a living just loaning out books. And I know enough about your people to know there's not an independently wealthy Flynn in the whole bunch to support you."

He was certainly right about that.

"I'm opening a new-and-used bookstore in the coffee shop. I see the lending library as a draw. Once people have read what's available to check out, I'm hoping they'll bring books in to trade, or purchase new books."

Bobcat fumbled with his pipe as she explained her plans, but his expression was sharp and his eyes were clear. Allie had not one doubt that his "crotchety old man" act had worked on more than one story source in the past.

She steered the conversation back to the business at hand. "If you're accepting advertising, I need to know what your pricing is. My funds are limited."

"What do you know about running a bookstore?"

With a sigh, she listed her qualifications—her love of reading, her six years of working her way up in the bookstore back in Waco—only to have Bobcat veer off into another question when she finished. And yet another after she answered that one.

Twenty minutes later, she made one more attempt at getting the information she needed.

"Do you maybe have your advertising rates printed out? I could just take a look at that, if you prefer."

"Rates?" Bobcat pushed his black-rimmed glasses back up on his nose and frowned at her. "Why are you worried about my rates?"

"Because, as I mentioned a while back, I don't have much of a budget for advertising."

Again he puffed on his pipe, grinning before he spoke. "Then it's a damn lucky thing for you that I'm doing a front-page feature on your little venture instead of offering you a spot on the classified page."

"A feature?" And on the front page! She could hardly believe her luck. Everyone who got that issue of the paper would know about her business and her need for books, even if they didn't turn past page one. She couldn't have imagined such wonderful publicity.

"I'm always looking for a good human interest story. I'll stop by soon to snap a few candids for the article." Bobcat rose from his chair and extended his hand.

Allie hopped out of her chair to grab his hand and pump his arm up and down. "You can stop by whenever you want to, Bobcat. Thank you. Thank you so much."

She hurried out into the bright sunlight, more excited than she could remember being in months. She needed to thank Papa Flynn for whatever he'd said to his friend. She needed to thank Katie for suggesting that she consider some kind of advertising.

And right at the top of her list, she needed to find a way to thank Logan for suggesting that she contact Bobcat in the first place.

His image floated in her thoughts as she hurried down the street toward the coffee shop.

This could be the perfect opportunity to find a way to see more of him. She could ask him out to have lunch. Just as a way of thanking him. They could eat and chat and catch up on one another's lives.

Her steps slowed as the reality of that scenario settled over her. What was she thinking? A full meal under the scrutiny of those penetrating brown eyes?

Coffee. Maybe she'd just ask him to join her for coffee.

As much as she liked having an excuse to spend time

with him, having to coordinate talking, chewing and swallowing was still quite a task when she shared a table with that man.

CHAPTER NINE

Allie had thought she couldn't be more surprised than she had been by Bobcat's offer to do a front-page feature about her bookstore.

She'd been wrong.

Two steps into the Hand and she realized the work on her bookshop area hadn't stopped just because she hadn't been there.

One wall was lined with bookcases and another bookcase was on its way down the stairs. She recognized only one of the two moving men—Cody O'Connor, Logan's older brother. The second man had to be Logan's friend, Tanner, because he fit Katie's description of "serious muscle definition" to perfection. Even though she didn't consider him in the same league of handsome as Logan, he was certainly the kind of guy you couldn't help but let your eyes linger over.

While Logan looked like he'd been born to wear

jeans and tees, this guy looked like jeans and tees had been invented specifically with him in mind.

No wonder Katie had wanted to be here to watch him lift heavy things.

As if on cue, Katie followed the bookcase down the stairs, carrying three books. When she noticed Allie, she smiled broadly, motioning toward the man in front of her.

Logan's sister was quickly proving herself to be someone Allie could enjoy spending time around.

"Allie," Katie called, stopping beside the two men as they attempted to set the heavy bookcase upright. "You remember Cody, right? And this is Tanner Grayson. He works with Logan at the firehouse."

"Pleasure to meet you," Allie greeted, extending her hand to shake.

"Pleasure's all mine," Tanner replied, accepting her greeting with a firm handshake and a slow grin that reminded her of Matt.

Great manners, killer body, and a devastating grin? Oh yeah, she could see why Katie might be attracted to this guy.

"Allie?"

She jumped at the sound of Logan's voice behind her, pulling her hand from Tanner's grasp as if she'd been burned.

"How'd it go?" Logan asked.

"Great!" She turned to find him staring at her, his face devoid of any expression. "Bobcat was wonderful. He's going to do a feature story on the lending library and come by to take pictures and… and everything."

She forced her tongue tightly up against her teeth to stop the inane chatter rolling out of her mouth. Why she allowed herself to get so rattled by Logan was simply beyond her understanding.

"That's great. That was the last of the bookcases," he said as he set down a large box. "We've brought down all the books we could find. You'll still need to choose which other pieces you want to use."

His tone was all business; the undercurrent of banter that she'd been so sure she'd heard from him on prior occasions was completely gone.

"I really appreciate all you've done to help me." If she was ever going to be brave enough to go through with asking him, this was her best chance. "In fact, I was hoping you'd let me take you out for a coffee or something. To, you know, say thanks for all your help."

Her face burned as if on fire as she waited for him to respond, though she could already tell from his expression what his answer would be.

"Thanks for the offer, but I think I'd better take a rain check for now."

The burning on her skin only intensified.

"Okay. No problem. I'm just going to..." *Escape.* "I should go have a look through the other furniture," she said, motioning toward the stairs.

Turning away, she hurried to the staircase. She couldn't get up the stairs and down the hallway fast enough. At the last room, she pushed open the door and slipped inside, closing it behind her to lean against it.

She pressed the heels of her hands against her eyes and sucked in a great gulp of dusty air. Where this urge to cry came from, she had no idea. It certainly wasn't because Logan had rejected her invitation. She didn't care that he had turned her down. She didn't.

So what if he'd brushed her off? A guy like that had better things to do than spend all his time with his best friend's little sister. He'd already given up a whole day to haul furniture and books around for her. She'd overstepped by asking him for anything more.

Another deep breath and she felt normalcy returning.

It was the stress of all the changes in her life. The stress of having to ask people she hardly knew for favors. She was an idiot for letting any of this get to her.

Besides, she still had the newspaper story to look forward to on Monday, and the hope that maybe someone would come through with a donation of books.

* * *

"What?"

Logan glared at his sister, who simply shook her head in disbelief.

"One of us must be adopted, because I refuse to be related to such a lame-ass." Katie pointed her finger at his chest to emphasize her last word — always a bad sign.

He didn't need this from his sister. Not now. Not after the way his stomach had tightened when he'd come downstairs and seen Tanner holding Allie's hand.

"Maybe you should stick to things you actually know something about, Kat. This isn't one of those things."

As usual, his sister was undeterred. "Well, I happen to disagree. I think I know you all too well. You like her. You know you do. How much easier could it be than to have *her* ask *you* out? You'll take a rain check? Seriously? What's with that?"

Unlike guys he'd heard complain about family who

tried to ruin their relationships, he'd been cursed with a houseful of matchmakers. And the worst of them was trying to bully him right now.

The thing was, he refused to be bullied by five feet, two inches of pure busybody energy, even if she did spring from his gene pool.

"I don't need you interfering in my love life. I've been handling it on my own for a good number of years now."

"Yeah. And how's that working out for you?" Katie's hands on her hips indicated she was prepared to argue for hours.

Logan wasn't.

"My private life isn't open to discussion. Stay out of it."

"Then try being reasonable for a change." An all-too-familiar stubborn expression settled over her face.

"I am. More reasonable than you know." He squeezed her shoulder and raised his voice for the benefit of the others still standing around. "Heavy work's done, so I'm heading out. I appreciate all of you coming by to help."

In spite of what Katie thought, she simply didn't understand. The last thing he wanted was to compete with Tanner.

Not again.

The memories of the last time were still too easy to dredge up whenever his psyche chose to torment him. He wasn't putting himself—or his friendship with Tanner—through that again for any woman. Not even a woman like Allie.

CHAPTER TEN

Allie's stomach churned with nerves as she guided her car into one of the freshly painted parking spaces at The Last Chance Ski Resort. She was grateful to have her brother along for company, even if he hadn't said a single word since they'd turned off the highway onto the resort drive.

"Do I look okay?" She turned to face Matt, licking her lips one last time.

"Way better than you need to for this bunch." Matt pushed opened his door and got out, his focus on the entrance ahead of them.

"I thought you said you were going to wait in the car."

"Changed my mind. I hear they have a nice bar up here. Don't forget that fancy bread you brought along."

That she had to turn back to get the loaf of caramel apple bread her cousin had sent with her could only be attributed to her nerves over this meeting with Helen Reilly.

Either that or the uncomfortable memories assaulting her from the last time she'd been inside this building. It had been just over eight years ago, the night of her senior prom. Thinking of it even now knotted her stomach and filled her mouth with a sour taste.

She couldn't let herself get worked up over that. It was history she couldn't change. The only thing she had any control over was her own actions and how they shaped her future. And, since it was her future that was on the line, she needed to focus on this visit, not that ill-fated one from so long ago.

"Okay." Allie tried to psych herself up. "Okay. I've got this. Are you still going to be in the bar when I'm done?"

Matt shrugged. "I'll be there or out here somewhere. Don't worry about me. And relax, for God's sake. It's not like you're party crashing. The old biddy invited you up here."

"Hush!" Allie cast a furtive glance around to make sure no one could have overheard Matt. "Geez. This is important to me, Matty. I'd appreciate your making an effort to be on your best behavior."

Bobcat's article had shown up in the paper yesterday, and within an hour Allie had received her first phone call — from the matriarch of the Reilly clan, owners of The Last Chance Ski Resort. Helen had invited her to come up to the resort for a chat about the lending library Allie planned for Chance.

Matt flashed a grin and a thumbs-up as he left her standing in the middle of the enormous lobby reception area. She thought she returned his grin, but she couldn't be sure. Her mouth felt frozen even though the rest of her face felt hot enough to fry eggs.

A look around to gain her bearing and she was ready. The information desk seemed the logical place to start.

This place was seriously elegant, even more so than she remembered. They must have remodeled since the last time she was here. From its rock waterfall stretching across one entire wall, right down to the cushy carpet she crossed soundlessly, the whole place screamed *exclusive* and *expensive*.

"How may I help you, ma'am?"

Ugh. The dreaded *ma'am* again.

"I'm here to see Mrs. Reilly, but I'm not sure where to find her." At the skeptical look on the face of the young woman behind the desk, Allie added, "She's expecting me. I have an appointment. My name is Allison Flynn."

"If you'll have a seat over there, Ms. Flynn." The woman behind the counter fluttered a hand toward a circle of plush seating in the lobby. "I'll call upstairs and let her know you're here."

Allie sat down to wait, her fingers aimlessly fiddling with the ribbons tied around the foil-wrapped offering she held. This whole meeting couldn't be over soon enough to suit her.

Against her will, her eyes wandered over the lobby, tracking toward the long hallway that led to the ballroom. Beyond that was the deck and patio, a place she remembered all too vividly, her last visit there etched in her memory by the acid of her humiliation.

She jerked her gaze back to her lap, to the warm bundle she held.

Let it go, she ordered herself. It was beyond stupid to continue to hang on to those old memories and the negative feelings they carried. It happened a long time ago, to a completely different person than she was now.

She forced out a breath to calm herself and allowed her gaze to roam the lobby once more.

Big mistake.

The knots that had tightened her stomach earlier took flight, leaving a full-scale assault of butterfly-fluttering nausea in their wake. If just being here had dredged up uncomfortable memories, the two women she spotted crossing through the lobby could easily rock her world right off its foundation.

Though they obviously hadn't recognized her yet, the Jenkins sisters, Shayla and Lacey, were headed directly toward her on their way to the front exit.

Of all the unpleasant possibilities in the world she would choose to avoid right now, in this place, an encounter with her ex-best friend sat right near the top of the list.

Allie dipped her head, focusing her attention on the ribbon she wound around her finger, as if her sanity depended on it. Maybe she could dodge this bullet. Maybe, with just a little luck…

"Allie Flynn!" The squealed greeting echoed off the rock walls and reverberated in Allie's ears. "Can that really be you? It is! Lacey, look who's here!"

So much for luck.

Allie stood, squaring her shoulders as she pasted an insincere smile on her face.

Lacey nodded a greeting as they approached, her eyes darting past Allie toward the door as if she'd much rather be escaping to her freedom than stopping to chat.

Shayla, on the other hand, acted as if she had nothing better in the whole world to do but to catch up with a long-lost friend.

"I thought I saw Matt at the dedication, but I didn't realize you'd come home, too. Lord, girl. You are the last person I ever expected to see back in Chance again." Shayla studied her as if she were trying to see inside Allie's soul. "And what on Earth could bring you up here to the resort?"

How rude would it be to tell her it was none of her damn business?

Much ruder than Allie could force herself to be, no matter how much she didn't want this conversation. Fortunately, she was saved the trouble.

"Allison?" A young woman approached from the other side of the lobby, her hand extended in greeting. "I'm Chloe Collins. If you'll come with me, I'll take you to see Helen."

Allie was so grateful for the interruption, she wanted to hug Chloe. Instead, she accepted the handshake, realizing as she did who this woman was. Helen's great-granddaughter. Danny's sister. No wonder she looked familiar.

"I'm sorry, but I really have to go." Allie did her best to keep the relief she felt off her face as she made her excuses and turned away from Shayla and Lacey.

"See you around," Shayla called out as Allie and Chloe headed toward the bank of elevators.

Not if Allie could help it.

"You're Matt Flynn's little sister, right?" Chloe touched her fingers to her forehead and chuckled as soon as the words left her mouth. "Duh. 'Little sister' makes you sound like you're ten or something. I was just trying to work my way up to saying that I don't know if you remember me or not, but I remember you. I remember seeing you with Matt, that is, when he and Danny used to hang out all the time."

Allie forced herself to smile again, fighting the urge to ask the other woman exactly what she remembered. Small-town gossip lasted forever, it seemed.

"I'm so sorry about your brother." Though the words sounded empty, Allie could hardly ignore the obvious connection between them.

"Thank you. Losing Danny has been the most awful thing you can imagine for our family. But tell me about Matt. How's he doing? Is he recovering?"

"He is, thank you. It's been a long, hard fight for him, but he's up and walking. In fact, he's waiting for me in the bar."

Chloe's head snapped around, her eyes meeting Allie's. "He's here? Now?"

Allie nodded. "He came along to keep me company on the drive. I'm a little nervous about meeting with your grandmother," she admitted, not sure why she'd shared so much.

"You don't need to be. Gigi is really interested in your plans. And before I forget, thank you for coming up here to meet with her. She stays so busy it's hard for her to get away. And, to be honest, though we'd never let her hear us say it, we like to keep her close to home when we can so we can keep an eye on her." Chloe grinned like she was sharing some conspiracy. "Not that she thinks she needs anyone to keep an eye on her."

"No problem. I don't mind at all."

Allie was so grateful at the possibility of getting help, she'd gladly have gone all the way to Denver for this meeting.

Chloe led her past the bank of elevators and down a long hallway before stopping in front of an unmarked door. She pulled a key from her pocket and inserted it into a small hole, and the door slid open soundlessly to reveal a mirror-lined elevator.

The ride up was silent and smooth, as if they'd hardly moved. When they stepped out of the elevator into another hallway, it felt as if the carpet squished up around Allie's feet; it was even plusher than in the lobby.

"Here we are," Chloe announced, stopping in front of a nondescript door that looked like every other door they'd passed along the hallway.

Chloe pushed the door open to reveal the most amazing room Allie had ever seen outside the pages of a magazine.

"Wow," she murmured, hardly aware she'd spoken aloud until Chloe responded, her own voice hushed.

"Pretty impressive, right?"

Helen Reilly waited on a white leather sofa, centered in a room carpeted in white. Behind her, showcased by a wall of sparkling windows, the glory of Chance Mountain served as a focal point for the room, dwarfing everything else.

Impressive felt like a major understatement.

Helen herself fit the scene perfectly. From her thick, white hair pulled back in a classic chignon to her soft gray suit and matching heels, she belonged in this room as much as the sprays of flowers or the glass tables.

"Welcome, Allison." Helen patted the sofa next to her. "Come sit down with me, my dear, so that I can have a look at you."

With effort, Allie relaxed her shoulders and crossed the elegant room to take a seat next to her hostess.

The last time she could remember experiencing this particular attack of nerves was the day she interviewed for her job at Books on the Brazos. In a way, this was as much a job interview as that had been. On that day, she'd had to sell herself as a salesperson. Today she needed to sell her idea.

"I appreciate you inviting me up here, Mrs. Reilly. I hope I can answer all your questions."

"As well you should if our collaboration is going to pan out. Now, what's that you're clutching there in your lap?"

"Oh!" If she'd squashed Dulcie's offering, there'd be heck to pay. "A gift. This is the special at The Hand of Chance Coffee Emporium this week. Caramel apple bread."

Helen accepted the foil package and lifted it to her nose to sniff. "Still warm," she murmured approvingly. "If it tastes half as good as it smells, I'll want my expert to have a taste, too. Chloe, would you have one of the girls bring up some coffee? And ask Chef Hyatt to join us, too."

With a nod, Chloe slipped out the door and left them alone.

"So, if Robert's paper is to be believed, you plan to start a bookstore in Chance. And a lending library. Very ambitious of you considering the high failure rate of independent bookstores, particularly in this economy."

Helen paused, her eyes piercing into Allie's as if she might read her thoughts.

Allie nodded, consciously forcing herself to clasp her hands together more loosely in her lap. "Having my own bookstore has been a dream of mine for a long time and, with the help of my family, I intend to make a go of it." What other choice did she have?

"Robert's article was a lovely piece of fluff," Helen continued. "But there were a few items that weren't covered to my satisfaction. I'd like to know who'll be eligible to borrow books from you and what kinds of fees you plan to charge."

Finally, an area of discussion where Allie felt confident. She launched into her plans, stopping only when the door opened and a young woman in a uniform that clearly marked her as wait staff at the resort restaurant entered bearing a large tray, followed by a man wearing a black chef's coat.

"I'd like to introduce you to one of the country's most promising chefs, Rio Hyatt. Rio, this is Allison Flynn. Allison's brother is—" Helen stopped mid-sentence and glanced down at her hands, as if inspecting her nails for some perceived flaw, before picking up again as if she'd never stopped speaking. "Was. Allison's brother *was* my grandson's best friend. She's brought us a treat that has my mouth watering just smelling it. I'd like you to give it a try with us."

The moment of raw emotion that slipped through Helen's steely mask squeezed at Allie's heart more intensely than if she'd seen the woman in tears. Impulsively, she reached out and gently squeezed Helen's hand. The older woman laid her free hand over the top of

Allie's, and Allie found herself holding her breath, waiting for the lump in her throat to clear.

Rio's head cocked to one side as he watched them, an instant of confusion passing over his face before all emotion blanked away. "My pleasure," he said, taking the bread from Helen to unwrap it and cut slices. "Both to meet your friend and to try her aromatic treat."

Helen patted Allie's hand before letting go to accept the small plate Rio offered.

"Back to the matter at hand, my dear. In the interview, you mentioned that you planned to offer the lending library free of charge to residents of Chance. Along those lines, I have a proposition I'd like you to think about. I have a substantial personal library that I would be willing to donate to your effort, to use however you see fit, in return for your agreeing to allow the guests and employees of Last Chance unlimited use of your facilities without charge."

"I don't have to think about that, Mrs. Reilly. Absolutely, they can." Allie didn't even need the lure of free books to help her with that decision. "I want everyone in the area to utilize the lending library. And, hopefully, to decide to buy books there, too. I think reading is a fundamental—"

"Is this your creation?" Rio interrupted. "Did you bake this?"

"Not me," Allie confessed. "My cousin is the baker."

"It tastes every bit as good as it smells, doesn't it?" Helen asked. "Do you think this might be the kind of addition you were looking for?"

"Possibly," Rio answered. "Where can I find this cousin of yours?"

This reaction was exactly what Desi had said she was hoping for when she'd insisted on sending her sister's bread along with Allie.

"In town, at The Hand of Chance Coffee Emporium. She's almost always there."

"Well." Helen stood up and brushed an imaginary wrinkle from her tailored skirt. "I suppose that concludes our business, Allison. I'll have my men deliver the books to your shop within the week."

The fact that Allie had just been dismissed couldn't be clearer if her hostess had told her to get out.

"Thank you," she responded, rising to her feet to be ushered across the room and out the door.

"So weird," she murmured under her breath, grateful that the elevator door didn't require a key on this floor, as it had in the lobby below. The whole experience had been somehow unreal, like something from a badly scripted foreign movie.

Stepping out of the elevator brought a sense of relief that the interview was over—and a rush of excitement. Her visit had been a complete success. Helen Reilly was giving her books and she'd managed to get Dulcie's bread in front of the resort's head chef, just as Desi had requested, without even having to ask her hostess if that was possible.

All in all, a most excellent day.

CHAPTER ELEVEN

"What burr got up your butt?"

Tanner Grayson waited in the doorway of the firehouse kitchen, arms crossed in front of him and a frown wrinkling his face.

"Don't know what you're talking about," Logan denied, refusing to look up from the sink he scrubbed. "No problems here."

"Right," Tanner drawled. "No problems. After all these years, don't you think I know you better than that? Something's on your mind. Otherwise, why are you so determined to scrub the enamel right off that spot? Because you *don't* have any problems? I'm not buying that one. You don't want to talk about whatever it is, fine. Just tell me so. But don't try to blow me off with BS."

His friend was right about one thing: Tanner did know him well. But hopefully not *too* well. He needed to throw the man a bone to divert him, because he wasn't ready to deal with his real issue. Not quite yet.

"What did you think of Matt Flynn?"

Though it wasn't Matt driving him to this fit of cleaning, his friend had been on his mind since he'd introduced him to Tanner at lunch yesterday.

"I liked him," Tanner said, his eyes narrowing as he focused his attention on Logan. "And I agree with your suggestion. We desperately need a med tech on staff and shouldn't have any trouble convincing the powers-that-be that he's the best choice. Once he's officially discharged and can get himself certified, that is. Seems like a good guy. I think he'll fit right in here."

"And his sister? What did you think of her?"

Logan wanted to bite his tongue off as soon as the words spilled out of his mouth. Allie was the last thing he wanted to discuss with Tanner.

"His sister?" Confusion crossed Tanner's face. "You mean the little blonde over at the Hand? Okay, I get it now. So she's Matt's sister."

"Yeah," Logan answered with what he intended as a nonchalant shrug, and turned back to scrubbing the sink before realizing what he was doing. "I'd noticed you talking to her the other day when we were moving furniture over there. Just wondered what you thought of her."

Behind him Tanner chuckled, and Logan turned to find his friend had relaxed, his arms above his head, fingers grasping onto the frame above the door, a typical stance for him.

"Seems nice enough. She's kind of short, though. Can't have more than an inch or two on Katie. And a little too bookish for my tastes." Tanner's grin widened. "That what you wanted to know?"

Tanner definitely knew him too well.

"I guess it is."

"Next time you should just ask, you know? Save a lot of wear and tear on the appliances."

Logan returned his friend's grin, shaking his head. No doubt. Likely would save a lot of wear and tear on the friendship, too.

"Okay then." Tanner smacked his hand on the door frame. "I'll be out running if you need me."

Logan dried off his hands, staring out the window toward the center of town.

When had he gotten so bad at this male/female interaction stuff?

The thought made him snort. When had he ever been good at it? He'd had little enough experience. First there'd been Shayla for five years, and after that fiasco, he'd sworn off relationships completely.

Maybe it was time to consider taking another chance on women. Another chance on life. Or at the very least, one small step forward.

Standing alone in the silent firehouse, the ticking of the big clock on the wall his only company, Logan found himself with a sudden hankering for coffee.

Maybe it was time he let Allie buy him that cup after all.

Not a date, he reassured himself as he headed outside, twirling his keys around his finger. Just coffee. Now that he'd talked to Tanner and learned he wasn't interested, there was no rush to think about anything as serious as a date.

His nerve almost faltered when he pulled into a

parking spot in the lot next to the Hand, but he forced himself to turn off the motor and get out.

For cripes' sake, what was wrong with him? He had no hesitation about running into a burning building or facing down a raging forest fire, so how could the thought of having coffee with one blushing, curly-haired blonde rattle him so?

It couldn't. He wouldn't allow it to.

"Hey, Logan. How's it going?" Desi greeted him with a smile as he stepped into the coffee shop. "Want your usual coffee to go?"

"No. I... um... I came to see Allie. Is she here?" He fumbled his way through the question, wishing his face didn't feel so hot.

"She's not. Sorry. She's up at the resort this afternoon and, if all's gone well, by now she's having herself a visit with that hunk of a chef they've hired themselves."

Allie had gone up to the resort to spend the afternoon with some guy?

"Oh. I didn't realize they'd hired a new chef."

"I guess he's new. I saw him for the first time at the dedication and, trust me, I'm pretty sure I would have noticed him if he'd been around before." Desi grinned and held her hands up in front of her, her wiggling fingers setting the chains she wore, draped from her fingers to her wrist, jingling like little bells. "He is what I would describe as one total looker."

"Afternoon, Logan," Dulcie called out as she entered from the kitchen. "Can I get your usual started for you?"

"No... yes," he amended quickly. No reason to hang out here now.

Dulcie had his coffee in the cup by the time he reached the counter and pulled out his money.

"Anything to eat with that?" she asked.

"No, just the coffee, thanks." The butterflies in his stomach wouldn't do well with food raining down on them.

"I'll let Allie know you stopped by," Desi said as he opened the door to leave. "Any message in particular?"

"No message," he answered.

He'd be delivering his message in person. Spending so much time fretting over whether Tanner was interested in Allie, he'd completely neglected to consider any other men in town. But his eyes were open now.

The next time he saw Allie, he was going to collect on that coffee she'd offered. In fact, it just might be time to consider asking her out.

"What burr got up your butt?"

Tanner Grayson waited in the doorway of the firehouse kitchen, arms crossed in front of him and a frown wrinkling his face.

"Don't know what you're talking about," Logan denied, refusing to look up from the sink he scrubbed. "No problems here."

"Right," Tanner drawled. "No problems. After all these years, don't you think I know you better than that? Something's on your mind. Otherwise, why are you so determined to scrub the enamel right off that spot? Because you *don't* have any problems? I'm not buying that one. You don't want to talk about whatever it is, fine. Just tell me so. But don't try to blow me off with BS."

His friend was right about one thing: Tanner did know him well. But hopefully not *too* well. He needed to throw the man a bone to divert him, because he wasn't ready to deal with his real issue. Not quite yet.

"What did you think of Matt Flynn?"

Though it wasn't Matt driving him to this fit of cleaning, his friend had been on his mind since he'd introduced him to Tanner at lunch yesterday.

"I liked him," Tanner said, his eyes narrowing as he focused his attention on Logan. "And I agree with your suggestion. We desperately need a med tech on staff and shouldn't have any trouble convincing the powers-that-be that he's the best choice. Once he's officially discharged and can get himself certified, that is. Seems like a good guy. I think he'll fit right in here."

"And his sister? What did you think of her?"

Logan wanted to bite his tongue off as soon as the words spilled out of his mouth. Allie was the last thing he wanted to discuss with Tanner.

"His sister?" Confusion crossed Tanner's face. "You mean the little blonde over at the Hand? Okay, I get it now. So she's Matt's sister."

"Yeah," Logan answered with what he intended as a nonchalant shrug, and turned back to scrubbing the sink before realizing what he was doing. "I'd noticed you talking to her the other day when we were moving furniture over there. Just wondered what you thought of her."

Behind him Tanner chuckled, and Logan turned to find his friend had relaxed, his arms above his head, fingers grasping onto the frame above the door, a typical stance for him.

"Seems nice enough. She's kind of short, though. Can't have more than an inch or two on Katie. And a little too bookish for my tastes." Tanner's grin widened. "That what you wanted to know?"

Tanner definitely knew him too well.

"I guess it is."

"Next time you should just ask, you know? Save a lot of wear and tear on the appliances."

Logan returned his friend's grin, shaking his head. No doubt. Likely would save a lot of wear and tear on the friendship, too.

"Okay then." Tanner smacked his hand on the door frame. "I'll be out running if you need me."

Logan dried off his hands, staring out the window toward the center of town.

When had he gotten so bad at this male/female interaction stuff?

The thought made him snort. When had he ever been good at it? He'd had little enough experience. First there'd been Shayla for five years, and after that fiasco, he'd sworn off relationships completely.

Maybe it was time to consider taking another chance on women. Another chance on life. Or at the very least, one small step forward.

Standing alone in the silent firehouse, the ticking of the big clock on the wall his only company, Logan found himself with a sudden hankering for coffee.

Maybe it was time he let Allie buy him that cup after all.

Not a date, he reassured himself as he headed outside, twirling his keys around his finger. Just coffee. Now that he'd talked to Tanner and learned he wasn't interested, there was no rush to think about anything as serious as a date.

His nerve almost faltered when he pulled into a parking spot in the lot next to the Hand, but he forced himself to turn off the motor and get out.

For cripes' sake, what was wrong with him? He had no hesitation about running into a burning building or facing down a raging forest fire, so how could the thought of having coffee with one blushing, curly-haired blonde rattle him so?

It couldn't. He wouldn't allow it to.

"Hey, Logan. How's it going?" Desi greeted him with a smile as he stepped into the coffee shop. "Want your usual coffee to go?"

"No. I... um... I came to see Allie. Is she here?" He fumbled his way through the question, wishing his face didn't feel so hot.

"She's not. Sorry. She's up at the resort this afternoon and, if all's gone well, by now she's having herself a visit with that hunk of a chef they've hired themselves."

Allie had gone up to the resort to spend the afternoon with some guy?

"Oh. I didn't realize they'd hired a new chef."

"I guess he's new. I saw him for the first time at the dedication and, trust me, I'm pretty sure I would have noticed him if he'd been around before." Desi grinned and held her hands up in front of her, her wiggling fingers setting the chains she wore, draped from her fingers to her wrist, jingling like little bells. "He is what I would describe as one total looker."

"Afternoon, Logan," Dulcie called out as she entered from the kitchen. "Can I get your usual started for you?"

"No... yes," he amended quickly. No reason to hang

out here now.

Dulcie had his coffee in the cup by the time he reached the counter and pulled out his money.

"Anything to eat with that?" she asked.

"No, just the coffee, thanks." The butterflies in his stomach wouldn't do well with food raining down on them.

"I'll let Allie know you stopped by," Desi said as he opened the door to leave. "Any message in particular?"

"No message," he answered.

He'd be delivering his message in person. Spending so much time fretting over whether Tanner was interested in Allie, he'd completely neglected to consider any other men in town. But his eyes were open now.

The next time he saw Allie, he was going to collect on that coffee she'd offered. In fact, it just might be time to consider asking her out.

CHAPTER TWELVE

"You have no idea what you're getting yourself into, Dulcie. I'm the only person I know who can screw up boiling water."

Allie's hands shook as she dropped the apron over her head and tied the strings around her middle. Her cousin might think she was kidding, but this was no joke. She really couldn't cook anything that didn't come frozen out of a box and go directly into a microwave.

"You'll do just fine," Dulcie assured her. "But you don't have to do this if you don't want to."

Allie had offered to do whatever she could to help out at the Hand until her first order of books arrived and she could get down to business. She'd just never dreamed that the help her cousin would want would be in the kitchen.

"No, I'll do whatever you need me to. I really don't mind. I'm just warning you."

Dulcie laughed, grasping Allie's hand to pull her over to a long table. "We'll keep it simple. No following recipes or anything like that. I need onions sliced for the soup I'm doing for today's lunch special. It's a horrible task, but if you seriously want to help, this is what I need done most. You'll see. We'll make a cook out of you before you know it!"

It was Allie's turn to grin. She highly doubted her cousin's claim, but she was willing to give it a go. "Even a kitchen klutz like me should be able to do something as simple as slicing stuff."

Dulcie demonstrated exactly what she needed Allie to do before pulling off her plastic gloves and heading back to the front of the shop. "I'll leave the door ajar. If you need me for anything, just yell. And don't forget the gloves."

Allie nodded and pulled a pair of gloves from the big box above the work area. Once she'd slid them on her hands, she picked up the big knife and made her first cut.

Not bad. This wasn't so hard. All you needed was a sharp knife and some good concentration.

Another cut and her eyes began to sting from the fumes.

And maybe a gas mask. But no problem. It was going really well and the pile of slices had already doubled in size. All her slices were so neat and uniform, if she didn't know she'd done them herself, she'd swear someone else had been working at this spot.

Maybe she wasn't a lost cause as a cook after all. She certainly felt like she belonged here now that she'd donned her new apron and completed her official uniform—black T-shirt with a sparkly clip-on bow tie, white apron with a big black hand and *The Hand of Chance Coffee Emporium* emblazoned on it in fancy black letters. It was as if she'd found her niche in Chance.

She continued working, the background of voices a steady hum outside the open door, her pride in her accomplishment growing as the minutes passed.

"Afternoon, Tanner. The usual for you, Logan?" Dulcie's perky greeting floated in from the other room.

Logan was out there, just on the other side of the door. Had he come back to see her? Desi had told her that he'd been in asking for her yesterday afternoon.

Her stomach did a nervous little flip and she fought the desire to check her hair. But, since brushing down the flyaways with hands covered in onion goo would hardly be an improvement, she'd just keep working. If he were here to see her, someone would come get her.

Surely they would. Wouldn't they?

She leaned forward, continuing with her work, straining for any sight of him through the small crack of open space where Dulcie had left the door ajar. If she could finish the pile of onions quickly enough, it would only make sense for her to go out there to ask Dulcie what she should do next. If she hurried, she might even get out there before Logan left.

Not that she wanted to see him if he didn't want to see her. But he had asked about her yesterday.

Maybe if she worked a little faster…

A sting shot across her finger, as if a wasp had attacked, and she jerked her attention down to her workspace.

The loose plastic covering her pointer finger was slowly filling with some dark red liquid and it took her shocked brain a moment to understand that the liquid was blood. Her blood.

How bad could it be? After that initial sting, it didn't hurt at all. That had to be a good sign. Likely it was no worse than a paper cut, and she'd had plenty of those.

"Dulcie?" she called out, her voice sounding detached and robotic to her own ears.

"Just a sec, hon," her cousin called back.

Blood welled up against the slice in the plastic and dripped onto the cutting board in a dime-sized splash. Paper cuts didn't bleed like this.

"Dulcie!" Was that a ring of panic in her voice?

Allie gripped her other hand around the injury and squeezed, while blood spilled out between the fingers she'd closed around the wounded digit.

"I'll be right—" Dulcie began.

"Now!" Allie yelled, no longer wondering whether she was panicking as the feeling returned to her injured finger. Pain surged with each pounding beat of her heart and the blood continued to drip.

If she could only hold it tightly enough, maybe she could force it to stop. Until then, she just needed to keep it together. She wasn't a kid anymore. She'd outgrown those old fears.

Hadn't she?

Dulcie stepped through the door, her hands filled with plates and a cup. "What's so urgent that I can't even…" Her words died off as her eyes fixed on Allie. "Oh, criminy. What have you done?"

"I lost my focus, I guess."

Dulcie hurried over, dropping the dishes onto the edge of the counter to grab for Allie's hand. "Let me see it.

Holy crap, you're bleeding like a stuck pig. Did you slice all the way through?"

Allie was only vaguely aware of a clattering crash of china as the plates toppled onto the floor. It was all she could do to keep her grasp locked around her injured finger even as Dulcie tried to pry open her grip.

"No," she murmured, her eyes fixed on the blood pooling in her hand.

Tighter. She had to grip it tighter to make it stop. Or was it that she needed to find a pressure point? She was sure she'd read something about tending wounds in the past, but the knowledge eluded her now.

Matt would know. This was the sort of thing he dealt with all the time as an emergency medical tech. Though how he could stand all the blood was beyond her. The sight, the smell, everything about it made her brain want to shut down. This sort of thing was exactly why she worked with books, where the worst injury she was likely to see was a paper cut.

She'd never seen a paper cut that bled like this.

"You have to let go, Allie," her cousin encouraged. But she couldn't let go. The fear from so long ago, the panic she'd always experienced at the sight of blood, crawled up from somewhere deep inside, wrapping its sharp claws around her lungs and squeezing.

* * *

Logan might have consoled himself that it was only his imagination that Allie's voice sounded strained, if not for the crash of breaking dishes when Dulcie disappeared through the door to the kitchen.

He was off his seat and vaulting over the counter before he even had time to think about what he was doing.

Tanner followed so closely behind that he bumped into him when Logan came to a stop after he burst into the kitchen.

Dulcie hovered over Allie, pulling at her cousin's blood-covered hand.

"Perfect example of why we need that med tech on staff," Tanner muttered.

Logan hurried to Allie and gently nudged Dulcie aside as he took Allie's hand from the other woman.

"Open your hand, Allie," he encouraged. "I can't fix it if I can't see it."

"I can't," she murmured, her gaze fixed on the injury.

"You can," he assured her. "Just relax and let me take over. I've got this."

Her reaction concerned him as much as the pasty-white color of her face. He'd seen this sort of behavior a few times before, in fire victims. She seemed to be suffering an acute stress reaction. He needed to get a good look at her hand to see just how bad the wound really was.

"There's a guy in the dining room who's staying out at the fishing lodge," Dulcie said from her spot at the sink. "I think Desi said he told her he was a doctor of some sort."

"I'll get him and the med kit from my pickup," Tanner offered, already running for the door.

Logan led Allie over to the sink, trying to break through the shell that she seemed to be locked inside.

"Look at me. Eyes right here." He pointed to his eyes as he lifted her chin until her gaze met his. "Now, take a big breath for me and let it out slowly. Everything's going to be okay."

"It's okay," she repeated, her voice shaky and unsure.

He turned on a small stream of cold water and pulled her hands toward it, almost getting there before she tensed again, clamping her hold on the wound tighter than ever.

"Your friend said someone back here was hurt?"

"Yes!" As the stranger who'd been sitting in the corner headed toward them, relief washed over Logan, leaving in its wake an empty hole in the pit of his stomach.

He stepped aside to allow the doctor to take his spot next to Allie.

"What happened?" the doctor asked.

"She apparently cut herself," Dulcie answered. "Not sure how bad, but you should know she has this thing about blood. Has ever since we were little kids. It totally freaks her out."

"Blood-injury phobia," he murmured. "This isn't exactly my field of expertise." He turned a reassuring smile in Allie's direction.

"More your field than ours," Dulcie responded, giving him a little shove toward Allie.

"I'm Dr. Gallegos," the stranger said quietly, his full attention on Allie as if she were the only person in the room. "I'm going to take this glove off now, Allie, and I want you to give your free hand to…" He turned to Logan. "What's your name?"

"Logan," he answered, moving closer.

"Okay, Allie. Now, I want you to hold on to Logan's hand and squeeze it as tightly as you need to." Dr. Gallegos placed Allie's free hand into Logan's. "You might want to give her some support there," the doctor said.

Logan braced an arm around Allie, realizing that the

perspiration speckling her pale skin could be a warning sign that she was close to fainting. He should have recognized that on his own.

He would have if it had been happening to anyone other than Allie. For some reason, he was having difficulty maintaining the emotional detachment he needed to do his job.

"Squeeze it tightly." She murmured the doctor's words back to him, her gaze still fixed on her injury.

"I'm just going to have a look at this, Allie," the doctor said, his head bent to study her wound.

Her breathing quickened and, if possible, she appeared even paler than a second before.

"Distract her," the doctor ordered quietly as he allowed the water to wash over the injury.

Distract her? How was Logan supposed to do that? Though he held her free hand, he wasn't sure she even knew he was in the room.

"Distraction, Logan," the doctor said again, more firmly than before.

Distraction. Right.

"Allie? Allie! I'm here to collect from you. You owe me a coffee and your debt is past due."

Like a woman emerging from under water, she blinked several times and slowly turned her gaze in his direction.

"What?"

"You owe me a coffee." It was the only thing he could think to say to get her attention, and she seemed to be responding. "For all the work I did to help you. And if I can't have my coffee right now, I'm afraid I'll have to insist that you go out with me to pay me back."

"You're asking me out?"

So it seemed. Even if he hadn't consciously made the decision to take that step yet, he was committed now.

"I don't think you'll actually need stitches," the doctor interrupted. "It wouldn't be a bad thing to have them, and definitely your doctor should be the one to make that call, but, if it were me, I'd say a good butterfly bandage or tight adhesive strip could do the job just as well. All the same, you should see your regular doctor."

"We have some of those," Tanner offered, setting the first-aid kit on the counter and popping open the lid.

"There isn't a doctor in Chance," Logan said. "So, if Allie were one of your regular patients, what would you do next for her?"

"If she were one of my regular patients?" Dr. Gallegos chuckled. "I'd likely prescribe an e-collar and give her a treat for being so brave."

"An e-collar?" That was what his mom had called that lampshade thing her dog had worn after surgery. "What kind of doctor are you, anyway? A vet?"

"I did warn you this wasn't exactly my field."

Logan would have said more, but Allie chose that moment to pull her free hand from his grasp and lay her palm on the doctor's arm.

"Thank you so much, doctor."

"Rafe," he corrected. "No need to stand on formality."

"Rafe," Allie repeated, the pink returning to her cheeks as she smiled up at the doctor. "I just want you to know how much I appreciate your help. I like to think of myself as a pretty together person, but I've always had an issue with blood and needles. You should see the problems

I have when I go in for physicals."

"I can imagine them well enough. My mother struggled with the same fear."

Logan backed away from the chatting couple. The vet's total focus on Allie — which had been reassuring when he'd been treating her — irritated Logan now more than he wanted to acknowledge.

Since Allie seemed oblivious to him and anything he'd said, it would appear that fate had decided to step in and rescue him from his hasty offer.

It was as good a time as any for him to make an unnoticed exit.

"Logan!"

He'd made it all the way to the parking lot before he heard her call his name. For a split second he considered getting in his truck as if he hadn't heard her, but he couldn't quite bring himself to do that.

Allie hurried toward him, a long strip of gauze trailing down from her hand as if she'd pulled away before Tanner had finished with the bandage. Her cheeks were a bright pink when she reached his side, evidence that she'd recovered.

"Didn't you forget something?" she asked.

"I can't think of anything."

"Really?" A dazzling smile lit her face, crinkling the corners of her eyes. "Well, your memory might be awful, but mine isn't. When you asked me out, you forgot to add when and where."

So much for fate coming to his rescue.

CHAPTER THIRTEEN

"That's where we're headed."

Logan pointed down the slope toward a little lake nestled in the most beautiful valley Allie could remember having seen in her whole life. With only the gentlest of urging from her, the big horse she rode followed Logan's mount down the trail.

Though she'd love to give herself a major pat on the back for making this moment happen, she knew it all had to be the work of chance. Had she not been high on whatever endorphins flooded her system after her freak-out, she'd never have been brave enough to follow Logan when he left the coffee shop and insist he make good on his offer.

It was as if this day were meant to be.

No matter. She was thankful that she had taken the risk. Maybe this wonderful day was a sign that she should try being assertive more often.

Logan's invitation turned out to be for a picnic, and he'd promised to take her someplace very special. He certainly had delivered on that promise.

"Not a bad spot for a first date, right?" he asked as her horse pulled even with his.

"It is gorgeous here, but do you really think this still counts as a first date?"

He'd taken her to coffee twice since that eventful day at the Hand, and they'd even shared a table at the Main Street Café for lunch yesterday.

"Sure it does. First official date, anyway," he assured her before allowing his horse to amble into the valley at a slow walk.

They rode in a comfortable silence, which allowed Allie time to appreciate the beauty of their destination. The only structure she saw in the entire valley was a good-sized lean-to at the edge of a stand of trees, and that was where they appeared to be heading now.

Logan drew his mount to a stop next to the shed and dismounted. When he lifted his arms to help Allie down from the horse she rode, her heart thudded in her chest. She placed her hands on his shoulders and he lowered her to the ground; though his grasp remained on her waist after her feet touched the earth, their eyes locked on one another.

For a split second, Allie was transported back to that night in the Hand, when they'd stood like this, face to face, just before Logan had dipped his head as if to claim her lips, their hearts racing together, beating as one in a moment of sheer—

"I'd better see to the horses," he murmured, crashing her imagination back to reality as he stepped away from her.

She accepted the blanket he handed her and hurried toward the water, anxious to put some distance between them. Anxious to give herself a moment to straighten out her thoughts.

How stupid of her. How utterly, ridiculously stupid of her to think he was going to try to kiss her. To actually expect it! The last time they'd been that close to a kiss had obviously been a total fluke. The two of them, alone in the dark, late at night, their emotions already off kilter. She was just an idiot for letting herself think that almost-kiss was any more than a one-time thing.

Still, it wasn't all her fault. She couldn't very well control the fact that Logan had always had the ability to set her hormones raging with nothing more than a simple look. Of course, that wasn't his fault either. He hardly knew her. Just because she'd been fantasizing about him for half her life didn't mean he had any similar feelings about her. In fact, he'd said himself, not ten minutes ago, that he considered this their first date.

She shook out the blanket before spreading it over the ground, under a big shade tree, close to the water. With several deep breaths in and out, she concentrated on relaxing. It would be so nice to be able to turn off her inner critic, even if only for one day. She wanted to simply enjoy this wonderful scenery, the comforting noises of nature all around her, the beauty of this moment, all without analyzing and second-guessing every single move either of them made.

Logan had chosen a perfect spot for their picnic. The water babbled next to them and a few puffy clouds gathered on the horizon. This was the sort of place an artist would give anything to find.

By the time Logan joined her, she'd managed to get her frazzled emotions back under control. He placed the large wicker basket he'd brought in the center of the blanket and sat down next to her.

"It appears that my location for the picnic is a winner. Let's see how much I can impress you with the food I brought."

The first thing Logan pulled out of the basket was a bottle of wine, followed by two crystal glasses.

"Wow."

Allie leaned forward, curious to see what he'd pull out next. A loaf of bread wrapped in two lacy napkins. She looked up at him and back to the basket. The contents so far seemed... not at all what she would have expected a guy like Logan to pack for a picnic.

When he opened a plastic container to reveal crustless cucumber and cream cheese sandwiches cut in little diamond shapes, her suspicions doubled.

Logan simply stared down at the contents of the plastic container, shaking his head. "You have to give my sister credit. Kat doesn't do anything halfway."

"Ah ha!" Allie accused, laughing as she tapped a finger to Logan's chest. "I knew it. I knew you wouldn't have packed food like that for lunch."

He favored her with one of those smiles that sent shivers down her whole body. "Remember now, in my defense, I never actually claimed to have made any of this myself. I only said I brought it."

He could have claimed anything he wanted as long as he continued to smile at her that way. She wouldn't mind at all.

"Thank God," he muttered, setting another container out on the blanket and gifting her with another grin. "Fried chicken. I was starting to worry that we might have to cut the picnic short to go find some real food."

By the time he'd emptied the basket, it was more than apparent that food wouldn't be an issue. Katie had prepared for them a feast that could easily feed several people.

After eating, Allie sipped her wine and leaned back on one elbow. The whole day had been picture perfect, from the moment Logan had picked her up, to the horses saddled and waiting for them when they arrived at his family's ranch, right down to the food and the location of their picnic. She couldn't have found a better setting in any book she'd ever read.

"It's so peaceful here," she said, turning to find Logan watching her. "It's like a whole different world."

"It is," he agreed. "I think it might be my favorite place on the whole ranch. My grandpa's favorite, too. He loved it so much, he brought my Nana Dot down here to this very spot to propose to her."

"How perfect," Allie whispered.

Sitting in the shade of the big stand of trees, with the mountains all around them and the clear stream bubbling down to fill the lake in front of them, it just might be the most romantic place she could imagine.

"As a matter of fact," Logan continued, "he planted every single one of those trees to represent their lives together. He started with one to celebrate her saying yes, and then kept adding trees for each anniversary and every kid and grandkid they had."

"Considering how your grandparents felt about this

area, I'm surprised they didn't build their home down here."

"He actually tried early on." Logan stood and held out a hand to her. "Come on, I'll show you where."

Allie accepted his hand, and somehow, as they made their way through the stand of trees, past stone tables and benches, and out into the grassy valley beyond, she simply continued to hold on.

His palm felt warm against hers, the pads of his fingers rough from working. For one silly moment she even allowed herself to imagine that their hands fit together as if they'd been sculpted to be together.

Her imagination was back in overdrive. She'd definitely read one too many love stories.

"Here." He pointed to the ground with his free hand, making no attempt to pull his other hand away from hers. "If you look closely, you can see the outline of the stones where he started the foundation."

Still holding Logan's hand, Allie led him to the center of the small, faint square and allowed her eyes to wander out over the landscape. What a view! No wonder J. J. O'Connor had chosen this setting for his home.

"It's perfect. I can so imagine sitting here on a porch, lulled by the babble of that stream, sipping my morning coffee. Why didn't he finish building it?"

Logan chuckled and squeezed her hand. "That's easy. Because in the spring, after a snow-heavy winter, that stream turns into a rushing river and the whole of this flat valley is waterlogged for days. You'd need to be wearing hip waders while you sat on the porch sipping coffee. Assuming your porch hadn't washed away, that is."

"Okay, then," she conceded. "That sounds like a

pretty valid reason for not continuing to build here. But what a shame."

"Yeah, it was just too unpredictable to try for anything permanent here. But it's also too great a spot to abandon completely. That's why Grandpa decided to plant his trees here and scatter the benches and tables. Sort of his version of an outdoor, waterproof family room. Even in the summer, the quick afternoon storms that roll in can swell that stream if it rains hard enough."

As if on cue, thunder rumbled in the distance as the gathering clouds rolled toward them.

"Speaking of storms." Logan gave her hand another squeeze and pulled her back toward the trees. "Guess we'd better get packed up if we don't want to get caught in one. I was concerned this would happen if we stayed too long."

There was nothing that quite matched a summer storm in the Rockies. When Allie had first moved to Texas, it had caught her by surprise how long it could take an approaching storm to reach her. But here in the mountains, storms moved fast and the speed with which this storm approached left no doubt as to where she was. By the time they reached their blanket, the first fat drops of rain had begun to splatter down.

Thunder shook the ground and Logan grabbed the blanket, scattering the remains of their lunch.

"Leave that stuff!" he ordered, and grabbed her hand as he turned to run.

He urged her toward the shed, their steps picking up speed as lightning crackled across the sky.

"We'll wait it out in here," he said as he spread the blanket over a bale of hay at the back of the shed.

He sat down and held out his hand in invitation for

her to join him on the makeshift seat.

A loud clap of thunder sent her scampering to his side. His arm slipped protectively around her shoulders and they huddled together, watching the storm that raged outside. In spite of the intensity of the weather, she felt safe here next to Logan.

Alone, together, his arm snug around her, it was the fulfillment of a dream she'd harbored for as long as she could remember. If only this interlude could last forever. If only she could turn off her brain and simply exist in this one perfect moment. Simply accept and enjoy it for whatever it turned out to be.

But even as the wish skittered through her mind, Allie knew she had never been good at turning off her brain. She was now, as always, her own worst enemy. Already her inner harpy dragged the reality of the moment to the forefront of her thoughts to intrude on her enjoyment.

The bliss she felt evaporated completely as a trickle of water rolled down her forehead and into her eye, its sting demanding her attention. She wiped it away, realizing as she did just how soaked they'd gotten in their race to the shed.

Her hair was dripping wet. A glance down confirmed that her white shirt had turned all but transparent as the rain had plastered it to her skin. And her face? The dark brown smudge on her hand where she'd wiped her eye left no doubt that her mascara was likely smeared everywhere on her face but where it belonged.

If anything, she must resemble a half-naked, waterlogged raccoon.

Picturing that description, Allie fought the urge to

giggle as best she could, but the whole situation struck her as beyond ridiculous. Here she was, cowering in a horse shed with the man of her dreams, waiting for some of the most spectacular lightning she'd seen in years to pass them by. The rain beat down in great, heaving sheets, hammering against the tin roof like a million tiny fists. Thunder reverberated in the ground under her feet and rumbled up in her chest. And yet, in spite of the best Mother Nature had to throw at them, she still managed to focus her worry on how awful she must look.

All too soon, the giggle refused to be stifled any longer.

"You okay?" Logan asked, his arm tightening around her shoulders as he looked down at her.

"I'm fine. As long as you don't count being an idiot as a problem."

"You're not an idiot."

"No? Then what would you call someone sitting here in the middle of a storm like this, stressing over how awful she looks?"

"Normally I'd call that person a typical female." With his free hand, Logan stroked a thumb and forefinger over her chin. "But in your case, I'd have to make an exception."

"What kind of an exception?"

Her breath caught in her throat when her eyes met his, and she felt herself transfixed, unable to break the connection between them.

"In your case," he said, his voice low and husky as his thumb traced a path over her lower lip, "I'd call that person beautiful."

"Beautiful?"

She echoed his compliment on a barely audible breath, unable to remember anyone ever calling her beautiful.

Electricity tingled through her body, but it had nothing to do with the lightning that streaked across the sky. His head dipped closer and his eyes held hers as if he'd ensnared her in some ancient magic spell. She held her breath, not even daring to blink for fear any movement on her part would break the spell that had fallen over them.

Was he going to kiss her, just as he had in every one of her dreams?

His lips brushed against hers, and she had her answer.

It was like that night on the stairs at the Hand, when she'd thought he was going to kiss her. It was like every dream, every fantasy she'd ever had, all rolled into one.

Only better. Much, much better, because, this time, his kiss was real. It lingered, his lips barely touching hers, his warm breath mixing with hers until she didn't know which of them breathed in or out.

Her imagination, even at its best, had never been half this good. This was the most erotic thing she'd ever experienced in her whole life and he was hardly even touching her.

His breath feathered over her cheek as his lips hovered a hair's distance above her skin, tracing a path to her ear.

"It would be so easy," he whispered.

Easy?

She should put a stop to this now. It would be simple enough to do. Just push him away and move to the other side of the shed.

Easy?

She was anything but easy. She should end this now and show him he was wrong.

Only problem was, she'd waited for this moment for most of her life. She didn't want him to stop. Not now that he was this close.

His lips brushed against her neck and her breath caught in a little gasp as his feathered touch tingled through every fiber of her body. Before she knew it, her fingers had twined themselves in his hair as if they operated independently from her conscious thought.

"So easy," he murmured again, just before his teeth grazed her earlobe.

She shifted toward him, her mouth seeking his.

The contact was exquisite. His lips, warm and tender, skimmed over hers in a slow tease, touching and withdrawing until she felt as if she could wait no longer.

She didn't care anymore. Didn't care what he thought of her. Didn't care who knew what they were doing. Didn't care what anyone in the entire world thought of either one of them. All that mattered was Logan and this moment with him.

"Logan? Allie?" A woman's voice called to them, drawing closer. "You guys up here?"

Katie!

Recognition pierced through Allie's need, shattering the lovely haze of desire that had cocooned them. They jerked away from one another and Logan was on his feet, backing away, putting distance between them.

A minute later, his sister's head appeared around the edge of the shed.

"Oh, good, you guys are in here. I hoped you would be considering how bad that storm was. That's why we brought the truck up here to check on you guys."

"We?" Logan turned his head toward his sister for the first time since her arrival.

"Yeah, we. Look who finally got home this afternoon." Katie's face broke into a big grin as her companion joined her.

Ryan O'Connor.

Allie's stomach felt as if it rolled, sending a weak-in-the-knees tingle through her whole body as the humiliation of her last meeting with Logan's brother marched front and center into her memory. That was what she got for tempting fate by declaring how little she cared for what anyone thought of her or her actions.

Obviously, she'd been wrong. Obviously, she did care.

She only wished she didn't.

* * *

It would be so easy…

This might be the first time in the history of his family when Logan actually was grateful to have his younger siblings interrupt him on a date.

Allie was a whole different level of woman for him. It would be so easy — much too easy — to allow himself to slip over the edge of just having fun, to pitch into the dangerous waters of a real relationship.

Without their even knowing it, Ryan and Katie had thrown him the life preserver he'd so desperately needed at the exact moment he'd needed it.

"Ryan! About time you came home."

He kept his back to his siblings, grabbing up the blanket he and Allie had sat on as soon as she stood up. He shook it out and fumbled with folding it up, stalling, praying the bulge in his pants would subside before anyone noticed.

A glance in Allie's direction confirmed that she looked as shell-shocked as he felt. Her skin blossomed with a dark, mottled red blush, as her fair skin frequently did. Whether that physical response was to what they'd been doing just before his brother and sister arrived or to Ryan's presence, he couldn't be sure.

She and Ryan had been an item in high school, at least according to Katie. And as annoying as his younger sister could be at times, she was rarely wrong when it came to town gossip, especially when that gossip concerned her own family members.

"It's been a long time, Allie. How have you been?"

Ryan's voice, always calm and quiet, held no hint of reproach. Maybe, if there had been something between him and Allie, it ended without any bad feelings.

"Fine," she answered, her tone clipped and her skin staining an even darker red. "And you?"

Then again, maybe not, based on her response.

"Did you hear me?" Katie asked, tugging on the back of his shirt, pulling his attention away from whatever his brother replied. "Several of the streams are swollen as a result of that downpour and there are more clouds rolling in. I think you guys should ride back to the house in the truck with us."

Logan nodded his agreement. Her suggestion did seem the safest choice. The horses they'd ridden were trained to follow along behind them and, after all these years, likely knew their way home as well as he did.

"I need to grab our lunch basket. We left it down by the water."

Katie shook her head. "If it was by the water, it's gone. The rain did its usual number on the lake out there. Ry and I had to hike in from the crest for fear of getting the truck stuck down here."

That explained why he hadn't heard the truck arrive. Well, that and his complete preoccupation with Allie at the time.

Meanwhile, the source of his earlier distraction stood near the back of the shed, her arms wrapped around herself, looking about as miserable as any one woman could.

"You okay?" he asked, knowing it was a stupid question even as the words left his mouth. Just looking at her confirmed that she wasn't okay.

"Absolutely," she lied. "I'm fine."

She said she was fine, but everything else about her told him another story.

"And you're okay with riding back up to the house in the truck?"

"Mmm-hmm," she agreed, her eyes fixed on her feet as she nodded. "No problem."

Right. No problem. Logan would be willing to bet serious money that Allie couldn't tell a lie if her life depended on it. At the very least, she couldn't do it convincingly.

He'd also be willing to bet that whatever was bothering her was more than simply what had passed between the two of them before they'd been interrupted. It had something to do with his brother.

Not that what had happened between her and Ryan all those years ago mattered. It didn't. Not really. Not to him.

He was just curious, that was all.

He slipped an arm around her shoulder and gave her a little hug. "So, I'm guessing as first dates go, this one has kind of bottomed out at this point, right?"

Her wavering smile left no doubt as to her answer.

"I'll make it up to you," he said. "I promise. The next time will be better."

"There'll be a next time?" she asked, meeting his gaze at last.

"Absolutely," he vowed, echoing her word choice back to her.

He slid his hand down her arm to catch her hand and lead her out of the shed and toward the slope where his brother and sister were already making their way back to the waiting truck.

In spite of the way she made him feel, in spite of how easy it would be to let his emotions get too involved, he couldn't very well end things like this. There was too much unfinished business hanging between them.

Absolutely, there would be a next time.

CHAPTER FOURTEEN

Allie and her mother waited in silence at the gate until her grandparents' truck turned the corner and disappeared. Matt hadn't been gone for five minutes and already everything seemed emptier without him here.

Maybe it only felt that way because they knew it would be months before they saw him again. Not even the knowledge that the next time he came home, he would be out of the military and finished with his EMT training helped to lighten the mood.

"You want me to fix you some lunch?" Allie laughed out loud at the look of apprehension on her mother's face and hurried to add, "Don't worry. We still have leftovers from the dinner Mama Odie cooked last night."

"Was I that obvious?" Susie shook her head, reaching out to clasp her daughter's hand. "I'm sorry, sweetie. I know you try and I do appreciate it. I'm just not real hungry right now. I think I might get comfy out on the back patio with a book. Take my mind off things for a while."

Allie couldn't blame her mother. Not for the unintended insult to her cooking abilities and not for wanting to escape in a book. She wouldn't mind doing that herself.

With Susie settled out back, Allie went inside to fix them both glasses of tea. By the time she returned, both her mother and Grainger, curled up at Susie's side, were sound asleep.

Quietly, Allie went back inside. Her mother needed the rest more than she needed the tea.

Since her grandparents had volunteered to take Matt to Denver to catch his flight, she'd taken the day off from the coffee shop to keep an eye on her mother. Susie had seemed to be doing much better for the last couple of weeks, which fit right in line with some of the things Allie had learned about chronic fatigue syndrome and stress. With Matt leaving, she wasn't sure how her mother would respond and she wanted to make sure someone was around to keep an eye on things, just in case.

While her mom napped, the next couple of hours were pretty much her own to do with as she pleased. She wasn't exactly sure what to do with herself since these moments came along so rarely.

Snagging a book off her keeper shelf, Allie strolled out to the front porch and climbed into the big wooden swing that hung from the eaves. This had always been one of her favorite spots to read.

Birds chirped in the tree out front and a soft, warm breeze wafted over her, carrying the scent of flowers blooming in the beds beside the porch. In spite of seeing

Matt off, this particular Sunday was shaping up to be a good one.

She hadn't read more than a couple of pages when the sound of a vehicle in the distance drew her attention. A pickup. Surely her grandparents hadn't returned before getting Matt to Denver.

She swung her legs to the ground and sat up, straining for a better look.

Not her grandparents, but definitely a pickup she recognized.

Logan pulled his truck to a stop in her drive and stepped out, heading up toward the porch where she sat.

Her body did that excited little internal shudder thing it always did when she saw him coming her way. So ridiculous. He hadn't even called her in the almost two weeks since they'd gone on their one official date, which should tell her something pretty important about what he thought of her.

That or Ryan had reminded him of her high school indiscretion. Either way, she needed to get him out of her system. There was nothing worse than liking a guy who didn't like you back, unless maybe it was a guy who told you he'd call and then didn't.

Now if she could just get her body on board with what her brain already knew when it came to the subject of Logan O'Connor.

"You missed Matt," she called out, rising to lean against the wooden post by the steps. "They left about half an hour ago."

Maybe she'd get lucky and he'd turn that beautiful jean-covered butt right back around and leave.

"I didn't come to see Matt. We said our good-byes

on the phone yesterday."

What was that old song about bad luck being the only luck somebody had? That should be her theme song lately.

"Okay, then. What can I do for you?"

He stopped about four feet away from where she stood, a lazy grin lifting the corners of his mouth. Lord, but he had to know how good he looked when he did that.

"Seems to me I owe you a makeup date."

After two weeks, what was this? Guilty conscience? Had Matt said something to him when they'd talked? The very idea made her stomach tighten in an uncomfortable little knot.

"You don't owe me anything. You're not obligated."

"That's not the way I remember it." The grin grew larger. "Official date number one was rudely interrupted, so I promised a better date number two. I would have come by sooner but we had our first fire of the season over in Vaca Valley so I didn't have much in the way of free time. I just got back home last night."

She'd heard someone in the coffee shop mention the fire and she'd seen the smoke hanging in the distance but, somehow, she'd just never connected it to Logan.

"I didn't realize you were gone." How lame did that sound? "That you got called out to other places, I mean. To fight fires."

"Ouch." He clasped a hand to his chest in mock pain. "Apparently, date number one not only didn't make a good impression, it didn't make much of an impression at all if you didn't even realize I'd left town. All the more reason to give me a chance with date number two. I'm thinking a nice dinner. Anywhere you choose. What do you say?"

While her brain and her body might be in constant disagreement when it came to Logan, one thing all her body parts agreed on was that you didn't turn down an invitation from a man who looked as good as he did. Especially not when he had such a good excuse for ignoring her for the past two weeks.

"I say yes. When?"

"Friday night, if that works for you. Where do you want to go?"

"Golddiggers?"

Since it was the only nice restaurant in town, it was the only sensible choice. And yet, a frown crossed Logan's face at the mention of the place.

"You sure about that? It can get pretty rowdy there on Friday night. I was thinking you might like to try the restaurant up at the resort. I hear their new chef is outstanding."

"No." Allie didn't even need to think about that one. No way. Not the resort. Too many bad memories associated with a fancy night out at that place. "The twins told me that they have live music at Golddiggers on Friday nights. I think it would be fun, don't you?"

"Sure." He shrugged one shoulder carelessly, but the impish grin he'd worn earlier had disappeared. "If that's what you want, Golddiggers it is. I'll pick you up at seven, if that's good for you?"

"Perfect. Friday at seven it is."

Allie felt as giddy as the proverbial schoolgirl as she watched Logan walk back to his truck and drive away, her thoughts already scattering to what she'd wear when she saw him next.

Five whole days to wait until Friday. It felt like an eternity.

* * *

Only five days until Friday. Already Logan could feel the time whizzing away from him at lightning speed. The next five days couldn't go by slowly enough to suit him.

Allie's choosing Golddiggers had caught him completely off guard. He hadn't set foot in that place even one time in the last two years. Not since the owner had died and left it all to his young wife, Shayla Jenkins.

Shayla Jenkins-Gold, he corrected himself. Her marriage to Harvey Gold had been the talk of Chance for a short time, surprising everybody.

Everybody but Logan. After the deceitful things she'd done while they were engaged, nothing she did could surprise him. Not even marrying a man fifty-five years her senior.

Old Harvey had named his restaurant and bar to honor the men who had founded Chance, miners who'd braved the Colorado wilderness to seek their fortune at the end of a pick and shovel. It was just blind, twisted coincidence that the name perfectly suited the new owner.

After the lies and the cheating that had ended his engagement to Shayla, Logan had sworn to avoid two things for the rest of his life: serious relationships and any encounter with Shayla Jenkins.

It hadn't been easy while living in a town as small as Chance, but he'd managed to avoid her for the last five years, and when she took over Golddiggers after Harvey's death, he'd avoided that hot spot too.

All that hard-won avoidance was coming to an end in

five short days. He had little hope of getting in and out on a Friday night without running into the queen of Golddiggers herself.

He pulled into the fire station parking lot and turned off the ignition, staring into his own past a few minutes longer before getting out and going inside.

Maybe it was just as well. Maybe it was time to let the past remain in the past.

"What the hell are you doing back here today?" Tanner tossed the kettlebell he'd been working out with to the floor and snagged a towel off the bench to wipe his face. "I thought you said all you wanted to do was sleep until it was time for your shift to start tomorrow. What's the matter, you miss me?"

"Yeah, that's it," Logan agreed, grinning as he walked into the kitchen and pulled a bottle of juice from the fridge. "I missed you."

In truth, Logan wasn't sure what he was doing there. Maybe he was just seeking out a good friend because he couldn't stand the idea of going home to an empty house with all these dark memories freshly exhumed.

He came back out to the area of the station garage they'd turned into their own personal gym and slouched down on the bench next to Tanner's abandoned towel.

His friend had moved on to the free weights.

"I stopped by Allie's place on the way home." He kept his tone light, casual, a simple opening to the conversation he needed.

"Oh yeah?" Tanner grunted with one last lift and let the weights drop to the ground. "You know, last time I checked, the Flynn place was the exact opposite direction from your way home. So what gives?"

Busted. It was hard to ease your way into a conversation with someone as observant as Tanner. Or as outspoken.

"I asked her out. For dinner on Friday night. Anywhere she wanted to go."

Tanner wiped his hands on the towel and crossed his arms in front of him. "And she said?"

"Yes."

"Then I don't understand what's your—" A look passed over Tanner's face as he balled up the towel and threw it against the wall. "Hell's bells. Don't even tell me. Let me guess. She picked Golddiggers, didn't she?"

Logan nodded, downing the last swallow of juice before tossing the bottle into the trash. "Bingo."

"So…" Tanner chuckled and drew out the word as if something else had just popped into his mind. "Does this mean that you're going to start pulling your weight around here when it comes time for fire inspections? No more avoiding the biggest firetrap in town?"

Logan hadn't even considered that. He hadn't allowed his thoughts to wander that far into the future. He chose to deflect rather than commit.

"Golddiggers is only one of the biggest firetraps. Chance is full of them."

"You got to let it go, man. It was a long time ago. Water way under the bridge. You need to get on with your life." Tanner watched him as if he expected some imminent breakdown.

"Yeah, I know." Logan stood and headed toward the door. Somehow, just saying it out loud to someone who knew the whole history made it feel a little better. "Too bad you're working tonight, Tan. I could use someone to have a beer with me."

"The story of our lives, right?" Tanner grinned, already reaching for the next set of weights. "It'll be good to get a third man in the rotation."

It would at that.

Logan headed back out into the fresh air. This time when he left the station, he was going straight home. Straight home and straight to bed. After seven days battling that wildfire, he felt like he could sleep for a week.

As Tanner had said, having Matt join them when he finished up his EMT training would be excellent. Just one more body to man the phones and hold down the fort would make all the difference in the world.

Too bad the time between then and now wouldn't go half as quickly as he expected the next five days to pass.

CHAPTER FIFTEEN

If anything, her high heels had grown even more uncomfortable after sitting in the closet for the past month. Apparently her feet were completely out of practice when it came to fancy shoes.

Allie turned this way and that in front of the long mirror, adjusting her dress and tucking the front together to hide her bra one more time.

Where had she put that tape, anyway? Maybe she should just change into something else. She'd worn this outfit the day of the community center dedication so Logan had already seen it.

But it was her best. She'd paid more for this than for any dress she'd ever bought just because it looked better on her than anything else she'd ever owned. And the day of the dedication, she'd worn a light sweater to cover up the skin-baring spaghetti straps and the plunge of the neckline.

No, this was what she wanted to wear tonight.

The tape must be in her underwear drawer. She was positive that was where she'd put it. It had to be there. Of course, she'd been positive about the last five places she'd looked, too.

This time she was right.

"Process of elimination," she muttered. When you run out of places, it has to be in the last place you look.

One strategic strip of tape and her wardrobe malfunction worries were over. Thank goodness she'd found it. The last thing she needed was to have the whole town see her half-naked.

The faint notes of the doorbell sounded and she gave herself one last quick examination in the mirror. Not bad. Not bad at all.

Logan waited by the front door, chatting with her mother. He stopped speaking mid-sentence when she walked into the room, a silly grin spreading over his face.

That expression alone was worth the fuss she'd gone to over wearing this dress tonight.

"You look great."

His words tickled down her spine and lodged somewhere near her heart. They must have, because her heart started beating a mile a minute.

"Thanks. You clean up pretty good yourself."

Did he ever! Here she'd spent all this time thinking the world had invented jeans and black T-shirts especially for Logan, only to find that he looked equally good in a tie and sports coat.

"We'd better get going. Our reservation is for seven fifteen."

"Great. I'm all ready." Allie gave her mother a quick

kiss on the cheek. "Dulcie is bringing your dinner over any minute now and she'll stay here until I get home. You need anything else before I go?"

"I'm fine. You kiddos go ahead and take off. Enjoy your evening." Susie settled into her chair in front of the television. "You two behave yourselves, you hear?" she added over her shoulder.

Allie walked toward Logan's truck, her face on fire from her mother's caution. After all these years of living on her own, she hadn't expected her mother to treat her as if she were a teenager again. More than that, she hadn't expected to feel like one.

"Your mom's sweet," Logan said, stepping in front of her to open the passenger-side door. "Worrying about you, and all."

So much for any hope that he might have missed her mother's admonition.

"Sorry about that. I guess it's hard for her to think of me in terms of being an adult now."

"No apology necessary. She's your mom. They're all like that. You'll always be her little girl, even when you're fifty. That's one of the awesome things about moms. They never give up on you."

He grinned again, just before placing one hand on her back and another on her arm to assist her into the pickup.

Her skin tingled where he touched her and her brain sizzled with his nearness, setting her heart pounding all over again. This close, the light scent of his aftershave wafted over her and she knew, without a doubt, had he not been supporting her, she would have stumbled.

It was the shoes. At least, that was what she chose to

blame it on.

She had a moment to collect herself while he made his way around to the driver's door and joined her inside the cab of the truck.

"Seat belt," he reminded as he turned the key in the ignition.

Good Lord. She was so frazzled she hadn't even thought about her seat belt. Maybe her mother wasn't so far off base in treating her like an inexperienced teen.

The drive to the restaurant passed in silence, leaving Allie only a short time to wonder whether Logan might be struggling as she was to find something to say.

The parking lot at Golddiggers appeared to be only about three-quarters filled, but Logan passed it by and turned at the corner heading down Miner Road. A few blocks down, he pulled the pickup to a stop in front of the abandoned assay building and stared out the window as the vehicle idled.

"Why are we parking here?"

A walk of this distance wouldn't be her first choice. Nor her second. Not in these shoes.

Another full minute passed before he unfastened his seat belt and turned toward her. "There's been something weighing on my mind ever since that day out at the ranch. I don't think I can sit through dinner with you until I've dealt with it."

This was it. Ryan had reminded him of how devious she'd been in dating him to get to his brother. It was so far in the past, it shouldn't matter anymore, but it did. It must. And if there was any chance for them even as friends, she needed to face her past.

"Then you'd best get that weight off your mind

now."

"I hoped you'd say something like that."

She steeled herself for whatever he might say next, but he didn't say anything. Instead, he lifted the console blocking the seat between them and slid toward her. Without a word, he slipped a hand under her hair and his warm fingers caressed her neck. Gently, he guided her forward until his lips met hers.

The unexpected kiss was exquisite. His touch was warm and caressing, and when his tongue traced the contour of her lower lip, it stole her breath and curled her toes. Only the seat belt snapping tight across her chest kept her from launching herself at him and defying her mother's final warning.

She opened her eyes when he lifted his lips from hers, not remembering when she'd closed them.

"Good," he said, a satisfied grin settling on his face as he slid back over behind the steering wheel. "I can enjoy my evening now that I have that out of the way. You can't imagine how often I've thought of doing that for the last two weeks."

Oh, yes, she could imagine. Two weeks? She could tell him a thing or two. Try fantasizing that move for half your life.

She still hadn't quite recovered when they pulled into the parking lot and he opened her door for her. She fumbled with her seat belt for a moment, stopping when he reached in to help her.

She climbed down from the truck, his hands around her waist, his body blocking her from moving anywhere except closer to him.

"Are you okay with what happened back there? Are

you upset?" he asked, his head dipping close to hers as he spoke.

"Not at all upset," she answered, her gaze meeting his. "Surprised, I guess, more than anything."

"Good surprised or bad surprised?" His words grazed over her skin as he all but whispered his question into her ear.

Though the night was unseasonably warm, chill bumps danced across her skin.

"Good surprised," she whispered in return. "Very good surprised."

"Excellent," he said, backing away and taking her hand to lead her toward the entrance of the restaurant.

A riot of noise assaulted them when Logan held open the door. But neither the crowd of people yelling at the band or even the loud music itself had any chance of denting the happy bubble in which she floated. Nothing could puncture this perfect moment.

Nothing except maybe a leather-clad Shayla Jenkins-Gold slithering toward them, her sultry gaze firmly fixed on Logan like some predator homing in on its dinner.

It wasn't until she was within touching range that Allie realized the woman held two menus in her hands. Too bad she didn't hold them a little higher so that they might cover the over-ample cleavage that threatened to spill out through the open buttons on her black silk shirt.

"Well, well," Shayla purred, lifting a hand to stroke Logan's arm. "Look who's finally decided to make an appearance at my place. I almost didn't believe it when I saw your name on the reservation list for tonight. Let me show you to your table."

Her place?

Allie's bubble burst with a huge, uncomfortable pop. Maybe that was why Logan had seemed reluctant to come here. She could kick herself now for having insisted.

Logan stepped away from Shayla's touch and fit his arm around Allie's waist. His movement put her squarely in between Logan and their hostess.

Shayla led them to a table in the dining room and handed over the menus she carried before positioning herself at Logan's shoulder.

"Spencer will be your server tonight." She lifted a hand to motion to a young man, who hurried to their table. "Take good care of my friends, Spence. Top shelf and don't skimp. Enjoy your evening, folks, and don't hesitate to ask for anything you want." With a wicked smile in Allie's direction, she leaned over Logan's shoulder to adjust the placement of the silverware in front of him. "Whether it's on the menu or not."

Allie doubted that the boob Shayla brushed up against Logan's cheek had been an accident. From the deep red stain creeping up Logan's neck, she'd be willing to bet that he didn't think Shayla's move had been an accident either.

Though she didn't usually drink, the evening's surprises just seemed to beg for a margarita, so when Spencer returned to their table, she ordered one.

"I'll need to see some I.D."

Great. Her purse, with all her identification, was hanging in the coat closet at home. She should have known to bring something along with her.

"She's over twenty-one," Logan pointed out. "You can take my word for it."

Spencer shook his head, shifting uncomfortably from

one foot to the other. "Listen, I'm sorry, but it's the rule. And breaking the rule could cost me my job. No identification, no drinks."

"It doesn't matter. I'll have iced tea."

"No." Logan stood up and tossed his napkin on the table. "Come with me, Spencer."

He led the waiter through the dining room, back toward the hostess stand where, if Allie scooted her chair back and leaned at an angle, she could see Shayla standing. When Logan and Spencer reached her side, she turned immediately, a big smile on her face.

Allie might not be able to hear anything she said, but she couldn't miss the hand that woman laid possessively on Logan's chest. She also couldn't miss that hand sliding inside his jacket.

Before tonight, Allie would have sworn on a stack of Bibles that she hadn't a single jealous bone in her body. Suddenly, all her bones seemed to have taken on a jealous life of their own.

It felt as if the temperature in the building had risen by twenty degrees, and she couldn't decide if she'd rather skip the drink altogether or make it a double.

By the time Logan dragged himself away from that woman's roving hands and returned to their table, Allie was leaning toward the double.

Though she knew very little about what had led to Logan and Shayla breaking up, she certainly hadn't expected them to still be on such... *friendly* terms. It was something she found herself desperately wanting to know about, but she was not quite brave enough to ask.

A few sips into what had to be the smoothest margarita she'd ever tasted, she found her courage.

"I didn't realize you and Shayla were still so…" No, she wouldn't say *hands-on*, even though that was the term that came to mind. "Such good friends." She washed the question down with the remainder of her drink.

"We're not." Logan tipped up his beer for a sip and set it back on the table, continuing to fiddle with it as if considering what to say next.

Or how to say it.

Before he could respond, the band returned from their break and the noise level amped back up to the point where conversation was almost impossible.

Another strike against Golddiggers, although the freshly refilled margarita that had mysteriously appeared to replace her empty glass was one of the best she'd ever had, especially on a night as warm as this one.

She was just thankful the drinks weren't very strong, especially since Spencer delivered her third to the table only moments before their dinners finally arrived.

"Do you smell that?" A frown creased Logan's forehead as he sniffed the air.

"Smell what?"

The aroma of the food sitting in front of her was all she could smell, and, considering she'd been too nervous about this date to eat all day, it smelled fantastic.

"I'm sorry. I know that smell." Logan folded his napkin and placed it next to his plate. "I'll be right back."

With Logan hurrying away from their table, Allie put her fork down to wait. She took a sip out of her drink and then pushed it away in favor of water, only to realize their waiter had never brought any water.

She'd have to ask for some. Because, although the drinks didn't taste too strong, she was beginning to feel a bit odd. Maybe while Logan was away from the table, she should sneak in a quick visit to the ladies' room.

Allie placed her napkin next to her plate and stood, only to find the entire room starting a slow spin around her. She fastened her hands to the back of her chair and waited, but the spin didn't go away. If anything, the room revolved faster.

Very carefully, very slowly, she let go of the chair and threaded her way toward the back wall where the door marked RESTROOMS waited. It felt as if the floor stretched out, making the journey twice as long as it ought to have been, but, finally, she pushed through into a long, cream-colored hallway.

Like something out of a horror movie, the hallway appeared to stretch out for miles in both directions. An arrow attached to an EXIT sign pointed to the right, so she chose to go to the left. She didn't want to leave the building. She simply needed to find the ladies' room and a spot to sit down before her legs gave out.

The door next to the ladies' room had a keypad affixed to it, and she spared only a moment's thought as to where it led or to how often people must have wandered in there for them to have gone to the expense of adding a keypad to keep it locked.

Inside the ladies' room, she stumbled to the sinks and turned on the faucet to splash cold water on her face. It didn't help.

This was horrible.

Behind her one of the stall doors opened and a young woman stopped at the sink beside her.

"You okay?" she asked as she handed a paper towel to Allie. "Too much to drink?"

"I don't think so." Allie's brain felt like it was turning to mush as she stared into the mirror. "I only had two."

"You must be drinking the Gold Strike Margaritas." The young woman chuckled. "Those things are, like, so seriously dangerous, they should come with warning stickers. Smooth as fruit juice going down but with an alcohol content that kicks your butt. You don't even feel them until you stand up the first time and then *whoosh!* I can only handle, like, one of those, even though I consider myself a drinker."

Butt-kicking margaritas. Who would have guessed? Allie only wished she'd run into this girl before she'd had that first drink. Or, at the very least, before she'd had the second.

"You here with somebody? You want me to send them back to, like, help you?"

"No." Lord, no! That was the last thing on earth she wanted. "I'll be fine in a few minutes."

She would be. Just as soon as the room stopped spinning and her brain quit trying to convince her she was viewing the world through a long, narrow tunnel.

"Okay, then," the other woman said, skepticism lacing her voice. "You take care."

Allie held the paper towel under the cold water before draping it over her face. After a minute or two, or maybe thirty, she pulled it off. Even her sense of time had deserted her.

She worked to focus on her reflection in the mirror, but it wasn't easy with the mirror hung so far away down that tunnel. When she finally did bring the world into focus, she wished she hadn't.

Great. Another date where she ended up looking like

a drowned rat. A drowned rat with her top wide open, she amended, fumbling to stick the two pieces of strategically placed tape back together. Thank goodness she'd worn her best lace bra tonight. Just in case that happened again.

A tiny giggle bubbled up, humming low in her throat as she tucked strands of damp curls behind her ears and headed for the door.

When she stepped out into the hallway, a strong, acrid scent burned her nose and she stopped to look around. The door that had been shut and locked when she'd first come down this hallway now stood ajar, a chair propping it open. A thin layer of white smoke wafted out through the open door and into the hallway.

A fire? Hey… that could be a good thing. If all the sprinklers went off at the same time, then everyone would look exactly like she did. Since she had no idea how long she'd been in the restroom, maybe it had already happened. And what a weird fluke of chance to have a fire start when she was on a date with a firefighter.

The giggle moved further up her throat, lodging at the back of her mouth, waiting for its moment to emerge.

Two steps brought her around the door, and the giggle that had wanted its freedom evaporated as if it had never had a reason to exist.

Ahead of her people bustled around a busy, smoky kitchen, avoiding a man and a woman. A man and a woman clutched together in an embrace, his hands on her black-silk-clad arms, her hands on his smoothly shaved face as her lips pressed against his.

"Shit me," Allie whispered, turning much too fast for her brain to handle. She twirled back against the wall and held out her hands to steady herself.

Shayla and Logan. Right there in front of God and the whole damn kitchen staff. And with her, his date, for crying out loud, waiting patiently at their table for him to return as if nothing had happened.

Only something had happened and she wasn't at the table.

She wasn't going to be there either. Ahead of her, down the mile-long tunnel of a hallway, the exit door stood wide open, beckoning her with its easy access to escape from this horrible excuse for a date.

Outside she paused, one hand on the wall, struggling to get her bearings. She must be at the back of the building. If she followed the alleyway in either direction to the street, she could easily make her way home. In Chance, no place was more than seven or eight blocks away from anything else. She grew up here. Even with her brain feeling this addled, even in these shoes, walking home was no big deal.

Getting dumped in the middle of a date—now *that* was a big deal.

"Big deal!" she told the light pole on her left. "Big freakin' deal. Leave me sitting in the dining room while he plays kissy-face in the kitchen? Oh, I don't think so. Not this girl."

She leaned on the pole for a moment longer before patting it like an old friend and starting forward, only to step squarely into a patch of squishy mud.

"Yuck."

She looked down at her foot, struggling to focus on the icky mess it had made on her shoe. Mud? Seriously? There hadn't been any rain for a couple of days, and if it wasn't from rain…

"Gross."

She wasn't going to allow herself to go there. Just the very thought of all the things it could be made her stomach tighten, and that was the last thing she needed right now.

What she needed was to keep moving and get home. Whatever it was, it wasn't anything half an hour in a hot shower couldn't erase from her memory.

Ahead of her, a large grate covered the sidewalk where one of the little gullies ringing Chance darted under the street. She paused at the grate and laid her hand on the rail to step cautiously across.

Not cautiously enough.

Her heel plunged into one of the metal holes and she toppled over sideways, saved from a nasty fall by the metal handrail slamming into her side.

There was no moving forward. Her heel was firmly lodged in the grate.

Fine. It wasn't like she needed to wear these stupid shoes again or anything. Obviously, not even shoes like these could win out over tight leather pants and a half-open slinky silk shirt.

"That you should button up!" she hissed as she leaned down to unbuckle her shoe and slip her foot out.

Two steps farther and she knew one shoe off and one shoe on wasn't going to work. Walking was difficult enough right now without doing it on a moving incline. She squatted down until she rolled onto her bottom in a full sit. That was better than what she'd planned anyway. Now it was much easier to get the remaining shoe off.

She stood and started forward again, finally dropping the shoe she carried. What was she going to do with one stupid shoe? She didn't need it. The night was warm and she was…

"Where am I? Wait." The words buzzed as she spoke and she licked her lips before repeating them again to test their feel. "Wait."

If only she didn't feel like she was wandering through a rotating fog machine.

"Wait."

This was ridiculous. She was in Chance, of course. No way she could get lost here, just a little turned around. She'd simply wandered to the end of the paved streets and past the area where the streetlights were even moderately close together. Everything was okay. Nothing bad ever happened here. Nothing bad, nothing out of the ordinary. Nothing even remotely—

"What the heck is that?"

In the distance, down the other side of the road, odd white lights danced up and down, heading in her direction. Odd little white lights with long yellow lights on either side of them.

Wings maybe?

In one of the books in her shop, it would be an alien. A benevolent alien, of course. Those were the books she preferred to read. Happy books. Or maybe a fairy.

"That's it. My fairy godmother," she murmured.

This she had to see, up close. Crossing to the other side of the hard-pack dirt road, she waited, hands on her hips, swaying just a little as the small, bouncing lights drew closer.

Was it her imagination or was her stomach doing little sloshing flips to keep time with the movement of that light?

Maybe it was magic. Maybe it really was a fairy. Maybe it was…

Someone she knew?

As the lights moved closer, she could see they were attached to a man. A man she recognized.

"Tanner?" she whispered as the rays of the light he wore hit her square in the face.

"Allie Flynn?" Tanner's deep voice held a note of surprise. "What are you doing out here? I thought you were supposed to be having dinner with Logan?"

"Two's company," she muttered, remembering her earlier ego-bruising dinner date as she walked toward him. "Three's a cloud. Crowd. Ow!"

A sharp, stinging pain assaulted her feet with every step. Trying to escape only made it worse.

"What's wrong?" Tanner was at her side, a hand on her shoulder. "Hold on while I… oh, geez. Sticker patch. Just be still for a minute."

Be still? Didn't he realize she had a million needles jamming into her feet?

"We can fix this. Let's just pick you up and get you back on the road. Hold still and hang on."

Tanner leaned down, grabbed her around the waist and hoisted her up over his shoulder.

"Like a sack of flour," she giggled.

It was an innocent enough movement. But the pressure on Allie's stomach, accompanied by the whirl through the air with her head hanging down his back, was more than the margarita slurry brewing in her stomach could handle.

"Sick," she groaned, any desire to giggle long gone.

Her brain had so much more to say but her body

simply wouldn't allow her mouth to cooperate. If she opened it again, it wouldn't be words coming out.

"Here's a clear spot. We'll just set you down and then we'll work on those stickers."

"Sick," she repeated, scrambling to her knees as he released her.

"Wait a minute," he said.

But why he wanted her to wait or anything else he might have to say was lost in the heaving contractions of her stomach emptying itself.

When she could stop, could finally catch her breath, she was aware of him crouched down next to her, one arm around her shoulders, the other across her chest, supporting her weight as the next wave of nausea gripped her and passed. His murmured, unintelligible reassurances were lost on her as one after another the waves hit and subsided until she felt as if she must have heaved up her stomach, her intestines, and maybe even her toenails.

"So sorry," she managed to say at last. "So, so sorry."

Somewhere along the way tonight she must have died and gone to hell. This was sheer agony. Complete and total misery, coupled with total humiliation. Her only consolation was that it couldn't get any worse than this.

"What the hell is going on here?"

She glanced over her shoulder to see Logan standing in the middle of the road, his wide shoulders highlighted in the rays of Tanner's headlamp.

Okay, she was wrong. It not only could get worse, it just had.

* * *

"Knock it off, Shayla." Logan peeled his ex-fiancée's fingers from his face and backed away, putting some physical distance between them.

"What?" she asked, holding her hands up innocently, fluttering her long, fake eyelashes. "I'm only trying to thank you for saving my kitchen. If you hadn't shown up when you did, we might have had an expensive tragedy in here instead of just a smelly little electrical fire. It's what you do, Logan. Accept it. It's who you are. Responsibility always was your middle name."

"Whatever," he muttered, making his way back to the front of the kitchen. "You need to get an electrician in here to take a look at that mess of wires. And, for the record, I'll be checking the files when I get to the fire station on Monday. Looks to me like your kitchen is overdue for a fire inspection."

His hope tonight had been to try to sneak in and avoid Shayla as much as possible, not to end up with her arms wrapped around him. The fact that she was right didn't help him feel the least bit better about the situation. And she was right, both about his saving her restaurant some major damage and about his actions defining him. When he'd smelled those wires burning, there was nothing he could do but track down the source.

He shook his head, as if he could physically clear away the last few moments. If he'd had any sense at all, he'd have insisted that Allie pick another place for their evening out.

But he hadn't.

Instead, he'd walked right into a predictably uncomfortable situation. On top of everything else, he'd ended up wasting a good chunk of their evening together dealing with the kitchen staff and the fire in the wiring.

A thread of guilt warned him he should have thought to send someone out to tell Allie what was going on, but he hadn't thought of it at the time. He hadn't really thought, period. He'd just acted, like he always did.

It didn't come as a total surprise when he reached the dining room and Allie was nowhere to be found. It was a disappointment, though. He'd hoped for better from her. Still, she had every right to be annoyed with how long he'd left her sitting there all by herself.

A quick check of the table showed that she hadn't touched her refilled drink or her dinner.

"Hey." He reached out to slow Spencer down as the waiter passed by. "Did you happen to notice when my friend left?"

Spencer, hands loaded down with plates, shook his head. "No, and I pay attention to anyone who heads for the door. Last time I saw her, she was headed back toward the restrooms. Oh, and somebody mentioned a lady back there not feeling well, so maybe that could be her?"

Logan rubbed a hand through his hair and headed for the area Spencer had indicated. This was great. Beyond great. First, his family descended on them to mess up their first date. Now, on their second — the one that was supposed to make up for that ruined first one — not only had he deserted her with no explanation, it appeared she might have gotten ill while he was gone.

Was there even a way to go about making up for a crappy makeup date?

He paused in front of the door to the ladies' room. After debating his next move, he chose at last to simply wait a few minutes. The Golddiggers bar was even busier than its restaurant. He doubted he'd have to wait long before another female showed up who could check behind the closed door to see if Allie was inside.

Sure enough, within minutes the door swung open and two giggling women stepped out into the hallway.

"Logan! What are you doing skulking around outside the ladies' room?" Lila Murphy grinned at him, looking very different from her normally prim and proper demeanor behind the counter at the post office. "Wait a minute. Is there a fire? I told you I smelled smoke, Gayle. Should we be getting out of here?"

Sure enough, though someone had thought to prop open the exit door, a thin layer of smoke still hung against the ceiling in the hallway.

"No need for concern, ladies," he reassured. "I've already checked it out and everything is fine. But could I ask you to do me a favor?"

"Anything you need," Lila said.

"Would you mind checking to see if there's anyone else still in there?" He nodded toward the door they'd just come through. "I seem to have misplaced my date."

"There's not," her friend answered. "We made sure no one was in there when we went in. Sorry."

"You know how it is," Lila said with a wink. "Girl talk and all. Chance is a real small town, Logan. Everybody gossips, but a little discretion on a Friday night can save a whole lot of apologizing come Monday morning."

The two women said goodbye and giggled their way back out into the restaurant, more than a little unsteady on their feet.

So Allie wasn't in the ladies' room. And, at least according to Spencer, she hadn't left the restaurant through the front door.

Maybe, like Lila and her friend, Allie had smelled the smoke and decided to get outside through the nearest exit.

Logan hurried to the end of the hallway and out through the door, where he paused in a pool of yellow light under the old light pole. The alley was empty in both directions.

If she came out this way, she could have gone anywhere.

He had almost decided to return to the pickup in case she'd gone there to wait for him when he noticed a footprint at the edge of the ring of light. It was smallish, spread out in the front where the base of someone's foot had squished into the mud, but with only a small hole where their heel should be.

High heels? Could be. Just as it could belong to anyone. Still, it was worth a follow-up.

Heading down the alley toward the edge of town, he waged a silent argument with himself with every step he took. Doubt over his decision to come this way gnawed at his mind even as images of Allie waiting for him at their table flashed through his head.

His night, like his life, was filled with second-guesses over choices he might have made differently.

His steps slowed to a stop and he scrubbed his fingers over his forehead. Was he just making a bigger mess of the evening than he already had? Surely Allie wouldn't have come this far out of her way. Why would she? Even if she'd thought the restaurant was on fire, surely she'd have circled around to get help.

He was about to give up and turn back when he noticed an odd shape on the grate crossing the dry streambed. A closer inspection revealed a shoe. Allie's shoe, if he wasn't mistaken.

Any doubts he'd had morphed into outright worry as he pulled the high heel from the grate. He couldn't think of any reason for her to have come this way or to have left her shoe behind.

He moved forward again, more quickly than before, his measured steps evolving into a jog. It was dark out here. Dark enough that anything could happen to a woman limping around in one shoe.

No shoes, he corrected himself as he found the second abandoned high heel, this one mud-caked, lying in the middle of the road.

Adrenaline washed into his system as he stood and surveyed the distance, the need to do something, anything, rising in his throat. Farther down the road, a couple of wavering lights caught his eye and he headed toward them at a full sprint.

Reaching the lights brought him to a faltering stop and sent his emotions, already high on adrenaline, plummeting over the edge.

Tanner knelt on the ground, his arms passionately wrapped around Allie, her dress gaping open, exposing her bra.

It was like some horrible bout of déjà vu played out in the open, on the ground, instead of in the back seat of an SUV. Only this time, the woman was Allie, not Shayla.

Not sure if he wanted to confront this little scene or turn and walk away, Logan rode the wave of his heightened emotions.

"What the hell is going on here?" he demanded.

"Where the hell have you been?" Tanner countered,

not making any attempt to move away from Allie or even to let go of her. "And where's your truck?"

"Where have I been?" Logan's head whirled at the accusation in his friend's voice. "I've been searching for my date. Who, apparently, is pretty damn comfortable there on the ground with you."

"You think..." Tanner growled something under his breath before standing up, lifting Allie to her feet like a ragdoll in the process. "Yeah. Right. That's it. I came out on a run tonight for the sole purpose of stealing your date. Because we all know I've always preferred my women puking their guts out. What kind of an idiot are you, O'Connor?"

Puking? As if a plug had been pulled, Logan's anger drained away, leaving him feeling weak and empty as the emotion morphed into guilt, all in the space of a heartbeat. Spencer had mentioned something about Allie being ill.

"The worst kind of idiot, apparently," he said in answer to Tanner's question. "What happened?"

"You tell me." Tanner guided a whimpering Allie the few steps toward Logan and propped her against his chest. "Though if I were a betting man, I'd guess that you were stupid enough to let her drink those margaritas at Golddiggers."

"Yup," Allie muttered, her head rolling against his chest. "'Ritas."

"You'll be better sometime tomorrow, darlin'," Tanner reassured her before turning back to Logan. "Even I can't handle more than one of those. Everybody in town knows about them. They go down smooth and come up hard."

Christ. This was his fault. He'd ordered the second

172

and the third ones for her himself while he'd nursed the same bottle of beer all evening.

"I had no idea."

He'd never considered this particular drawback to picking a spot he'd personally boycotted for the past two years.

"You'll want to do something about those feet of hers, too," Tanner advised. "She had an encounter back there with a sticker patch. You better get her home."

"Home? I don't think so." If Susie saw her like this, there was no telling what effect it would have on her condition. "Maybe over to the fire station until she sobers up?"

Tanner's head began wagging his disagreement before Logan's words were even out of his mouth.

"Bad idea. Very bad idea. You don't want Chance's early risers to see her coming out of there in the morning. That just opens all three of us up to a whole new level of gossip that we do not want." Hands on his hips, Tanner scanned both directions on the road. "Your place, maybe. Where's your truck?"

"Still parked at Golddiggers. Whatever I do, I should probably get ahold of Dulcie. She's over keeping an eye on Susie this evening."

"First things first. Let's get your little lady to the fire station. You can deal with the mess in her feet while I go get your truck and deal with Dulcie. Then you can take Allie out to your place until she's sober enough to go home. Sound like a plan?"

"Sounds like a plan," Logan agreed.

A plan, all right. Just a very bad plan.

CHAPTER SIXTEEN

The earth could shake until the planet fell apart for all Allie cared. The end of the world would simply have to happen without her participation.

She squeezed her eyes more tightly shut, but even that didn't help. The shaking would not stop.

Neither would the deep voice whispering in her ear.

"Come on, Allie." A voice from her dreams. "I know you want to sleep, babe, but we have to get going. I promised Dulcie I'd have you home by six."

Home by six? But she was home. She must be. If not, where could she...

Snippets from the past few hours began to fall into place, filling in the big, black hole that currently served as her short-term memory.

Her, staring at a pair of large pajama pants, trying to figure out how to get her feet to go into the holes while the whole world spun around her.

Her, face down on a sofa while someone gently rubbed her back.

Her, retching into a white porcelain bowl while someone held her hair back.

"Argh," she groaned, not wanting to face any of the memories coming back to her now.

All these years she'd comforted herself with the idea that, as bad as the night of her senior prom had been, at least the worst was over and she could go through the rest of her life knowing she'd never experience a more humiliating moment.

She'd been wrong.

Reluctantly, she blinked open her eyes to face the latest catastrophe she'd created for herself.

"That's a girl," Logan encouraged, helping her to sit before taking a seat on the rumpled blanket next to her. "Just take it slow and easy and you'll be fine."

She'd be fine? Only if the new definition of *fine* included the insides of her head pounding their way out through her ears.

"Where are we?" She didn't recognize anything.

"My house," he said, one large hand still rubbing comforting circles on her back. "Didn't want your mom to see you all, you know…"

"Drunk as a skunk," she filled in when he paused. "Thank you for that. Oh my God, did you say your house? Your family?" The very idea of bumping into his sister or, heaven forbid, his mother made her stomach threaten to empty itself again.

"Don't worry about it." His hands were on her shoulders squeezing rhythmically, soothing muscles she hadn't even realized needed soothing. "We're at my house, not the ranch house. No one else is here but us. I hate to rush you, Allie, but I need you to get dressed so we can get you back home, okay? Here, let me help you up. Careful."

He was handling her like some fragile china doll, and though she couldn't say she actually minded, she hardly needed such treatment.

Or so she thought until she stood and the bottoms of her feet throbbed as if she'd been beaten with sticks.

She groaned, a sharp, breathy noise forced out of her body, far beyond her ability to control. "What on earth did I do?"

"Your feet?" Logan swept an arm under her legs and lifted her, fitting her against his chest. "You took a stroll through a sticker patch after you abandoned your shoes. I'm pretty sure we got them all out, but you're going to be tender for a day or two."

She laid her head against his chest, listening to his voice rumble as he talked. There was no memory of the sticker patch, just some fuzzy, murky half-memories of wandering around in the dark. Maybe it was just as well. Maybe there were some things she didn't want to remember.

Unlike this moment. This moment she wanted to remember forever.

"You'll probably want to grab a quick shower," he suggested as he set her on her feet in front of the open bathroom door. "I tried to keep your hair out of the way through the worst of it, but I'm not sure I was totally successful."

But definitely not this particular moment. This particular moment she'd be more than happy to forget. As soon as possible.

She closed the door behind her, taking a moment to lean against it and look around the bathroom. Her clothes, a pair of jeans and a T-shirt, were neatly folded on the sink, right next to a big, fluffy towel.

A vague memory of his saying something about Dulcie giving them to Tanner floated through her mind, but it didn't really matter. She'd been too busy enjoying the feel of his words rumbling in his chest to worry about what he'd actually had to say.

Too bad Dulcie hadn't sent her toothbrush. Her mouth tasted like goats had been sleeping in there. A bottle of mouthwash caught her eye and she poured a hefty swig into a tiny paper cup and sloshed it around in her mouth until she couldn't stand the burn any longer.

She stepped out of the big pajama bottoms and pulled the overly large T-shirt over her head, wincing as she lifted her arms. A quick check in the mirror revealed a bruise the size of her hand on her side. She'd have to remember to ask if she'd wrestled any bulls last night. And what the bull won after winning the match.

Climbing into the warm shower, she allowed the hot water to flow over her face and into her hair. What a godsend! It felt so good, it was even worth the pain of standing on her poor, wounded feet.

Try as she might to remember, the whole sticker incident was a blur. In fact, a major portion of the evening was a blur, though some of it was coming back to her in bits and pieces. She remembered wandering down a dark alley. Remembered making her way down a hallway that could have been straight out of some old horror film. Remembered smoke. A fire, maybe? She did have a vague memory of being really upset when she'd left the restaurant, so that might make sense.

She leaned over to rinse soap from her hair, and the movement set her head pounding. At least it was only a headache now, not that awful, nauseous spinning she'd felt last night.

Not like when she'd come out of the ladies' room. Not like when she'd peeked into the kitchen.

Not at all like when she'd seen Shayla and Logan kissing.

* * *

Urging Allie to hurry up again was the last thing Logan wanted to do. She no doubt felt awful this morning considering the night she'd had. If only he'd known enough to warn her against that second drink, he might have saved her going through all this.

But he hadn't.

What he had done was spend the night rubbing her back and holding her hair as her body had rejected the alcohol she'd poured into it. But not even that was enough to make up for what she'd gone through. And now he needed to force her to move faster, because they were running out of time. The alarm he'd set would be going off soon to warn them they needed to get moving if they were going to get her home before six, like he'd promised Dulcie they would.

The water in the bathroom had stopped running quite a while ago, but he'd heard no other movement behind the door. Worry over her physical well-being began to outweigh any concern over getting her home too late to conceal the fact that she'd been out all night.

He rapped his knuckles against the door. "Allie? Everything okay in there?"

Slowly, the door opened and she stepped into the hallway next to him, a vision of steamy temptation. Barefoot, she wore only jeans and a tight blue T-shirt, both of which looked as though they'd seen better days a decade ago. Gold-blond curls that normally looked as if they were just barely held under control hung in damp, orderly waves, framing a face pink with the heat of the shower.

It took everything he had not to sweep her off her feet and race down the hall to his bedroom. Who did he think he was kidding? It took everything he had not to go at it right here on the floor in front of the bathroom door. One word from her and—

"No," she said quietly, looking up at him, her eyes darkened with emotion. "No, everything is not okay."

Those were not the words he'd imagined her saying.

"What's wrong?"

He moved toward her, but she backed away and held up one hand, as if to separate herself from any contact with him as she skirted around him and headed back toward the living room.

"What's wrong?" he repeated, following after her.

Allie stopped in the middle of the room, her arms crossed in front of her, her face clearly reflecting some internal debate she waged with herself.

"Where were you last night? At the restaurant, I mean? I remember sitting at that table, all alone, for what seemed like forever. What happened to you?"

The question was long overdue and certainly one that deserved an answer.

"There was a small electrical fire in the kitchen. I

smelled the smoke and went to investigate. Once I found it, I was focused on dealing with it. I'm sorry. I should have thought to send someone out to let you know what was going on but I was doing my job and I just got wrapped up in the moment."

"Wrapped up, yeah, that's a good description," she said. "At least from what I saw, it is."

"I was doing my job," he insisted, actually hearing what she'd said only after he spoke. "What do you mean? What exactly did you see?"

She lifted one shoulder in what appeared to be an elaborate show of indifference. "Not much really. Just you and Shayla. *Wrapped up,* as you call it. Sharing a moment, I guess. Well, a kiss more than a moment, but we're dipping into semantics territory now and, actually, it's not any of my business what you do anyway."

"No, you're right. It's not," he agreed, regretting the words the instant they left his mouth.

He didn't owe a justification of his actions to her or anyone else. But for some reason he didn't quite understand, he wanted to explain to her what had really happened. He needed to explain it to her. He needed to wipe that expression of hurt from her eyes.

"In spite of what you think you saw, I wasn't kissing Shayla."

"I know what I saw, Logan. Granted, I was totally sloshed, but that doesn't change the fact that I know what I saw. She was all over you." Allie looked away for a second, chewing her bottom lip. "Again, not that it's any of my business what you do with her. It just would have been nice if you hadn't been doing it with her when you were supposed to be having dinner with me. That's all."

That was hardly *all,* and both of them knew it.

"I didn't kiss her," he said again, slowly making his way across the room to where Allie stood. "She did kiss me. She wound herself around me like bindweed out in the pasture and I had to pull her off. But I didn't kiss her. I wouldn't do that whether I was having dinner with you or if I'd been there all by myself. What once existed between us is long gone."

Five years long gone, to be exact.

Her arms, held so protectively in front of her, seemed to relax a little, and he could almost see the images flipping past as she searched her memory.

"Okay," she said at last. "In fairness, I didn't actually see you kiss her. So, maybe I did jump to a conclusion or two. The men in my life haven't been all that trustworthy."

He was within reaching distance so he reached out, closed his fingers around her upper arm and gently pulled her to him.

"I'm not those other men, Allie."

"I know," she whispered in return, as if, being so close, she couldn't manage to speak any louder.

A whole new emotion filled her eyes as she stared up at him. An emotion he didn't mind being responsible for putting there.

He breathed her in as he dipped his head to cover her lips with his. She smelled like something that belonged in his house. She smelled like his soap, his shampoo… his woman? That thought, which a month ago would have scared him beyond reason, didn't seem to have the same power over him at this moment.

It certainly didn't have anywhere near as much power as holding her in his arms did.

Her skin was warm and responsive under his wandering hands, encouraging him to explore further. His fingers slid up her sides, pushing their way under the soft cotton of her shirt, and she shivered as his thumbs trailed along the undersides of her breasts.

Shivered, but made no effort to push him away.

He walked her backward until they bumped into the sofa, then slowly lowered her to her back, following her down, careful not to break the kiss they held.

It wasn't lost on him that her hands caressed his face before twining into his hair, her body pressing closer to his.

She gasped when he lifted his lips from hers. He traced one thumb over her lower lip before returning his hands to her waist to push her shirt up, baring her beautiful stomach and beyond to the lace above and the soft mounds encased in that lace.

She gasped a second time when he lowered his head to rest his lips against one of those lacy mounds. Her body lifted up toward him when he breathed out, his warm, moist breath flowing over her.

His fingers fumbled with the button on her jeans, and he silently cursed himself for ever thinking that he liked seeing a woman in tight jeans. From this moment forward, he was a confirmed loose-jeans guy. He quickly reconsidered that pledge when the button gave way and the copper tab of the zipper slid slowly down with only a little urging on his part.

He covered her lips once again with his own and swallowed her third gasp, the one elicited when his fingers slid between her smooth, soft skin and the lace revealed beneath the jeans.

She felt so good to him. This moment felt so right, so perfect. If only that damned beeping would shut up.

The alarm!

Reluctantly, he lifted his mouth from hers. "I can't begin to tell you how much I hate to put a stop to this."

"I know," she sighed. "We have to go."

Next time, he promised himself as he forced himself to stand and offered a hand to help her to her feet.

The next time he planned the perfect evening, it would be perfect. He'd see to it. No family, no ex-girlfriends, and not one single damned alarm in the entire house.

CHAPTER SEVENTEEN

"Would you like to explain to me how you can possibly call this our third date?" Allie grinned across the table at Logan, waiting for his response. They'd had breakfast, lunch, or coffee together two or three times a week, every single week since their disastrous night out at Golddiggers. "We have to be at number ten or fifteen by now, at the very least."

"Granted," he conceded, returning her grin. "But none of those are official dates. Tonight will be our third official date. To make up for—"

"Don't say it," she interrupted with a laugh. "Don't even think it. Let's not jinx ourselves."

She wasn't really a superstitious person, but so far, official dates hadn't worked out so well for them.

"Tonight will break the Official Date Curse. I've got everything worked out with no possible hitches in sight this time. I'll pick you up at six sharp, then we'll go back to my place. We can pop open a bottle of wine, relax on the deck while dessert is baking and then I'll grill steaks for us. How's that sound?"

"Sounds pretty good," she replied. "But how about instead of you coming to get me, you stay home and get things ready and I'll drive myself out there."

"If you're sure that's what you want to do. That gives me more time to run a few errands and still get a special dessert in the oven." He pushed back his chair and stood, leaning down to brush a light kiss on the top of her head before offering a reminder: "Don't forget, it's the second turnoff after you go through the cattle guard and then just keep hanging lefts at each fork in the road."

"Got it. See you tonight."

The kiss was something recent and she was sure he'd only felt comfortable enough for it now because there were no other customers in the Hand except for Lila Murphy, and she was out of sight back in the bookshelves.

"Getting serious, I see."

Of course, there was Dulcie, who seemed to see everything, even if you didn't see her.

"You think so?"

Allie had been so focused on simply enjoying her time with Logan, she hadn't allowed herself to stop and think about where the relationship was going. She hadn't even allowed herself to think of what was happening between them as a relationship.

"Trust me," Dulcie said as she sat down in the chair Logan had just vacated. "I've seen that man in the Hand almost every day since we opened. And I've known him my whole life. In all that time, I've never once seen him kiss anyone in public."

"Maybe," Allie conceded, a tendril of worry already beginning to wiggle around in the pit of her stomach.

"It is what you always wanted, right?" Dulcie asked. "What you always dreamed about?"

"Fantasized about," Allie corrected.

After so many years of wanting this exact thing, it was difficult to accept that it actually might be happening. She had no doubt that Logan was attracted to her. His physical reaction to her was too obvious to miss. But actually liking her? There was a huge difference between physical attraction and an honest-to-goodness relationship. Though it had always been her fantasy that one day this would happen, it certainly hadn't been her expectation. Especially not after all these years.

If Dulcie was right, this changed everything. If Logan's feelings for her were more than just a simple case of lust, if what was happening between them was more than simply hanging out and having fun together, she couldn't afford to ruin any chance they might have for a future together.

"If what you say is true, if we're going to have any chance of building a halfway-decent relationship together, I'm going to need to come clean with that man."

Just saying the words out loud made her want to throw up.

"What the heck are you talking about?"

Dulcie's puzzled expression appeared genuine, though she, of all people, should understand. The twins had been Allie's confidantes from the time they were little girls walking to grade school together. They knew all her deepest-held secrets.

"You know what happened between me and Ryan.

I'm sure Logan does, too. I have to deal with that. I have to get it out in the open and explain my side."

If she didn't, it would always be there, festering, like a splinter under her skin.

"I can*not* believe you just said that!" Dulcie shook her head, her eyes narrowing before she continued. "You're talking about your big prom night breakup after Lacey Jenkins ratted you out, aren't you? Are you a complete crazy woman? That was in freakin' high school, Allie. I can't believe you'd still be carrying that kind of useless baggage around with you after all this time. Don't you understand that not one other soul on the entire planet cares about what happened eight years ago? Literally, not one. Let it go and move on with your life. The only thing standing between you and happiness is having the courage to forgive yourself. If you don't love you, how can you expect anyone else to?"

If Dulcie didn't understand the impact that incident had had on Allie, the bits and pieces of angst she'd carried around with her for eight years as a result of it, there was no point in arguing with her about it. Logically, she might even be right, but it didn't matter. Allie would always feel the weight of that uncomfortable little piece of her past if she didn't at least address it with Logan.

Tonight they'd be together, relaxed and alone. Tonight she'd be able to find the perfect moment to bring it up and have done with it, once and for all. Either Logan would laugh it off and tell her how unimportant it was what she'd done all those years ago, or their relationship would be all over before it really even began.

Either way, tonight was the night.

* * *

A thrill of forbidden excitement rippled through Logan's chest as he picked up speed after passing by the wide spot in the road known as the Vaca Vista Inn.

He could have stopped there and found exactly what he wanted because it was the kind of place where people didn't check in for more than a few hours at time. But everyone in three counties knew what went on at the inn, so having his truck spotted there didn't sit well at all with him. Gossip moved more quickly through the valley than wildfire.

Feeling like he was sixteen again, he pressed down on the accelerator and let the miles fly beneath his wheels. An hour's drive to Grand Junction was the last thing he had planned for today. This trip was carving two hours out of his already tightly planned schedule.

But it was two absolutely necessary hours. Driving to Grand Junction was the only way he could guarantee himself the anonymity he wanted.

It was surreal to feel this excited about a shopping excursion. He couldn't remember the last time he'd been this excited about a trip into town.

Or this nervous.

It fit, though. He also couldn't remember the last time he'd felt this excited about a date.

He looked in his rear-view mirror and caught a glimpse of himself, grinning like some puberty-plagued adolescent.

No matter. The sensory part of his brain could battle all it wanted. He'd already made up his mind that he wasn't going to allow either his common sense or his overdeveloped sense of guilt to drive away this joyous awareness of anticipation.

It felt too good. Anticipation had been missing from his life for far too long. Now that it was back, he intended to grab it with both hands and hold on for the ride.

As he approached the outskirts of town, he quickly decided to bypass any of the stores where he regularly shopped. He also passed up at least two chain drugstores before settling on a superstore he'd never frequented.

Pushing a large cart around the enormous store was overkill, but no way was he going to hit the checkout stand with only one item. Besides, there were a couple of things he still needed for tonight's dinner.

He hurried through the grocery area, picking up what he could use. Bittersweet chocolate. Butter. Fresh strawberries. Some greens for a salad. A quick detour to choose a couple of tall tapered candles and that should do it. He'd stalled as long as he could.

Nerves stretching tight, he crossed to the other side of the store and entered the pharmacy area.

Two women chatted in the middle of the aisle, carrying on for a ridiculously long time about some swimming instructor who couldn't recognize how much raw ability their toddlers displayed.

Logan impatiently passed up the aisle, turning down the next one to stare sightlessly at six feet of shelf space devoted to tooth care.

This was a ridiculous waste of time. It wasn't like he didn't have as much right as those women to be in that particular aisle, shopping for any damn thing he pleased. It was none of their business.

In spite of his logic, he couldn't quite force himself

to enter that space while they were there. Couldn't manage to walk past those women to stop and study the contents of the shelf next to where they stood. And even if he could make his legs carry him to their location, he knew he wouldn't be able to make a selection from the variety of boxes and put one into his cart. Not with the two of them watching him.

So he circled past the toothpaste, the painkillers, and hair products, back to the end of the aisle he wanted to go down. And then he circled one more time, trying to build his courage for the task.

How foolish was it that he could face down a burning house or a wind-whipped forest fire, but the idea of two gossiping housewives passing judgment on his behavior intimidated him, making him feel like a badly behaved adolescent. His mother should be proud. She'd instilled a sense of guilt in him to always be a *good boy* that he'd likely never overcome.

Finally, on his third pass, one of the talented toddlers threw himself against his mommy's leg in a fit of impatient rage.

Logan didn't blame the kid one little bit, sending up his thanks as, at last, the women parted ways and he was left to make his choice in privacy.

Selection made, he tossed the nondescript box into his cart. He almost whooped in joy when he discovered the self-checkout lanes, and within minutes he was loading his purchases into the truck and getting back on the road toward home.

Thanks to Allie's offer to drive herself out to his place tonight, he still had plenty of time to bake the dark chocolate chess pie he was sure would wind its way straight into her heart.

The night would be perfect. Good food, a bottle of excellent wine, and a beautiful woman to share them both. And, if events should follow the natural path they always seemed to wander down when he and Allie were alone together, thanks to the contents of the little box he'd gone to so much trouble to procure, he'd have the protection he needed to follow through.

Tonight was the night.

CHAPTER EIGHTEEN

"More wine?" Logan lifted the bottle from its ice bucket home as Allie began to shake her head.

"Nope, no more for me. Your dessert put my taste buds in heaven and I don't want to drag them back down to earth with that wine." Her eyes rounded as she heard her own words, and she hurried to add, "Not that the wine is bad or anything. Don't think I'm saying that. It's just that nothing tastes better than chocolate. Not in my book, anyway."

He might argue with that, especially since he was looking forward to sampling her lips soon. He intended to test for himself her theory of whether the chocolate taste lingered.

After settling the bottle back in its bucket, he edged closer to her on the blanket where they lay, ostensibly gazing up at the stars.

"See that one over there?" He pointed up at the

sparkling night sky. "That's Venus. And that one, that's Mercury."

"Really? Mercury? But it's so tiny. I'd expect one of the bigger planets to be easier to see than that little thing."

If she wanted a bigger planet, he could accommodate. Astronomy had been one of his favorite hobbies as a kid.

"Bigger. Okay then, let's see..." He scanned the sky to get his bearing, leaning a fraction closer to her as he looked. "It should be... yeah. Look over there, to the south. You see that bright one over there? That's Saturn."

She shifted her weight to her right elbow as she looked in the direction he pointed, bringing her cheek close to his lips. He resisted the temptation to touch, breathing her in instead. Her hair, so soft against his chin, smelled of fresh, green, growing things.

"It's so amazingly beautiful out here," she said quietly. "I'd forgotten how brilliant the sky is at night this far from the city lights."

"Beautiful beyond words," he murmured in response, noting her shiver as his breath ruffled her curls. "Just one more reason to avoid the city."

"Oh, I don't know about..." Her words trailed off as she turned, as if ready to debate the issue until her lips brushed against his.

He hadn't the strength to resist the temptation of her lips a second time. Seeking to satisfy the desire curling low in his stomach, he indulged himself in a kiss she willingly returned. Though it was as wonderful as he remembered, there was no satisfaction of the need he felt. If anything, her kiss, her touch, only strengthened his desire for her.

Planets forgotten, his tongue explored the contours

of her lips until they parted, inviting him inside to deepen the kiss. It was as if nothing in the world could satisfy the fire stoked deep inside him, except more of Allie. Nothing less than all of her.

After blocking all his feelings for so long, it was as if the dam had broken and he was being flooded by them all at once.

"I can't believe this is happening."

"What?" she murmured, her eyes opening slowly, blinking, like a woman waking from some erotic dream.

He'd done that. He was responsible for that look on her face. Him. His kiss. He suddenly understood why the peacock strutted. He felt a little like strutting himself.

If a kiss could make him feel like this, what would he want after they'd done what he expected was getting ready to happen between them? It felt as if the relationship he'd been running from all these years had finally caught up with him.

And, considering the way he felt, holding this woman in his arms, he was finding it difficult to remember exactly why he'd avoided a relationship for so long.

Maybe it was because he'd been waiting for Allie to come along.

A breeze wafted past, blowing a golden strand of hair across her face, catching on her eyelash. He drew his finger across her forehead, brushing away the unruly curl to tuck it behind her ear.

"How is it possible for me to have known you my whole life and yet never have known you at all?"

Allie's teeth scraped over her bottom lip and her eyes darted away from his for an instant. "You know me. I'm the same person I've always been."

"No," he said, tracing that same kiss-swollen lip with the pad of his thumb. "I feel like an explorer, venturing into undiscovered territory for the first time. I want to know all of you. Everything about you. I don't want any secrets between us, Allie."

She covered his hand with hers, stopping his caress. "Is it really so important to you, what's happened in the past?"

It could be. For him, at least. He needed to banish his demons if he was going to have any chance at happiness with Allie.

"The things we've done, the choices we've made— they're what's made us who we are."

"I don't know if I totally accept—" she began, but he brushed his thumb over her lips to stop her mid-sentence.

"You asked me once what had happened to end my relationship with Shayla. I didn't answer you then."

He had, in fact, gotten up from his chair and disappeared to put out a fire, deserting her. Maybe not the best moment to remind her of that.

"You don't have to tell me about it. It doesn't matter to me."

But it did matter. It mattered to him. In spite of everyone who'd told him over the past five years to let it go and move on, what had happened between him and Shayla had wound itself around the core of his psyche, carving an open, cancerous sore. Until he bared that malignant growth, until he ripped it out by its roots, he wouldn't be able to move on. And right now, holding Allie, he wanted to move on more than he could ever have imagined.

"Shayla and I never stood a chance. Our whole

relationship was built on dishonesty. We weren't even looking to travel the same road in life. She never loved me, she simply wanted a ring on her finger. Her goal was money and somebody to take care of her."

"I'm sorry she was dishonest with you."

How easy it would be on his ego to leave it there. But leaving Allie with that impression wouldn't cure what ailed him.

"It wasn't only her dishonesty. It was mine, too. I wanted the kind of relationship I saw at home. What my parents and my grandparents had. I wanted it so badly that I ignored our reality and convinced myself that no matter how rocky things were between us, no matter how different our goals in life, things would get better. I thought that once I finished college and came home to Chance, we would change somehow, *she* would change somehow, and everything would be perfect."

"But that didn't happen."

Logan shook his head, picking through his most painful memories to offer an explanation.

"She didn't want to wait."

Shayla had lied to him. Deceived him by telling him she was pregnant. And, because the stakes had been so much higher than at any other point in their relationship, he'd confronted her for the first time ever. He'd confronted her lie and her cheating and then he'd confronted the truth of their relationship for the first time ever, and it had ripped the ground from under his feet.

"She left you?"

"No. That would have been much easier to accept. She did much worse. She deceived me. Lied to me. In the end, I was nothing more than an easily interchangeable tool she used in an attempt to get to what she really wanted."

Just as he'd been using her to get to what he really wanted, only he couldn't yet bring himself to give voice to that admission. Saying those words would lift the guilt from Shayla's shoulders and place it squarely on his own.

Where, in truth, it had belonged all this time.

"So, it was the lie that ended things for you?"

"Not the actual lie, no, but the deception intended by the lie. It was her letting me think she cared about me, when I wasn't at all what she wanted. It was the using, the deception, that I couldn't forgive."

Shayla's sin was topped only by his own. She might have told the lies, but he'd allowed himself to believe them because he'd wanted to believe.

This time, he wanted everything to be different.

"I feel like we're opening the door to something special between us, Allie. But I need you to know that I have a history that makes commitment to a relationship difficult for me. I needed you to know that history. To understand. So that if—when—I get weird about the whole thing, about us, you'll know it's not you. And maybe, if I'm lucky, you'll be patient and not give up on me while I work through it."

He leaned into her, covering her mouth with his, tasting her lips with the tip of his tongue. He hadn't meant to deprive her of her opportunity to respond, but with the moonlight sparkling in her eyes, it felt like the right moment.

And, as rarely as moments like these came along, who was he to quibble? Especially not when she returned his kiss with equal intensity.

* * *

Allie's heart lodged somewhere near the base of her throat, beating as wildly as if she'd run a hundred-yard dash with no warm-up.

After what Logan had just confided to her, there was no way she could tell him about her dating his brother for no other reason than to try to get close to him. He would think she was no different from Shayla.

Maybe she wasn't. She didn't know anymore.

What she did know was that she was in love with Logan O'Connor. She had been for as long as she could remember and nothing — not her leaving Chance, not her proof of the infidelity of all men, not even her own personal experiences—had changed that. He was all she wanted and here he was, practically admitting that he wanted her, too.

There was no way she intended to mess up a chance like this. She would do anything, say anything, *be* anything to be the woman Logan wanted.

"I'll wait for you forever, if that's what you want," she said when he lifted his lips from hers.

"I'm not asking you to wait forever," he whispered before dipping his head for another brief kiss. "In fact, right now, waiting for any amount of time sounds like the worst idea I've ever heard."

To show him that she couldn't agree more, Allie rolled to her back, urging him to follow.

Logan didn't require much urging. He hovered above her, his dark eyes alive with emotion. She lifted a hand and threaded her fingers through the hair at the back of his neck, pulling his lips to hers.

He kissed her softly, his lips barely brushing over hers before they moved to her cheek, her chin, the sensitive skin at the base of her throat. His warm, moist breath wafted across her chest, leaving a ripple of cold bumps in its wake.

He lifted his head and smiled. "Have I told you how very much I like this shirt you're wearing? I think it's possibly my favorite out of all the things I've ever seen you wear."

Her mind floundered, at a loss to understand what he could possibly like about this plain, featureless shirt. Then the first button slid out of the embroidered hole which held it.

"I see," she breathed, understanding dawning.

A second button slipped free. Followed by a third. And a fourth. She lay motionless, barely able to breathe as the soft cotton slid away to expose her skin to the night air.

"Another clothing choice I like," he murmured and, with a touch, the clasp on the front of her bra popped open.

His warm hand on her cooled skin was a sensory delight. When his mouth replaced his hand, it turned into sensory nirvana. Beyond her ability to control, her body arched into him, seeking the pleasure of his tongue circling her breast.

She slipped her hands under his T-shirt, savoring the passage across the solid planes of his chest and up to his strong shoulders.

His fingers slipped beneath the waistband of her jeans, and after what seemed like an eternity, the soft denim began to slide over her hips and down her legs. She lay there, bare save for a small scrap of lace, as he pulled away from her hands to sit up, his admiring stare saying what he didn't speak aloud.

When he pulled his shirt over his head and tossed it to one side, her breath caught in her throat. When he popped open the button on his jeans and lowered the zipper, she thought her heart might burst right out of her chest. She'd dreamed of this moment so many times, for so many years, and now, at last, it was actually happening.

"I can hardly believe this moment is real," she whispered as he lowered his body back over hers. "That I'm really doing this."

"That *we're* doing this," he corrected, brushing a loose strand of hair from her face before his hands trailed down her throat to begin a slow, sensual journey along the contours of her body. "The two of us. Together."

A shiver of anticipation rippled through her as his knee gently spread her legs and he fit himself over her. His hands, large and warm, explored her eager body as his lips closed over hers again.

This was it. Nothing could stop them now. They were in the homestretch. They were going to—

Oh no! Panic and disappointment warred in her chest before she managed to pull away to voice her distress. "We can't do this."

"What?" His voice had a faraway edge to it, matching the dreamy expression in his eyes. "What's wrong?"

"I'm not on any... I'm not prepared for..." She fumbled for the words she wanted, her face burning with embarrassment even as her body burned with frustration. "No protection," she finished lamely.

"No worries." Logan chuckled, rolling away for an

instant to reach for the jeans he'd tossed next to their blanket. "Got it covered," he said confidently, twirling a small foil packet in his fingers.

How perfect was this man of her dreams? Handsome, strong, a great cook, and well prepared. Absolutely perfect.

Now, truly, nothing stood in their way.

Nothing except the jangling noise coming from that same pair of jeans he'd so recently discarded.

"Oh, not now," Logan groaned, his body tensing over hers.

"Ignore it," she breathed, the sensations he'd created with his hands still vibrating through her body.

"Can't ignore that phone, love. It's the station house. Tanner wouldn't call if it weren't an emergency." He rolled away, snatching up the phone from his jeans. "O'Connor here."

Allie knew he was right. Knew he had no other choice. But that knowledge did nothing to lessen the disappointment and frustration coursing through her body.

"I hate to end our evening like this, but I have to go, babe." Logan pulled his shirt on over his head, muffling his words for a second. "Structure fire out at the Webster place. You okay?"

He leaned over her, a hand outstretched to help her up.

"I'm good." She smiled up at him, forcing her lips to curve even though she didn't feel the least bit happy. The Official Date Curse had struck again. "Hazard of dating a firefighter, I guess, right?"

"You hold my place, okay? We'll pick up where we left off next time." Logan grinned, grabbing the blanket they'd laid on to wrap it around her shoulders even as he kissed her cheek. "I gotta go now. I'm so sorry."

"I understand. Should I wait here?"

"Probably not. Sounds like this could take all night. Outbuildings are already engulfed. They're just trying to save the barn and house now. You okay with locking up for me?"

Allie nodded, not trusting her voice as he turned his back and broke into a run.

She tightened the blanket around her and gathered her clothes, feeling more sorry for herself by the minute. In fact, the only thing in the world she could imagine that would be worse than being her right now would be being the Webster family and watching that fire eat everything you owned.

"Big baby," she grumbled, heading into the house to get dressed. Here she was feeling sorry for herself when she should be counting her lucky stars. Her wonderful evening might have been interrupted at a most inopportune time, but at least she knew now that it wasn't simply lust driving Logan's actions. He thought they had a chance together.

She double-checked that everything in the kitchen was turned off and the house was secured before heading to her car. Good thing she'd driven herself out here tonight.

Nothing happened the first time she turned the key in the ignition but, after counting to twenty, she tried again and her car started up as if nothing were wrong.

Yep, she was definitely living under a lucky star lately. Her dream man had been dropped in her lap, she loved her work, her mom seemed to be getting better and even her car was mostly working.

Coming back to Chance just might be the smartest thing she'd ever done.

CHAPTER NINETEEN

Cheery summer sunlight filled the room when Allie awoke, but a foreboding sense that all was not right nagged at the back of her mind like some half-forgotten memory. A sound, maybe? A sound that might have awakened her?

She sat up in bed, closing her eyes and concentrating to listen. There it was again! Something in the distance. A wail? Her mother!

"Oh my God!" she whimpered as she hit the floor at a run. "Mom? Where are you?"

This was the exact thing she was supposed to be here to prevent.

Allie ran through the house, calling for her mother as she checked each room on her way to the back door. Outside, on the deck, heart pounding, she tried once more.

"Mom? Are you out here? Mom!" She paused, breathless, listening for any sound in response.

Birds, the wind and, somewhere in the distance, a

dog. Then, finally, the one sound she'd sought.

"Allie? I'm out here, honey!"

Allie spotted her at last, way out in the field, headed away from seemingly anything. No wonder she hadn't spotted her earlier. Susie appeared to be sitting in the weeds!

"I'm coming!"

Allie jumped down off the deck, running as quickly as her bare feet would allow through the wild growth in the far field. By the time she reached her mother's side, Susie had rolled to her stomach and was struggling to get up on her hands and knees.

"What's wrong? What are you doing out here, Mom?"

They'd made so much progress in the past months. Allie had begun to believe her mother's illness was improving.

"It's Grainger," her mom answered. "He took off this direction and wouldn't come back when I called. Naturally, I came after him, but then I stepped in that damn prairie dog hole over there and twisted my ankle. Put me right on my butt."

"You're hurt, then."

Allie dropped to the ground by her mother's feet, examining the swollen ankle. She hated that her exclamation had come out sounding so relieved, but the idea that her mom was on the ground because she'd hurt herself was so much easier to deal with than that she'd collapsed from exhaustion as she'd been doing several months back.

"Yes." Susie sucked in her breath as Allie pressed on her ankle. "And by now, because I'm such a klutz, those damned coyotes are probably feasting on my poor baby for their dinner."

"That's not happening." Not on her watch. Not after all that old dog had done for her mother. "I'll go find him. We'll get you back into the house and get some ice on that ankle and then I'll go find Grainger and bring him home for you."

She helped Susie to stand on one foot and, wrapping her mother's arm around her neck, acted as a crutch to help with the trip back to the house.

"Did it seem like we'd come this far from the house to you?" Allie asked, doing her best to keep her mother's spirits up when they stumbled.

Susie gave her a strained smile, perspiration popping out on her forehead with the effort she exerted. "No, but I was a little more nimble on the way out."

When they finally reached the deck, Susie waved toward one of the folding chairs. "This is good enough. I just want to get my foot up."

Allie hurried inside and quickly returned with a pillow to put under her mom's foot and a bag of ice to place on top.

"There. I'll get dressed and then I'll go hunt for Grainger."

"Thank you, sweetie. I do love that stubborn old dog. Losing him would be like losing a part of me. I don't know what I'd do."

That was exactly what concerned Allie.

"Try not to worry, Mom. I'll take care of it."

Minutes later, she was ready, armed only with a bottle of water and a vague idea of the direction in which Susie had last seen the dog headed. She kissed the top of her mom's head and hopped off the deck for the second time that morning.

"Could you call over to the Hand and let the girls know I won't be in?"

"I will," Susie called after her. "Wait a minute! Don't you want to take the shotgun along with you? I know for a fact there's coyotes out there. I've seen them myself."

Shotgun? Not a good idea at all.

"Did you forget which of your kids you're talking to?" Allie shook her head, sending a disapproving look her mother's direction. "Sending me off with a gun is just begging to get your dog shot. Or your daughter. Or, more likely, both of us."

"And just what do you think you'll do if you run into a pack of those beasts?" Susie struggled to roll herself off the chair where she sat.

"Sit down, Mom," Allie ordered, backtracking up the steps. "If it makes you feel any better, I'll take that old walking stick Mama Odie gave me when I used to go on walks with her and the twins. I saw it in the storage shed the other day. One good smack with that should give pause to any creature that comes my way."

"Better that than nothing, I guess," her mother grumbled, resettling herself in the deck chair. "And you take your cell phone, too."

Allie nodded her agreement, knowing that the phone would be worthless once she got up into the canyon. They were lucky to get reception here in town, and, unless things had changed drastically from what she remembered, there would be little chance of service back in those hills.

"You don't know how much this means to me, Allie. I can always count on you. You're so take-charge and independent. I wish I'd been more like you when I was your age. I really admire you for never being too timid to just do what needs to be done."

Allie considered asking her mom once again if she'd forgotten which of her offspring she was speaking to, but settled for a grin instead.

"Thanks, Mom. I won't let you down."

A few minutes later, her mother placated, she set off again, determined to bring her mother's faithful companion back.

An all-day hike into the backcountry tracking an ill-behaved old dog was the last thing she'd planned for herself today. But there was no way she was going to let anything bad happen to that dog. She didn't want to think about what kind of relapse her mother might suffer from an emotional jolt like losing Grainger.

Damn stubborn dog. If he simply would have returned when Susie called him, they wouldn't be worrying themselves sick about him right now.

Allie pounded the walking stick she carried into the ground with each step she took, pleased that she'd brought it with her. It was turning out to be a good means of releasing some of the pent-up frustration bubbling inside her this morning.

She felt as if she'd reached another turning point in her life. The elusive, shiny, gold-wrapped chocolate of happiness was so close to her grasp, she could almost taste it. It was dangling there, just out of her reach. And every single time she tried to grab it, some fresh new turmoil swirled around her to keep her from her goal.

From Shayla's flirting with Logan, to his confiding his issue with deceit, right up to Grainger's running away this morning, there always seemed to be something blocking her from moving forward to capture what she wanted in life.

"And who has the power to change that?" she asked the rocks and bushes around her. "I do, that's who!"

It was time for her to attempt to be that take-charge, independent woman her mother thought she was. Past time, in fact.

The whole jealousy/trust thing she struggled with might take some time, but she was determined to work on it. As far as stressing over how Logan would react to what she'd done in the past, there was only one way forward. She would clear the air with him the very next time she saw him, no matter what the circumstances. No more stressing over what he'd think or what he'd do. There were only two things that could happen. He'd either accept it or not. And either way, she could finally stop carrying that old baggage around with her, once and for all.

But first up on her Taking Charge list was finding Grainger and getting him home safely.

She stopped, hand raised to shield her eyes from the bright sun, and called the old dog's name.

"Grainger!"

Closing her eyes, she concentrated on listening, hoping for some sound to guide her.

Nothing.

Her only course was to continue to follow the worn trail she was on, honed out over the years by elk and other animals coming down from the backcountry. Her hope was that Grainger had chosen the easiest path rather than forging out through the weeds that would have been higher than his head in many places.

A few steps ahead, on a small, prickly bush that jutted out into the pathway, a fuzzy brown clump caught her eye.

Fur!

Allie squatted by the plant and pulled the fur off, carefully avoiding the thorns. She rolled it between her fingers and lifted it tentatively to her nose.

The smell of dirt tickled her senses, and three sneezes later, she was forced to laugh at her inept tracking abilities. Like she even knew why she was smelling it—other than that was what they always did on television.

Without any real tracking abilities, she would simply have to rely on logic. The fur was the same color as Grainger's. It was caught at a height that would have been about right for the old dog wobbling along the path. It was all she had to go on, so she was taking it as a sign. She was on the right trail.

The sun shone brightly overhead now, beating down, making her glad she'd opted for shorts instead of jeans. Poor Grainger must be melting out here in his heavy fur coat.

She stood and scanned the distance, seeing and hearing nothing more than a few birds in the trees ahead of her. One quick sip from her water bottle and she was off again, convinced now that this hunt was going to take all day.

* * *

"Maybe she let the battery on her phone run down."

"Maybe," Logan halfheartedly agreed, casting a doubtful look in Tanner's direction.

That didn't seem like something Allie would do. In his experience, she was more than a little obsessive when it came to details like that. But there had to be some reason she wasn't answering his calls or returning his messages for the last hour.

"What? You think she's just not answering?" Tanner paused to scrub his face and hair with a towel before continuing. "I'd find that pretty hard to believe based on how the two of you have been getting along. Why not run over to the Hand and check it out? I could use some decent coffee after the night we had."

Coffee sounded pretty good to Logan, too. It had taken until well into the wee hours of the morning to get the fire out at the Webster place. And several more hours for the cleanup. They'd been lucky to hold the damage down to just two outbuildings. Most of that rundown ranch was little more than piles of tinder. He'd have to remember to talk to Cody to see if there might be something the sheriff's office could organize to help that old couple get the weeds and rubble close to the main house cleaned up.

But all that would have to wait until later today. Right now, all he wanted was to hear Allie's voice. He needed to satisfy himself that she was okay with his running out on her last night. Especially since his departure had come at a rather... inopportune time.

With all the grime of the night's work showered away, he grabbed his hat and followed Tanner out to the parking lot.

"You want to take separate rides?" Tanner grinned and slapped him on the shoulder. "In case you want to stay longer or take off to finish your interrupted dinner date. Since it is, you know, technically your weekend off and all?"

Logan returned the grin. *Weekend off* was always a relative term when you were the second man on a two-man team. When the fire call came in, they were both on duty.

"Yeah, that might be a good idea."

He pulled into the lot next to the coffee shop only a minute ahead of Tanner, but he was out of his vehicle and through the front door in record time.

"Hey, Logan!" Dulcie greeted as he stepped inside. "You want the usual?"

"Yes, thanks." He needed that coffee today. "Might as well set one up for Tanner, too. He's on his way in. Allie around?"

Dulcie shook her head as she poured the coffees. "There was some kind of problem with Grainger this morning that kept her home. As a matter of fact, I was going to run over there in a few minutes to take Aunt Susie a sandwich. You want me to give Allie a message?"

"I have a better idea. Make my coffee to go and I'll be your delivery boy. How's that?"

If Allie was ignoring his calls, she might ignore any message he sent along with her cousin, too.

"That's excellent," Dulcie replied with a grin, handing over the coffee and a sandwich she'd already wrapped. "Coffee's on the house for saving me a load of time. You can just go round back when you get there. Aunt Susie said she'd be out on the deck. Oh, since Allie's not there, could you remind Aunt Susie not to forget her meds?"

Since Allie's not there...

If she wasn't at work, and she wasn't at home, then something must be very wrong. Logan shoved the sandwich into his shirt pocket before he climbed into his pickup, his mind already a few miles down the road.

He found Susie on the back deck, just as Dulcie had said he would. Her eyes were closed, her face red and blotchy, leaving him no doubt she'd been crying. His stomach tightened and the few sips of coffee he'd managed to swallow on the way over here threatened to reappear. Something awful must have happened.

"Susie?"

Though he called her name softly, the woman sat bolt upright, her fingers clinched around the arm of her chair.

"Oh, Logan, it's you. I thought Allie might have come back."

"What's going on? Where is she?"

"She's gone to find my baby." Fresh tears rolled down Susie's cheeks unchecked. "Or what's left of him after the coyotes have at him. He got away from me this morning and headed for the backcountry."

It was the dog in trouble. Only the dog, not Allie.

"But she's been gone so long, I'm starting to lose hope we'll ever find him."

The pressure that had been dissipating in Logan's chest slammed back at full force. "How long?"

"At least three, maybe four hours."

He'd need water. He ran back out front to his pickup and pulled his rescue pack, with its freshly filled canteen, from behind the seat and strapped it around his waist before returning to the back deck.

"Which way did she go?"

Susie pointed toward the hills behind their property. "Same direction Grainger went, up Papa Flynn's hunting trail. You'll want to hurry, though, Logan. Looks like there's an afternoon storm building to roll in over the mountains."

Her description of where Allie had gone told him all he needed to know. No wonder she hadn't returned his call. That trail wound its way into some rough mountain backcountry where there was no hope of cell service. He'd traveled into that area many times with Matt and Danny. Back in high school, the three of them had camped up there one weekend in an old hunting cabin Harley Flynn had built several decades ago.

Logan placed a quick call to Tanner to advise him of the situation before he got too far in and lost his cell service. This wasn't the sort of thing you did without letting someone know where you were going.

"I just heard on the scanner that they're tracking a big-assed storm headed our way. Dropping temps, high winds, heavy lightning, the works. If we get the kind of rain they're predicting, there could be some local flooding, too. At the very least, you're going to find some treacherous footing if you're up there too long. Coming down after dark could be a serious mistake," Tanner warned.

"Don't worry. I won't try to make it back down after the sun sets. If worst comes to worst, I... *we* can spend the night in Harley's hunting cabin." It would be *we*. There was no way he wasn't going to find Allie. The problem would be finding her and getting back before dark.

He remembered a shortcut or two to hasten his trek up the hill. At least, he hoped he could remember the way to find the shortcuts. They were his best hope for catching up with Allie. No matter. Shortcuts or no, if Allie had stayed anywhere close to the trail, he'd find her.

And when he did, he intended to give her a damn good piece of his mind for taking off into the wilderness like that all by herself.

CHAPTER TWENTY

Thunder rumbled in the distance and Allie halted her progress once more. The sky looked even more threatening than it had only minutes before.

"Just great," she grumbled, taking a moment to lean against a big tree.

It wasn't bad enough that her stomach was rumbling almost as loudly as the approaching thunder or that she was out of practice hiking in this altitude, leaving her with just about zero energy, or that she still hadn't found Grainger. Now, on top of everything else, it was going to storm.

"Just freakin' great," she said, louder this time.

No doubt about it, before long she would be one miserable woman. Rain in the high country almost always meant a big drop in temperature, so these shorts that she'd been so pleased with herself for wearing were very quickly going to become something she wasn't the least bit pleased to have worn.

She briefly considered turning around and trying to beat the approaching storm, but there was really no chance she could do that. So, since she hadn't found the dog yet, and she was going to get wet no matter which way she went, she might as well keep going the direction she was headed.

She pushed off the tree and started forward again, glancing down in time to find another clump of fur snarled around another little bush. This was the fifth time she'd made such a find and, while it gave her hope she was still on the right trail to find Grainger, she was beginning to picture her mother's little dog as being bald when she did finally catch up with him.

Her only consolation at this point was that a bald Grainger was going to be every bit as cold and miserable as she would be when those rains hit.

"Grainger!" she yelled for what felt like the millionth time.

She'd been at this for hours. If the coyotes didn't finish off the contrary little half-bald furball, she just might be tempted to do it herself if she ever found him.

"When, not if," she muttered, angry that she'd allowed doubt to creep into her thoughts.

She couldn't afford to doubt her success now. Not with her mom counting on her to bring Grainger home, safe and sound.

Another boom of thunder rolled through the sky, and in the seconds of silence that followed the ominous noise, Allie could swear she heard something like a whimper.

"Grainger," she called, more quietly this time. "You

out here, baby dog?" It sure had sounded like him.

Slowly, she moved away from the trail, pushing through the thick underbrush with her feet, searching. If she ended up with ticks on her bare legs because of this, she was going to...

Another rumble of thunder, followed by another whimper. And a rustle in the underbrush just ahead.

Slowly, cautiously, she extended her walking stick to push aside the branches and leaves. There, in a small depression under a web-covered juniper bush, she found a bundle of shivering brown fur.

It would have to be a juniper, testing her last bit of reserve. She hated the spreading green spider-houses, hated the thought of having to reach her hands in there, but the little terrier obviously was in no shape to come out of his hiding place on his own.

Forcing back her own fears, she reached inside and snagged Grainger, pulling him out, expecting the worst. To have crawled off into a hole like that, he must be hurt.

He didn't resist when she cuddled him close, but he was shaking like an aspen leaf on a windy day. Thunder rumbled once more and he shook even harder.

How could she have forgotten? This little guy was brave enough to face down a bull elk. He had, as a matter of fact, done exactly that years ago, chasing the massive beast right out of their yard. But thunderstorms? Thunderstorms terrified him senseless.

"We all have our failings, don't we, big guy?" she soothed, scratching behind his ear as he pressed his body against her chest. "Don't you worry. You're okay. I've got you now and you're going to be just fine. I'll take care of you."

"Really?" a deep voice rumbled from the trees behind her. "And just who is going to take care of you?"

* * *

The forest was no place to be with that storm so close, but it wasn't like Logan had much of a choice. Tanner had said they were warning of heavy rain. Fingers crossed, that meant he could eliminate the worry of fires started by dry lightning. The regular stuff was dangerous enough. If he hurried, he might be able to make it to Harley's hunting cabin before the worst of it hit. He just prayed that the hunting cabin was still standing after all these years.

Heading directly for the cabin would mean postponing his hunt for Allie. It would mean leaving her out here to face dropping temperatures and lightning strikes on her own, and that simply wasn't acceptable.

In the distance he heard something he'd been hoping to hear for hours.

"Grainger!"

He'd found her. The shortcuts had worked.

Forging through the trees, he spotted her at last, off the trail, standing in underbrush up past her calves. Wearing shorts.

"What the hell were you thinking?" he muttered.

For a woman who'd been born and raised in these mountains, she sure didn't seem to have the bare-bones knowledge of a native. He'd seen wet-behind-the-ears tourists, who'd never spent a single day of their lives in the mountains, who had better sense than to head off into the back country dressed like that.

"You're going to be just fine," she said to the creature in her arms as he approached. "I'll take care of you."

That from a woman whose legs already sported a network of scratches and who was going to be freezing her ass off in about fifteen minutes.

"Really?" he asked. "And just who is going to take care of you?" Because it was obvious to him that she wasn't capable of doing it.

Something sounding like a high-pitched squeak came out of her and she jumped, literally, a good two inches off the ground, twisting toward him at the same time.

"Jesus, Logan!" She clutched the bundle of fur she held to her chest, her eyes open wide. "You scared me half to death."

"Only fair," he answered, ignoring how this wasn't the first time she'd said those words to him. "Because you had me worried half to death. What were you thinking heading up this far all by yourself? Without a plan and without even telling anyone where you were headed?"

He was fully aware that it was fear sparking his anger, but that knowledge didn't change how he felt. His heart still pounded at the thought of all that could have gone wrong with this scenario. He'd been called out on too many rescue operations for hikers in trouble who thought they knew what they were doing and who had been much better prepared when they'd set out than Allie had been today.

"Well, sorry." Her tone was anything but contrite. "But Grainger didn't bother to leave a detailed itinerary of his travel plans for the day, so just how was I supposed to tell someone where I was going? And what I was thinking was that I needed to find this damn dog before he ended up as a coyote snack. The absolute last thing I need from you is—"

Thunder boomed overhead, obliterating her words. Apparently he'd have to live a while longer without learning what she didn't need from him. Right now, he had more important concerns. A glance to the sky told him all he needed to know. The rain would be miserable, but not life threatening. It was the lightning that presented the greatest danger.

"We can't stay out here." He crossed the distance between them, taking her by the elbow as he spoke. "This is only going to get worse."

In typical Allie fashion, she pulled her elbow away. "I don't see what choice you think we have. It's not like we can outrun this. It's taken me all day to get here."

"Your grandpa's hunting cabin is just a little farther up this trail. If we keep moving, we might get there before the worst of it hits."

"Then again, we might not," she muttered as the first big, wet drops splattered against the foliage around them.

She grumbled, but at least she followed along with him when he started forward.

The cold rain was pelting down in earnest by the time they made their way to the little cabin. Logan's relief at finding the place was short-lived when he spotted a lock hanging through the latch on the door. He didn't remember that being there the last time he'd been to the cabin.

"Damn."

Neither the knife nor the small flashlight he carried would be heavy enough to break the lock, and in spite of his many skills, he had no abilities as a lock-pick.

"Here," Allie said from behind him. "Try this." She slipped the leather strap of her walking stick off her wrist and offered it to him.

"Lock looks too new for me to be able to break it."

"Maybe," she conceded. "But that latch thingy looks like it must be at least a hundred years old. I bet a couple of really good whacks will knock it out of that wood, screws and all."

It was worth a try. The first hit reverberated up Logan's arms and into his shoulders, but barely budged the rusted metal. The third hit bent it out far enough that he could slide the heavy walking stick under it to use as a pry bar to pop the old metal loose.

Within minutes the door swung open and he scanned the interior with his flashlight before ushering Allie inside.

The place was a cabin in name only. Harley hadn't bothered with any of the amenities that modern-day hunters might consider a necessity. Two bare army surplus cots, a table and two chairs made up the furnishings, along with an open shelf built along one wall. An old coffeepot sat on the top shelf, next to some neatly stacked metal cups and plates and, on the shelf below, a kerosene lamp that was likely older than Harley. That was it. Bare bones. There weren't even any windows, though the cracks around the door served the purpose pretty well.

"F-fireplace," Allie said as his light swept the interior again, her voice shaking as she shuddered with the cold. "A-and dry wood. Th-thank you, Papa Flynn."

Now that they were safe from the immediate danger, survival instincts kicked in and Logan set about doing what needed to be done. First things first. They were all soaked to the skin, and both Allie and the dog were shivering with the cold.

Logan pulled one of his two silver emergency blankets from his pack and wrapped it around Allie's shoulders before he set about building a fire. A quick check of the chimney assured him that, though spiders had been busy building webs inside, there were no obstructions that would prevent them from starting a fire.

Once the fire roared to life, he pulled off his T-shirt and hung it over a chair to dry. Behind him, Allie clapped her hands. Whether her applause was meant for his action or for the fire, he wasn't sure. He turned around to ask, and found her pouring the last of her water into a bowl she then set in front of the dog... the dog that she'd wrapped in the blanket he'd given to her to warm her up.

"Allie, the dog has fur to keep him warm. He's going to be fine." Whereas she was still shivering.

"I know. But he's so wet right now. And frightened out of his little head by the storm. He feels safer all cuddled up inside that blanket. I can hang out by the fire."

He started to tell her how ridiculous she was being, but the words dried up in his mouth when she walked toward the fire, pulling her T-shirt up and over her head to hang on the chair next to his. When she began to unzip her shorts, he suffered a major coughing fit as the words that had clumped in his mouth backed up into his throat. Or maybe it was just his own saliva drowning him rather than dripping out as drool.

She paused, shorts halfway down her legs, to send him a look. "What? It's not like you haven't seen me in my underwear before."

True. He'd also seen her *out* of her underwear, and

that was the memory flooding his mind—and all his blood vessels—as he watched her now.

"You should peel out of your wet pants, too, if they're going to have any chance at all of drying." She wiggled her eyebrows as a big grin lit her face. "I won't attack you. I promise."

That made him smile.

"Okay, then. As long as my chastity is safe."

"It is. Though I can't promise the same for your blanket."

"I knew it!" He sat down close to her and looped his arm over her shoulders, drawing her close within the shelter of his blanket. "I finally find the perfect woman and she only wants me for my body heat."

Next to him, she stilled. "I want a lot more from you than body heat, Logan."

Him too. But it was as good a place to start as any. He turned into her, intending to lower her to her back but, for the first time, he met with resistance. Her open palm pressed against his chest and she scooted a few inches away from him.

"What's wrong?"

"I want more," she repeated, "but not under any false pretenses. I have something I need to tell you."

* * *

This was the moment Allie had promised herself. The moment she would take a chance on total honesty. She'd just never imagined they'd be sitting together in their underwear when it arrived. All she had to do was open her mouth and let the truth roll out.

224

She took a deep breath and began. "You know that I dated your brother, Ryan, right? Back in high school."

"So I'd heard."

What was that tone she heard in his voice? Suspicion? Disapproval?

"Did he ever tell you why we broke up?"

"He never even told me you'd dated, Allie. Katie's the one who mentioned it. Right after you first came back to Chance."

Okay, this is it. Tell him. Just say the words.

"I need to tell you about what happened between us. About why Ryan stopped seeing me. You need to know."

"I don't care why you broke up with Ryan. What happened between the two of you when you guys were in high school doesn't matter to me in the least." In spite of his words, that same suspicious look still knitted his brow. "Not unless you still like him and that's why you're seeing me."

Something close to a hysterical giggle bubbled up in the back of Allie's throat, burning until tears clouded her vision. "No, that's not it. In fact, it's more like the other way around."

"I don't understand where you're going with any of this, Allie."

One more deep breath to calm herself, to stop the shivers of dread, and she forced herself to confess.

"My senior year, I decided to stalk Ryan. Nothing else had worked and I felt like I was running out of chances. I hounded him until he asked me out. I made myself the perfect girlfriend so he'd continue to see me."

She paused, her heart pounding so hard in her chest she expected that any minute the sound would drown out her words.

"And then he dumped you? For some other girl?" Logan reached for her hand but she pulled away.

The last thing she deserved was his pity.

"No. Then he found out that I'd betrayed him. Lacey told him my secret. That I'd been dating him in hopes of getting closer to you."

"Me?" Genuine surprise replaced the suspicion in his eyes. "Why would you... I wasn't even in Chance then."

"I know. That was why I thought dating Ryan was my only way to get to you. It was stupid and deceitful and wrong. I really liked your brother as a friend. And letting him think otherwise was awful of me. I've regretted it ever since." Allie paused again, drawing in a long, shuddering breath. "But that's what I did. And I couldn't let us get any closer without making sure you knew what kind of person I really am."

"What kind of person you *were*," he corrected, a soft smile curving his lips. "You were worried I'd be upset about something you did when you were seventeen?" He cupped her face in his hands, his thumb stroking against her cheek. "Oh, babe, that would never happen. So you did something stupid at seventeen that you regret. We all regret the stupid stuff we did at seventeen."

"But you said the thing you hated most was deceit, and that's what I did. I deceived Ryan, and knowing how you feel about something like that has been eating at me. I was the definition of stupid."

Logan slid his hands to her shoulders and pulled her to him, her head resting on his chest. Underneath her ear, his heart pounded almost as hard as hers.

"No, Allie, you weren't. If either of us was the

definition of stupid at seventeen, it was me. I proposed to Shayla at seventeen. You think you deceived Ryan by dating him because you had some fleeting little crush on me. But I did something much worse. I deceived myself. Because I wanted to find that perfect girl to settle down with. Because I wanted what I saw between my parents every day of my life, I convinced myself that Shayla was the one." He stroked his hand down her hair and gave her a quick hug. "It took me a long time to realize you have to let go of the stupid stuff you did when you were a kid. It doesn't matter. It's what you do with your life now that matters."

He didn't care what she'd done in the past. As if some huge pressure had been lifted, the tears that had only threatened earlier spilled out and rolled down her cheeks. Relief settled over her and she wrapped her arms around his neck, snuggling closer to him.

"It wasn't a *little* crush," she said at last. "And it wasn't fleeting. Since we're clearing the air and all."

His hand stilled on her hair. "What are you saying?"

"I'm saying that I've felt this way about you since my eleventh birthday, when you gave me a Nancy Drew book all wrapped up in shiny silver paper."

"I remember that." A chuckle rumbled through his chest beneath her ear. "You do realize I had nothing to do with that gift, right? I didn't even know it was your birthday. I was just coming over to hang with Matt and my mom handed me a gift to give to you. I just delivered a package."

"You did more than that," she said, remembering the moment as if it had been yesterday. "You walked in the door and smiled directly at me, as if you'd come just to see me and then you tugged on my braid and wished me a happy birthday."

"Yeah? And then I took off with Matt and never gave it another thought. So that's why you thought you liked me? Because I brought you a book?"

"I didn't say that was *why*. Who knows why? I said that was *when*. And I didn't say I liked you. I said…"

Her words trailed off as she gathered her courage to speak of the feelings that would expose her vulnerability. She'd gone this far, she might as well go all the way.

"What?" he asked, his eyes searching hers.

"What I meant was that was when I first realized I loved you. Was in love with you. I always have been."

"And now?" he asked, his voice barely more than a whisper.

"Now more than ever," she replied, closing her eyes as his head dipped close and his lips claimed hers.

"Knowing that makes what we're about to do all that much sweeter," he said, rolling her to her back, one hand protectively cushioning her head as she lay down.

Thunder rumbled overhead and rain beat down on the wooden roof at a constant tattoo, isolating them from the rest of the world. No people for miles, no phone service, nothing to interrupt them.

Cocooned in their own private ecstasy, Allie relaxed into Logan's embrace, eager to finish what they'd started the night before.

His hands roamed over her body, slowly, possessively, filling her with a whole new level of desire for him.

"Now," she whimpered, lifting her hips into him.

"Time doesn't matter here," he whispered into her

ear. "We're taking it slow. I want you to remember every minute of this."

This was one experience she intended to savor, tucking every single minute of it into her memory. But memories or no, slow wasn't working for her. Slow was a game of torture.

A game two could play.

When she slid her hands between their bodies and wrapped her fingers around the length of his hardened shaft, slow apparently stopped working for him, too.

An involuntary groan of pleasure burst from her lungs when he entered her, plunging deep before he paused, his body hovering over hers.

"You're beautiful," he said, his voice cracking as he slowly pulled out before driving in again. "Beautiful lying under me, your eyes filled with surrender."

"You don't read eyes very well, do you? That's not surrender you're looking at." She pushed against him, rolling until he was on his back and she sat atop him. "That's triumph you're seeing, pure and simple. It works like this."

She began to move back and forth in an undulating motion, until he grabbed her waist, stilling her. Twining her fingers through his, she encouraged his hands up to her breasts while she resumed her movements from before.

Her body tensed with pleasure only moments before his did, and when it was over, she lay down, curled next to his side, his arm cushioning her head. Never in any of her fantasies had she felt this wonderful.

Logan lay on his back, his eyes closed. His chest rose and fell in a steady cadence, his slow, rhythmic breathing the most relaxing thing she'd ever imagined. By turning her head only slightly, she was able to study his profile.

That she was here with him now was almost beyond belief. She had no more secrets to carry around. And nothing she'd told him had changed his mind about how he felt about her. At least, she assumed it hadn't. It would be easier to be sure of that if she actually knew how he felt about her. But other than that one minor issue, everything was perfect. Almost perfect. Perfect would have involved him replying to her declaration of love with a similar admission.

She trailed a tentative finger across the muscles in his chest and his eyelids fluttered open. When he turned on his side and pulled her close, the lazy grin on his face left no doubt as to his intentions. Intentions she was more than willing to play an active role in fulfilling.

Soon enough, they'd have to get themselves together and head down the mountain. But for now, she was more than happy to settle for almost perfect.

CHAPTER TWENTY-ONE

With a sense of confidence Logan hadn't felt in a very long time, he pulled the clipboard from under the seat of his pickup, adjusted his cap, and headed up the sidewalk to Golddiggers.

"I'd like to see your manager," he announced to the young woman standing just inside the door. "I'm here for your fire inspection."

He could thank Allie for his being here today. It was as if in finding her, he'd found a missing piece of himself. A missing piece that had kept him from getting on with his life. His relationship with her had made him whole again.

"Well, well, if it isn't Logan O'Connor surprising me yet again." Shayla walked toward him, her hand extended in welcome. "When Carla told me someone was here for the fire inspection, I expected it to be Tanner. What's up with that?"

Though he'd known he was likely to run into her

today, this wasn't at all what he'd expected. Rather than the slinky, satin-clad vixen version of her he'd prepared himself to encounter, this was a thoroughly scrubbed, makeup-free, jeans and T-shirt version. He hoped for her sake that this was the real Shayla.

He shook her hand, only mildly surprised to find that the action carried with it absolutely no emotion whatsoever. The past just might be behind him, where it belonged.

"Strictly a business call, Shayla. Your number came up on my list instead of Tanner's this year."

Not exactly a lie, but close enough that he found himself scanning over the form on his clipboard rather than making eye contact with the woman. Coming here had been more of a test he'd set up for himself. A test he was happy to realize he was passing.

"All righty, then," she said with a smile. "Let's hit the kitchen and get this over with. You can see for yourself all the exits are marked. All my extinguishers are up to date, and I want you to know, I called in an electrician from Denver to go over all the wiring the day after our little fire incident."

"Do you have documentation for that?"

She laughed and held open the kitchen door for him to enter first. "You want to see the paperwork to prove I'm telling the truth? What happened to my sweet, trusting Logan?"

You happened. That being his first thought meant that he hadn't yet completely put the past behind him. But the fact that he didn't say it out loud convinced him that he'd come a long way.

"I'd like a copy to attach to the inspection report

since I witnessed firsthand that there was a problem."

"In that case, yes, I have paperwork on it, from a fully licensed company. I'll make sure you have a copy in your hot little hands before you leave." She leaned back against one of the kitchen workstations, her arms crossed in front of her. "Let's get one thing straight up front, Logan. Regardless of what you might think of me, I don't cut corners when it comes to my business. I have big plans for Golddiggers and taking shortcuts won't get me where I want to be."

"Understood," he said, still not completely convinced she was being honest with him. "I'll try to make this as quick as possible and get out of everyone's way."

The kitchen was a hive of activity, with what appeared to be a full staff busily cleaning and prepping food. He had specifically waited until the afternoon so that he'd arrive after their lunch rush and before they began preparations for the dinner crowd, but, from the looks of things, he'd miscalculated.

"Shay?" A young woman pushed through the kitchen doors, her expression strained. "Thank goodness. The liquor distributor is here and the order is short."

Logan didn't recognize the newcomer, and in a town the size of Chance, that said something.

"Not again!" Shayla snapped, already moving toward the door. "Sorry, Logan. I have to deal with this. Staff in here will be heading out shortly, but there should be someone left around to answer any questions you might have until I return. I'll be back as soon as I can."

Within minutes of Shayla's departure, exactly as she'd predicted, the kitchen staff began to drift away until only a couple of people remained.

Logan filled his lungs and exhaled the stress that had built since he'd entered the building, relieved to continue his work out from under Shayla's watchful eye.

The inspection progressed quickly, with no concerns of note. At this rate, he'd be back at the station by the time Allie called to check in. He glanced at his watch, reassured that she'd had time to reach Grand Junction by now and would likely be wandering through one of the stores she had planned to visit at this very moment.

Thinking of her enjoying her shopping trip almost made up for his disappointment that he couldn't have gone with her. The timing hadn't worked out, though, since he wouldn't be off until tomorrow and she had to get her mom's meds today. But the day wasn't a total loss. She'd agreed to join him for dinner at the station tonight, so he'd still get a chance to see her.

"It's all good," he muttered, scanning over his checklist to make sure he hadn't missed anything.

He had almost finished when he noticed a cluster of what appeared to be liquid-filled gallon glass jars sitting on top of some high metal shelving. Normally he would have ignored storage items, leaving that sort of thing to the health inspectors. But these particular items fell squarely under his area of concern, since they were all tall enough that they butted up against the fire sprinklers. One had even been placed so that a sprinkler head hung down inside the jar. A definite violation he couldn't ignore, but one he'd give any business owner a chance to correct.

"Fire code stipulates that you can't store anything in a manner that impedes the function of the sprinklers," he said to the young man cleaning the stove. "You'll need to move those."

"Not me," the employee replied. "Chef Roberto stuck that stuff up there. No way I'm messing with anything of his."

"Look"—Logan paused to read the name on his uniform—"Joey, we need to clear that shelf to meet fire code. Simple as that. I'm sure your boss would approve."

"No way. Shayla might be fine with it, but she's not the one who'd have to deal with Chef. That would be me. You don't know what he's like to work with. I'm not doing it. No one here in the kitchen will." Joey bent back to the oven he was cleaning, clearly indicating that, as far as he was concerned, their conversation was over.

Frustrated by the unhelpful teenager, Logan started to mark the infraction on his sheet, but stopped, knowing he'd handle this situation differently for any other business in town. If he was ever going to be rid of his past with this woman, he had to deal with her exactly as he would anyone else.

"Okay, then. You got a stepstool somewhere around here?"

The kitchen staff might be intimidated by their chef, but Logan wasn't.

"Only that little one by the walk-in," Joey mumbled, his head still inside the oven. "But I wouldn't touch any of that stuff up there if I were you."

Logan retrieved the small metal stool and looked it over before dropping it in front of the shelf. It looked sturdy enough to hold him, though it only added about six inches to his reach. Either the chef was one giant of a man or there was a ladder around here this kid wasn't telling him about.

Stepping up on the stool, he extended his arms above

his head and hooked the very tips of his fingers onto the base of the first jar, inching it forward toward the edge of the shelf in short side-to-side jerks. The lip of the jar snugged up against the sprinkler and he shoved the base to the left, sloshing some of the liquid inside over the edge and onto his hands.

Please don't let it be vinegar.

The thought of smelling like a salad for the rest of the day wasn't appealing in the least.

The last shove brought the jar close enough for him to get his finger under the front and pull it forward, just as the skin on the back of his hands began to itch.

"What's stored in these jars?" he asked, tightening his hold on the bottom of the glass as he at last edged it off the shelf.

A question he should have asked earlier, he realized too late.

In spite of his best effort, the wet glass slid through his grasp, tipping forward and dumping its contents on him. He jerked his head back, avoiding a direct-face hit, but his entire front, chest to knees, was soaked.

The itching in his hands intensified as the cold liquid pasted his uniform against his skin.

"What's going on in here?" Shayla had returned, standing only feet away. "You're soaked. What is that stuff?"

"Smells like that drain cleaner Chef was using yesterday," Joey said. "I think he might have stuck it up on that shelf when he finished with it. He was in a pretty big hurry to get out of here."

"Oh, Christ," Shayla said, dropping the folder of papers she'd carried and grabbing the buckle on Logan's equipment belt. "You have to get out of those clothes. Right now. That crap is toxic. Caustic. Whatever you call it. It'll burn right into your skin. You need to get that rinsed off of you before it's too late!"

"What's in it?" Logan asked, reluctant to peel out of his clothing here in the middle of the Golddiggers kitchen, in spite of the skin irritation he was already feeling.

"Roberto made up his own crap. Lye and... what was that other thing he said he used, Joey? Oh!" She snapped her fingers and grabbed for his belt again. "Sulfuric acid. Strip, Logan. This instant."

Logan didn't know a lot about chemistry, but what he did know convinced him he needed to get this stuff off of him as soon as possible. He made no protest when his equipment belt slid from his waist and dropped to the floor and Shayla began to push him forward.

"Use the dishwashers' station. The hose is long enough to reach out onto the floor and you can hose yourself off. Don't worry about the mess. Joey, go get one of the kitchen uniforms we'd give a new hire. Hurry up!"

By the time they reached the dish-washing sinks, Logan's reluctance was gone. His hands felt like he'd run into a fire without his protective gear and his chest was beginning to itch just as his hands had.

"What the hell were you thinking when you took the lid off that jar?"

"There was no lid," he told her as he stripped off his shirt. "All the jars are wide open."

"Son of a... I should fire his ass the minute he walks in. I would if I didn't need a halfway decent cook tonight. Oh—" She stopped speaking as he unzipped his pants and she turned her back. "You need any help over there?"

MELISSA MAYHUE

"I got this," he assured her, grabbing the sprayer and turning the nozzle on full blast, allowing the cold water to blast over the front of his body. All that mattered right now was getting the chemicals off his skin before they did any real damage.

If she said anything else after that, he couldn't hear over the rush of the water, and he didn't bother to look back to see if she remained where she'd been. It didn't matter to him whether she stayed or left.

He realized with a shock that his past with her no longer held any importance to him. None of her actions mattered to him anymore. He simply didn't care what she did.

He didn't care, that is, until he turned around and saw her holding his equipment belt in one hand and his cell phone up to her ear.

* * *

Few emotions tasted sweeter to the soul than accomplishment. So far, Allie's day tasted like it had been made of pure spun sugar and dipped in honey.

She wore a smile that she could feel stretching her face as she left the big pharmacy and crossed the parking lot to her car. This was the sort of day that made all others fade into misty memory.

Logan had awakened her with an early phone call, inviting her to join him for dinner this evening at the firehouse. The knowledge that even on his duty nights he wanted to spend time with her warmed her heart.

Her drive to Grand Junction had been without incident, other than a fun sighting of a herd of elk wandering through one of the valleys she'd passed by. The natural foods store where Dulcie ordered her dried fruit had given Allie a moment's concern when she'd arrived and they'd had to hunt for her cousin's order. But they'd located the bags of specialty fruits at last and sent her on her way. She'd had a lovely lunch and two glasses of her favorite sweet tea. Even the pharmacy had cooperated, and she was in and out with her mother's prescription much more quickly than she'd expected. At this rate, she'd be home in plenty of time to take a nice, relaxing bath and get all fixed up before dinner with her man.

Her man. The words fairly sang through her mind as she slipped into her car seat and tossed her bag and purse into the seat beside her.

Her business was on the verge of turning a profit, her mother's illness seemed to be moving toward remission, and she'd managed to find the one man in the world she might actually be able to trust.

"Life is good," she announced to the world with a little chuckle.

She'd done everything she needed to do on her trip except for one thing. She'd promised Logan she'd give him a quick call when she was on her way home so he'd know everything was okay. He'd told her he worried about her and wanted her to check in. How lucky was she? Clever, handsome, a great cook, *and* he worried about her. The list of reasons why Logan O'Connor was the perfect man continued to grow.

She slipped her cell phone from her purse, remembering as she did that she'd forgotten to charge it. One check assured her that her battery was almost dead, but perhaps she could sneak in one more call before it pooped out on her. With a silent prayer to the telephone gods, she pressed the speed-dial button under Logan's smiling face.

One ring. Two.

There was no way he wouldn't answer. She'd called his work phone, just as he'd asked her to. As she knew all too well, he never missed a call on that phone.

Three rings.

"Logan O'Connor's phone," a feminine voice lilted from the little machine in her hand.

Logan's phone maybe, but not his voice.

"Hello?" the voice said when she didn't respond. "Anyone there?"

Not Logan, but a voice she recognized all the same. Shayla.

Time slowed to a crawl as shock seethed through Allie's system. It tingled through her chest and tightened her throat, preventing her from doing anything other than listening to the sounds issuing from the little red piece of technology in her hand.

She listened as Shayla confirmed to someone — Logan? — that, yes, she'd answered his phone and that maybe he should put on some pants and come get it from her if he wanted it that damn bad.

Put on some pants?

Allie's good sense returned at last and she pressed the button to end the call, holding it until her phone turned off.

Lightning wasn't supposed to strike the same place twice, but it had. She'd lived through an almost identical phone call once before. She could just as well have been standing in front of a hospital in Texas as sitting in a parking lot in Colorado. Her life had just served up an enormous helping of hideous rerun.

Only this time, she didn't feel the detached nothingness she'd experienced before. This time it hurt like hell. Pain lanced through her heart, ripped through her guts, doubled her over with the agony of realization.

No wonder he'd wanted her to call before she came back. He hadn't cared about her. He'd only wanted time to make sure he didn't get caught. Too bad he hadn't been more careful with his phone.

In spite of what she'd thought, in spite of how she'd deluded herself, Logan was no different from Drake. No different from her father. The realization did nothing to lessen the pain buffeting her with every breath. If anything, knowing she'd allowed this to happen all over again only made it worse.

"Hold it together," she whispered to encourage herself.

Just hold it together for a couple of hours. Just until she could get home, get into her room. There, away from the prying eyes of the rest of the world, there she could safely break down.

With shaking hands, she reached for her key and stuck it in the ignition. When she turned it, nothing happened.

"Of course you won't start," she said, her voice shaking as tears pooled in her eyes. "Why would I expect anything else?"

Deep, breath-stealing sobs clawed their way up from her chest. Large, salty drops rolled down her cheeks, plopping onto her lap as she cushioned her head against the steering wheel and gave in to the misery that threatened to crush her.

CHAPTER TWENTY-TWO

Doc Gillsap, the only medical doctor in the valley, had come as soon as Tanner had called. Logan hadn't wanted to call the doctor. The whole incident hardly seemed worth the old man's travel time all the way to Chance.

But now, almost two hours after the initial incident, Logan was grateful his friend had been so insistent. Even with the extra strength lotion their local store carried slathered on his skin, the itching on the back of his hands and at the very center of his chest had intensified to the point of serious discomfort.

"We need to get an antibiotic cream on the backs of those hands. That little spot on your chest, too," Doc Gillsap said, wrinkling his nose as he tilted his head to see through his reading glasses. "I'm calling in a script for some pills that will help the itch, as well. Looks as though you got most of it off in time to avoid the worst of it, but

243

you're gonna feel this for a while, boy. Chemical burns are nasty buggers. They don't really show the extent of their damage for a couple of days. If it gets any redder or blisters start to form, you call me right away, you hear?"

"I'm sure I'll be fine," Logan answered. "Just as soon as I go pick up the meds you're calling in for me."

"Oh no you don't," Tanner said, stuffing his cell phone back into its holder on his belt. "I'll go get them. You don't need to be out on the highway with your hands all messed up like that. I need to head over that direction anyway. You take it easy like Doc said. You want anything before we go?"

Logan shook his head and leaned back on the sofa, feet up. Tanner had hovered over him like some old woman ever since Logan had first called him about the accident. He hated being treated like an invalid. Especially by someone like Tanner. His partner was about as far from a coddler as anyone could be, so to have him acting like this was something serious only made Logan feel guiltier.

The entire afternoon had been a disaster of his own making. He should have been smarter than to pull an open jar down on his head in the first place.

Then there was the problem with Allie. She hadn't checked in. Not once since she'd headed out for Grand Junction this morning. No calls for a whole day wasn't at all like Allie. At least, it wasn't like her now that they had this relationship.

Funny that the word *relationship* had sprung to mind so readily. But that was what it was, this thing that had grown between them. A fully realized relationship. And, after all the years he'd spent avoiding entanglements and the idea of a relationship, he couldn't quite imagine life without this particular one.

Where was she?

He closed his eyes, struggling to recall every word of their early telephone conversation. She had planned to make the trip to pick up ingredients for Dulcie and a prescription for her mom. Then she'd be back here to join him for dinner.

Only she wasn't here. And, in spite of her promise, there'd been no calls. Even if she'd stopped for lunch, she should have returned by now.

He'd tried to reach her multiple times but couldn't get through to her and now worry ate at his gut.

His phone lay on the table next to him and he reached for it to call her once more. Still no answer, so he left another message. What was that? Number five or six? Granted, she might not be comfortable answering while she was driving, and there were dead spots through parts of the canyon. But she'd promised to call him before she left the city for home and there hadn't been a call all day.

Unless...

A memory of one particular moment from this afternoon flashed into his mind, carrying with it a trickle of sick dread. There had been that one call. The one that had come through while he was washing off the chemicals. The call that Shayla had answered because he hadn't heard his phone ringing. The call she'd said had no one on the other end of the line when she'd answered.

In the flurry of activity that followed his accident, he'd dismissed the incident from his mind, chalking it up to nothing more than a wrong number.

But now? Now, with a thousand fears gnawing at his brain, that call took on an ominous feel.

Could it have been Allie?

He scanned through the options on his phone, hunting for the list of calls. Sure enough, there it was, Allie's number recorded as incoming right after his accident this afternoon.

The call Shayla answered. The one where no one had responded and she'd yelled at him to get his pants on and come get the phone.

Christ! He could only imagine what Allie must have thought was going on when she heard that. She'd told him all about what had happened with that guy back in Texas. And the whole town knew what her father had done. With her history of bad experiences, there was no way she wouldn't have jumped to the worst possible conclusion. He certainly would have.

Logan pushed up off the sofa, hunting for his keys. He had to find her. He had to explain. Before it was too late. Before he lost her for good. If that happened, the afternoon wouldn't be just a disaster. It would be a complete and total disaster of epic proportions.

* * *

How long she'd sat in the parking lot, Allie had no idea. She knew only that her head hurt and her tears were all used up. She wiped her hands over her cheeks and tried to decide what to do next.

She had to get her mother's prescription home to her tonight, even if that meant calling someone to come get her. The realization that two hours ago that *someone* would have been Logan started a fresh trickle of tears in spite of her thinking there could be no more.

No! She wouldn't let herself dwell on this anymore. Not right now, anyway. Her heart might be broken, but it would mend, even though she suspected it would never be the same again. She would sort all of that out later, after she got home.

There were more immediate concerns for her to deal with first. Her grandmother would be the logical one to call for help. Or Dulcie. Except one glance at her cell phone reminded her that the battery was completely dead, so she'd have to find a phone to use to make that call.

The sudden *plink, plink* of raindrops peppering down only added to her frustration.

"Perfect," she ground out between clenched teeth. "Just perfect. Any other crap you want to dump my way today?"

According to Mama Odie, tempting fate was never a smart thing to do, but Allie briefly wondered how many days like this her grandmother might have faced. Few, she'd guess, considering the woman's always optimistic outlook.

Just for the heck of it, she tried the ignition once more and the car purred to life as if it had never had a problem. Maybe fate needed a little tempting every now and then to shake things up.

She pulled onto the road and turned toward home, feeling every bit as gloomy as the skies above her. The gentle peppering of raindrops continued until she was on the highway, at which point the skies opened up and the rain poured down in great, heaving sheets.

The rain persisted and Allie slowed her speed, hands clasped tightly around the steering wheel. Navigating the winding canyon on rain-slicked roads required her full attention and frayed her nerves like little else could. Eight years away from the mountains had made her doubt her ability to drive in them.

"Bull pucky," she whispered, and then louder: "I call bull pucky!"

This was her home. She'd learned to drive on these roads. She'd be damned if she'd be intimidated by them now. Not the road and not any of the other roadblocks thrown in her path today.

"You better have more than that if you think you're going to knock me out of the game," she said aloud, leaning forward to look up at the gray sky. "I might be down, but I'm a long way from out."

She pressed her foot down on the accelerator, surprised when the car didn't speed up as she'd expected. For the first time, she realized that the car was quieter than usual. Remarkably quiet in fact. Quiet like a car whose engine had been turned off.

Fighting the panic rising in her throat, Allie struggled to turn the unresponsive steering wheel. It felt as if she were trying to drive her grandpa's ancient tractor. At the same time, she pulsed her brake in an attempt to bring the car to a stop without running off the road. Considering the sheer drop into the canyon, off the road would be bad. Very bad.

After several long minutes of braking, the car rolled to a stop, but slid at least another foot on the slick pavement before coming to a complete halt in the gravel at the road's edge.

Allie sat where she was, hands frozen on the steering wheel, breathing deeply. When she could finally make herself let go, she removed her seat belt, opened her door and stepped out into the rain to survey the damage.

Another couple of inches and her worries would have been all over. Permanently. As it was, anyone getting out the passenger side would need a parachute to survive that first step.

It would appear her grandmother had been right about tempting fate, after all.

"You win," Allie whispered, staring over the edge of the cliff.

In one afternoon she'd lost the only man she'd ever wanted and very nearly lost her life in an accident all to similar to the one that had claimed her father. She couldn't hope to stand up to such a formidable power.

She trembled, teeth chattering, as she backed away from the road's edge. She had to figure out what to do next. Had to figure out what she could do. There was maybe an hour left before it started getting dark, and dark out here, with no houses or people around, was a whole different dark than in town.

Vaca Vista Inn was only a few miles down the road. She could walk that far, even in this rain. Once there, she'd call Mama Odie and this nightmare would be over.

Her eyes stung with tears as she reached inside the car to retrieve her purse and the little white prescription bag. The boxes of dried fruit would just have to wait to be rescued by someone else.

The storm began to slack off as she walked, turning into a slow, steady drizzle. A few cars passed, but none stopped or even slowed. A part of her was grateful they didn't. She could only pretend her face was wet from the rain for so long.

She heard another vehicle in the distance, coming

toward her, and, once again, she scooted to the far edge of the road. Only this one didn't zoom past. This one slowed and came to a stop in the middle of the road.

"Allie?" Tanner Grayson swung open the door and climbed out of his truck, walking toward her. "What the hell are you doing out here in the middle of nowhere? Are you okay?"

"No," she whimpered, humiliated that she couldn't fake it for even one minute.

"Come on," he encouraged, wrapping one arm around her shoulder and all but lifting her up into the passenger side of his truck. "Jesus, you're soaked to the skin. What happened?"

"Car died," she answered, unable to say more without completely breaking down in the face of his kindness.

"Okay then," he said as he climbed into his seat. He spoke in that all-business way of his that seemed to indicate he was already marking items off a checklist. "Did you talk to Logan? He's been trying to call you for the last couple of hours."

She shook her head, not trusting herself to say anything. Fortunately, Tanner's phone rang, giving her a reprieve.

He glanced at the little screen before answering, and a frown creased his brow. "Goddammit, Kat, I already told you he's fine so—" Tanner stopped speaking abruptly and a mottled red color crept up from his neck to his face. "Sorry, Mrs. O'Connor. I saw the number and assumed it was Katie calling. Again." Another pause. "Yes, ma'am, I know what assuming does. And, yes, you'll be my first call if there's any problem. Good night." He clipped his phone back into the holder on the dashboard and shook his head before turning toward Allie. "Well? Have you spoken to him?"

"No. My battery died."

"Okay then," he said again. "Logan had a little accident this afternoon. A minor chemical spill, but there's no need to worry. He's okay. I'm heading into Junction to grab some stuff the doctor prescribed for him and then I'll get you home. How's that sound?"

Her heart missed a full beat at hearing Logan had been hurt, but she pushed the feelings away. He didn't need her. He had his sister and his mother to worry after him. And Shayla. Let her nurse him back to health. Apparently that was what he wanted.

She just wanted to get home.

"Would you mind dropping me at the Vaca Vista Inn first?" When he looked as if he were going to refuse, she tried again. "I had two really big glasses of tea at lunch, Tanner, and I've been walking forever. If I don't get to a bathroom soon, I'm going to embarrass myself. Please, can we go to the inn?"

"Fair enough," he answered, turning the truck around to return in the direction he'd come from. "You want to use my cell to call Logan and let him know what's going on?"

"No."

She didn't want to speak to Logan. Not on a cell, not in person, not at all. Not now. Not ever.

"You want me to call him for you?"

"No."

Tanner didn't ask any more questions and she didn't offer any more information, choosing instead to stare blindly out the window until they reached their destination.

After another ten minutes, they pulled into the inn's parking lot, and Tanner came around to her side of the big truck to open the door and help her down.

Rather than stepping away, he blocked her path with his body and placed both hands on her shoulders. "You want to tell me what's wrong? I might be able to help, you know. I can be a pretty helpful guy sometimes."

"Not this time, I'm afraid," she answered. Rising up on her tiptoes, she kissed her rescuer on the cheek. "Thanks for saving me back there. I owe you one."

"Hey, that's what I do," he answered in his usual flippant tone. "You want me to come in with you?"

That was the last thing she wanted.

"No. You go on and get the stuff you need for Logan. I'm going to call my grandmother to come get me."

"If you're sure that's what you want," he said, his gaze focused on her like he was trying to read her mind. "You want me to have Logan call you at home?"

"No. But you can give him a message for me. Tell him not to bother calling me. I don't want to talk to him or to see him again."

"You sure you don't want to reconsider that?" he asked. "Logan's not going to take that message very well, you know."

"I don't care how he takes that message." Any more than he'd cared about her when he took his pants off at Shayla's this afternoon. "Whatever I thought we had between us, I was wrong. It's over. I don't care anymore."

"If you're sure that's what you want." Tanner continued to study her for a moment longer. "You gonna be okay?"

"Eventually," she answered honestly, as the damned unstoppable tears started to leak down her cheeks again.

He gave her a big hug, patting her back like a man unused to comforting anyone. "You can call me if you need anything, okay?"

"Okay," she answered, knowing she never would.

She turned her back and walked away, not waiting to see him get back in the truck and leave.

She had meant what she said about being okay. She had every intention of putting this all behind her. Eventually. It was only that right at this moment in time, she felt as though *eventually* might take centuries to get here.

CHAPTER TWENTY-THREE

Logan felt as though he'd been punched in the gut.

There was no mistaking Tanner's pickup, not even looking through the drizzle-covered windshield. No one else in the valley drove a huge white beast of a truck with red lightning bolts racing down either side. Curiosity as to why his friend would have stopped at the Vaca Vista Inn on his way to Grand Junction drew Logan off the highway and into the parking lot.

Within minutes, he had all the answers he could stomach. A deft U-turn had him back on the highway, headed home.

Tanner and Allie. At the Vaca Vista Inn, known for miles to be *the* place to go for a quick afternoon rendezvous. If he hadn't seen them with his own two eyes, he wouldn't have believed it—the two of them huddling so close together, the kiss, the embrace.

He'd left then. He couldn't bear the thought of

watching them walk into the inn together, knowing what would come next.

It all made sense now. The repeated calls Tanner had received while the doctor was there, his insistence on going to get Logan's meds, his comment about already planning to head that direction—everything fit.

Everything except how sure he'd been that Allie was the one. Everything except the way she'd gazed into his eyes as he'd held her in his arms last night and all the nights before. Everything except the genuine happiness he'd been so sure he'd heard in her voice this morning when he'd called to invite her to meet him for dinner.

He pulled his truck to a stop in front of the fire station and slammed his palm against the steering wheel. No, it didn't make sense. None of it. At least, it wouldn't have before Allie's call this afternoon.

It might make sense if she believed he'd cheated on her. If he'd let her down like all the other men in her life had, that might explain her running to another man.

But it didn't make sense that Tanner would agree to be that other man.

Logan climbed out of his truck and walked slowly back into the station, holding his chest as if his heart had sustained a physical wound.

It hurt. It hurt that she hadn't trusted him enough to ask him what had happened. It hurt that she'd jumped to a faulty conclusion without even giving him a chance to tell her the truth. It hurt that she'd had so little faith in him.

He stood in the shadows for several minutes, staring at the bag of groceries he'd left on the table this afternoon, canned goods for the meal he had planned for tonight. Like a child possessed by a temper tantrum, he crossed the room and swept the bag to the floor. Overcome by the utter helplessness of his situation, he watched as the cans rolled in all directions.

A perfect metaphor for his life at this moment. Chaos. Out of control.

He gripped the back of the wooden chair and closed his eyes, sucking in a deep breath before letting the air out slowly.

Too bad he was working tonight. A full bottle of something 80-proof sounded like the only thing that might dull the misery plaguing his heart. Instead, he headed for the counter and poured himself a cup of strong black coffee. It wouldn't dull his senses or strip the memories from his mind, but it might occupy his hands long enough to keep him from digging them raw.

It wasn't right that Allie had judged him solely based on what she'd been through in her past. She should have trusted him, just a little. If he'd been able to talk to her, he could have explained what had really happened. He could have assured her that he would never let her down. He couldn't. He couldn't because he was in love with her. But without even giving him a chance to defend himself, she had tried him and found him guilty.

Halfway to his mouth, his hand paused, splashing hot coffee over the edge of his cup as realization settled over him.

He *was* guilty. Guilty of doing the exact same thing he accused her of doing. Seeing her with Tanner, he'd judged her actions based solely on his own past experiences. How could he criticize her for having so little faith in him when he'd just demonstrated how little faith he had in her?

But it wasn't too late—*please, God, don't let it be too late!*—He wasn't giving up. He was in love with her. He knew that now. He loved her and he would fight for her. He would fight for them. He would do whatever it took, for as long as it took, to get her back.

CHAPTER TWENTY-FOUR

"Up and at 'em, sweetie. You can't hide under the covers for the rest of your life. Believe me, it won't help." Susie lifted the blankets in a large, sweeping move, exposing Allie to the bright light streaming in her windows. "I speak from experience, you know."

"Ugh," Allie responded, rolling to her stomach to bury her face in her pillow.

Staying in bed might not make things any better, but it kept her from having to deal with any of it, and that alone was worth retreating from the world.

"Logan called again yesterday. He wants to talk to you."

"No!" She opened one eye to glare in her mother's direction. "Absolutely, positively no way I'm having anything to do with him. Not now, not ever."

Her mother's skeptical look expressed what she didn't need to say in words. Allie knew it would be impossible to avoid Logan forever in a town the size of Chance. But she intended to give it her best shot, and hiding in her room, under her covers, was one heck of a good start.

"Your call, I suppose," her mother conceded. "But I would ask you to get up and get dressed. I need you to help me with something I can't do myself."

Allie sighed and rolled to her back before pushing up to sit. Her mother so rarely asked her to do anything, she could hardly refuse now. Wallowing in her own private misery would just have to wait for a little while.

"What can I do for you, Mom?"

"I've decided to rent out the apartment over the old garage, so it has to be emptied out."

That explained why her mom needed help. The old garage had been Allie's dad's space, housing his office in what was originally built to be an apartment. Susie hadn't set foot in the place since before her husband's death.

"What brought this on?"

"A desire to pay bills, mostly," Susie said with a sheepish smile. "I ran into Brent Corey yesterday when I went to the post office and we got to talking. He's just sold the old Cheevers building and the woman who bought it is going to need a place to live until they can get some renovations done. I offered up the garage. But before she can move in—"

"We need to move all that old crap out," Allie finished for her.

"Exactly. I have a stack of boxes I'll take out there for you while you're getting dressed, and then I'm going over to Mama Odie's to pick up some more. I left a sandwich on the counter for you."

"Thanks, Mom. You want me to pack it all up?" Heaven only knew how much stuff her father had stored in there.

Her mom shrugged, her expression veiled as she headed for the door. "Keep whatever you want, or anything you think Matt might want, and toss the rest. I don't want any of it."

And yet her mom told *her* not to hide under the covers. Allie shook her head and climbed into the shower.

"Maybe that's how she knows it doesn't work," Allie mused before sticking her head under the hot water.

After two days of hiding out in her room feeling sorry for herself, the shower felt heavenly. Her heart might be broken, but that didn't mean life wouldn't go on.

She grabbed the sandwich on her way out the back door, stopping to admire what a beautiful, warm day she had to attack this task, though it must have been cool earlier this morning because the smell of wood smoke wisped in the air if she breathed deeply. Another month or two and they'd all be firing up their woodstoves.

She headed out across the field toward the old building halfway between their house and her grandparents' home, the two-story garage apartment. When she'd been little, she'd often imagined that one day, after her dad had retired and didn't need an office anymore, she would move into this apartment and fill the walls with shelves of her beloved books.

Of course, she'd also imagined that soon after that she'd marry Logan and live happily ever after.

Life hadn't worked out at all like she'd imagined.

"But I do still have my books," she said, grunting as she put her shoulder against one of the big doors to push it open.

Dust lifted on the air currents, sparkling like little jewels floating thorough the air as the tiny bits drifted through a sunbeam. A short coughing fit later, Allie amended that mental picture to tiny, fuzzy floating jewels.

Along with the stack of collapsed boxes, her mom had left a pair of plastic gloves, a box of trash bags, and a set of keys.

"Good call, Mom," she said, slipping on the gloves.

Considering how long the rooms had remained untouched, there was no telling what kind of creepy-crawlies she'd bump into. That thought gave her pause, but not for long. If she didn't clean it out, they'd have to hire someone to do it and there was no money to hire anyone to do anything. It was her or nothing.

With the boxes tucked under one arm and the trash bags under the other, she climbed the stairs and fit the big antique key into the lock. When she walked inside, she felt as if a memory capsule had been unlocked, and for just a moment, she wished more than anything that Matt were here with her to keep her from facing this on her own.

Not that she'd spent much time up here. This had always been Dad's special place, and no one was allowed inside except when he invited them in, which wasn't often.

Maybe that was why it felt so strange to be in here now, as if she were creeping around like a trespasser.

She dropped the boxes in the center of the room beside his old desk and steeled herself to peek into each of the adjoining rooms. Surprisingly, this job might not take nearly as much effort as she'd imagined. The bedroom was completely empty, if you ignored the huge spider web in the corner, which was exactly what she was going to do until she could drag a vacuum cleaner up here to deal with any eight-legged beasties.

A quick scan of the bathroom revealed only a few personal items in the drawers and medicine chest, so she tossed a trash bag in there to fill later. The kitchen was equally sparse—a coffeepot, one cup and a couple of hand towels.

That left the one bookshelf and her father's desk.

The books were a no-brainer. She boxed them to take to the Hand. They could all go into the used-book sales area.

Her father's desk was another matter. It felt almost like an invasion of his privacy to sit in his chair, preparing to go through his things, but this had to be done. It would be easier if she kept it impersonal. This needed to be a ruthless cleaning, as if it belonged to someone she'd never met. If it didn't have some obvious sentimental value, it went straight in the trash.

The top drawer was filled with pens and notepads and plastic letter openers, all bearing the logos of various companies, no doubt advertising giveaways her dad had picked up at the sales conferences he'd so frequently traveled to attend. As a business supply store junkie, these were the sorts of things she could dither over all day if she allowed herself the luxury. Keep, don't keep?

"Ruthless," she reminded herself, and dumped the entire contents of the drawer into a large black trash bag.

There. She'd set the tone. It should be easier now.

The first big filing drawer was stuffed full. File after file that looked like they were filled with copies of orders and correspondence from her father's years as a salesman. If no one had needed this stuff up to now, they'd likely never need it. She dumped all the files into a second bag, intending to shred or burn these papers since they might contain personal information about his customers.

It was apparent to her by now that her father hadn't been the type to keep photos or knickknacks in his desk or on his bookshelf, so this whole task was going much more quickly and painlessly than she'd imagined it might. One more drawer full of business files to toss and she'd be done.

This last drawer appeared to be stuck, so she put some muscle into it, realizing as a twinge of pain shot up her arm that it wasn't stuck. It was locked.

"Weird," she muttered, reaching for the ring of keys to search for one that might fit the drawer.

The third one she tried worked, and she pulled open the last drawer.

Not files. Stacks of letters, bound with rubber bands, redolent with the aroma of perfume even after years locked away in the drawer. Love letters? And one bulging envelope filled with photographs.

So her dad had been a sentimental man, after all. A man who'd loved his wife and children before he'd turned into that cheater who drove off the side of the mountain with some woman half his age sitting beside him.

She fingered the smooth paper of the top envelope on one stack, considering whether her mom might want to keep these letters. Her father had obviously valued them, keeping them up here in a locked drawer. Maybe they would remind her mom of all those good years before her husband had gone middle-aged crazy.

It was odd that there were so many of them. How had her mom managed to write so many in the short time they dated? She must have written to him every single day. And if not then, why would she write them later, once they were married? The only times he'd been away from home had been for a day or two at most when he'd traveled to sales conferences.

Not that it really mattered. The letters were private moments that belonged to her mother.

She skipped over the stacks to reach for the brown envelope filled with photos. Carefully, to avoid bending them, she dumped the contents on the desk in front of her, her heart pounding. That her father had kept photos of his family close at hand tugged at her heart, and she prepared herself for an emotional moment or two when she flipped over the photos to leaf through all his old family memories.

Her first emotions were anything but the pleasant ones she'd expected.

These weren't family photos. They weren't even photos of anyone Allie recognized. All women, all in various states of undress.

Allie quickly slapped the envelope down on top of the photographs, feeling as if she'd walked into a room she shouldn't have.

A glance to the stacks of letters left her with an uneasy feeling of dread, and she reached for the first one, setting it on the desk in front of her.

Not her mother's handwriting. Addressed to her father at a post office box in Denver. She reached for another stack and found they were the same. All addressed to her father at the Denver address, all with different handwriting, none of them her mother's.

Thank goodness she hadn't taken these down to her

mother!

How her dad had managed to meet so many women in the last year or so of his life was beyond her, but it didn't matter now. She'd burn all of these so her mother wouldn't have her husband's final infidelity rubbed in her face again.

Allie picked up a third stack and the aged rubber band snapped, scattering envelopes into the drawer and on the floor. She shoved back the chair and got down on her knees to pick them up, noticing as she did some of the dates on the letters.

This one was postmarked the same year she was born.

How was that even possible?

A closer look at the stacks showed dates that ranged over a thirty-year period. Here was one dated the same year her parents had married. And one from the year before that!

"What the hell was he doing?"

"I forgot about those."

Allie dropped the letters as if they burned her fingers, looking up to see her mother standing in the doorway, her face pinched in sorrow.

"I came as soon as I remembered. I thought maybe I could get here before you found them."

"You knew about these?" Allie asked, unable to believe her mother understood the depth of what her husband had done. "All of them?"

"All of them," Susie confirmed. "Some men are addicted to alcohol or drugs. Your father suffered from a different kind of addiction."

"I don't understand," Allie said. "You seemed like

you were devastated by the circumstances of his death. By his being found with that woman in his car."

"I was devastated. Jimmy broke our agreement. I was to turn a blind eye and he was never to humiliate me by carrying on his little indiscretions anywhere near home."

Susie approached the desk and lifted one corner of the envelope covering the photographs, as if to confirm what she already knew she'd find. With an expression of disgust, she scooped up a handful and shoved them into the black trash bag sitting on the floor.

"Why did you put up with it for all those years?"

Susie continued to stuff handfuls of letters and photographs into the trash, pausing for only a moment to fix her daughter with a stare. "What would you have had me do? Leave him? By the time I learned about Jimmy's little problem, I had no family to go back to. I'd used what little money my parents had left me in my first year of college, where I met your dad. Mama Odie and Papa Flynn treated me as if I were their own daughter. I didn't want to lose the family I had found here. And,"—she shrugged, a sad smile curving her lips—"I was pregnant with your brother. At the time, staying here, making the best of my situation seemed to be the smartest thing for me to do."

Allie shook her head, wanting to reject everything her mother had told her. "When I first heard about the accident, about him going bad like that, I didn't want to believe it. But to know it had been going on forever—"

Susie cut her off with a snorting sound of sheer derision. "Going bad? Good grief, Allie. Are you listening to yourself? Your dad wasn't a month-old bag of celery. He didn't *go bad*. Jimmy had a dependency he couldn't shake. He even tried seeing a therapist for a while, but, in the end, it was who he was."

"I always thought you guys had the perfect story. I wanted to be just like you. To find my perfect story. I thought I had," Allie said, her last phone call to Logan playing through her head. "But I was wrong. They all go bad sooner or later, don't they?"

Susie came around the desk, dropped to her knees beside Allie and cupped her hands on her daughter's cheeks. "Is that why you're refusing to speak to Logan? Because you think he's gone bad? Baby, men don't go bad. They either are or they aren't. Logan isn't anything like your dad."

Her mom pulled her close, stroking her hair like she had when Allie had been a little girl and had come home crying over one hurt or another. In spite of her best efforts, tears prickled in Allie's eyes, threatening to fall in the face of her mother's kindness.

"A long time ago, Allie, you told me that you had to leave Chance because Logan was the love of your life and you couldn't stand being here and not having him. Do you still feel that way? Do you still love him?"

Fighting back the tears, Allie nodded. "More than anything. But when I called him, Shayla answered his phone. He was with her."

Again. Like history repeating itself, she had lost him to Shayla once more.

"Then don't cut your nose off to spite your face." Susie pulled away from her, reaching out to tuck a strand of her daughter's hair back behind her ear. "You're so much stronger than I ever was, Allie. You're a fighter. If you love Logan, don't let your wounded pride keep you from going after what you really want. Talk to him. See if there isn't a way to work things out. Don't flounder around trying to recreate someone else's perfect story. Take a chance and create your own. I've seen the way he looks at you, baby. I don't think you'll have to fight too hard."

"You really believe that?"

"I do," her mother assured her. "You've never been afraid to work hard for what you wanted. It would be pretty sad to see you start being afraid now."

Her mother was right. She was rolling over like some pathetic quitter. She was dealing with Logan in exactly the same way she'd dealt with Drake. Only Logan wasn't Drake. Logan was the man she wanted for the lead in her perfect story.

"Thanks, Mom," she said, kissing her mother's forehead before standing and walking to the door. "Will you be okay finishing this off by yourself?"

"Go!" her mom answered, flapping her arms in a shooing motion.

Not that Allie needed any more urging. Talking to her mother had opened her eyes. If Shayla Jenkins-Gold thought she was just going to waltz in and steal Logan out from under Allie's nose, she had another think coming. That wasn't happening. Not without a damn good fight, anyway.

Allie loved Logan. She always had. And right now, she was going down to the fire station to tell him that. She was going to do her best to convince him that he loved her, too.

Ten minutes later, she turned into the parking area at the fire station and hopped from the old pickup she'd borrowed from her grandmother. Though Logan's pickup was parked outside, she knew the minute she opened the door to the darkened station that she wouldn't find him here.

The big red fire truck was gone.

Back outside, she stood by her car, trying to decide what to do next. If she knew where he'd been called to, she'd have a better idea of how long he might be gone. She could call him, but private calls had no place in a firefighting scenario. She'd never risk distracting him when he might need to have his full attention on his work.

Besides, what she needed to say needed to be said in person.

As she buckled her seat belt, she noticed a haze on her windshield and flipped on the wipers. With their first swipe, a fine gray powder floated into the air and quickly settled back on the glass.

Though it had been years, she'd seen this stuff before. Ash.

"Oh, Lord," she muttered, rolling down her window to stick her head outside.

Wood smoke. What a fool she'd been to even consider that someone might be using their fireplace on a day like this. From the strong scent, she'd bet everything she had on a forest fire. A quick scan of the sky and she spotted what she'd totally ignored earlier. A huge white cloud billowed on the western horizon, unmistakable proof that she would have won her bet.

A big one, from the looks of all that smoke. And wherever it was, she had no doubt that her Logan was right smack dab in the thick of it.

Cody would know. As sheriff, Logan's brother would be well aware of any emergency in the county.

By the time Allie reached the sheriff's office, Cody was just getting into his SUV. With a spray of gravel, she pulled across the driveway, blocking his exit. She jumped from her truck before the engine had even stopped knocking.

"Where's Logan?" she asked breathlessly as she reached the spot where he waited, engine idling. "He's at that fire, isn't he?"

"It's a big one," Cody said, confirming her worst fears. "All departments in the county responded after they lost control of it with the winds the first night. The out-of-state guys started arriving this morning and they're hoping to have the big sky-tankers making drops later today if the wind dies down."

"Will he be back tonight?" she asked, fearing the answer she'd get.

"I wouldn't count on it. They've set up a forward command at the mouth of the canyon but they're closing down the highway to keep traffic out just in case. That's where I'm headed now, to man the roadblock."

If the fire made it to the highway, there was no telling how long it might take to get it under control.

"Is there anything I can do?"

Cody patted her shoulder. "Go home, Allie. All you can do is wait. Chance should be fine, but it wouldn't hurt to check the emergency reports every so often. Just in case. And try not to worry. Logan is good at what he does."

Allie returned to the pickup and backed it out of the driveway to allow Cody to leave, lights flashing as he headed for the highway entrance.

Cody's reassurance did little to calm her nerves. She'd lived in the mountain community long enough to have witnessed the power of the big forest fires. Over the years those infernos had taken down more than one firefighter who was good at his job.

All she could do now was wait. Wait and pray that Logan wouldn't be added to that list.

CHAPTER TWENTY-FIVE

The noise of a crowded dining room met Allie's ears before she reached the front door of the Hand.

Good. Lots of people to distract her might be just what she needed.

After talking to Cody, she'd dropped off the borrowed pickup and walked home. She'd done her best to take her mind off her worries, but to no avail. Not even her favorite book could distract her for long. Vivid images of Logan, shrouded in smoke, battling the monster blaze in the canyon, kept invading her thoughts, pushing away any story she hoped to lose herself in.

After a couple of stomach-twisting hours, she gave up even trying. She slipped into her work uniform and headed for the coffee shop, hoping a brisk walk would help rid her of the nagging fear that wouldn't leave her alone.

It hadn't.

"Could you use an extra pair of hands?" she asked as she approached the counter.

Dulcie's grateful look was all the answer she needed.

"They're all worried," Dulcie said quietly, placing slices of her latest bakery treat on plates.

"Worried and hyped up on way too much caffeine," Desi added as she swooped up three of the plates to carry out to customers. "But it's supergood for business."

"You okay?" Dulcie asked as Allie stepped behind the counter to stand next to her. "He's going to be fine, you know. He and Tanner both. They're professionals."

"Yeah," Allie agreed, biting her tongue to keep from blurting out how little respect a fire like this one had for professionals. "I need to stay busy. What can I do to help?"

"I've got goodies in the oven I need to tend to," Dulcie said. "If you'd just man the counter and see that the cups are all kept filled, that would make my life so much easier."

"You got it, boss. I'm a good coffee-cup filler," Allie joked, forcing a grin. "Coffee's one of the few things I actually know how to make in the kitchen."

Bantering with the locals, racing from one end of the counter to the other to keep on top of refills, was exactly what she'd needed. The worry didn't disappear, but it did dull. By the time she looked up at the sound of the bell announcing more customers, she was feeling closer to normal than she had for a long time.

"Now there's a purty waitress if I ever did see one," Papa Flynn greeted. "You know, Bobcat, they don't advertise it, but they got the best-lookin' gals in town at this coffee shop."

"Only reasons I come here," Bobcat agreed. "Pretty women and tasty treats."

Her grandfather and his best friend slid onto the last two seats at the counter, both grinning at their own cleverness.

"House coffee?" Allie asked, knowing her grandfather's preference. "You want something to eat?"

"Does a bear..." Bobcat paused, winked, and changed what he was going to say. "I'll take some of whatever that is that Dulcie has baking right now. The smell is making my mouth water something awful."

Allie hurried to fill two cups for the men before slicing off two healthy servings of the still warm lemon bread her cousin had just brought out of the kitchen.

"... not good at all," her grandfather was saying as she set the plates in front of them and picked up the coffeepot. "By the looks of that plume, the beast is growing, too."

Bobcat nodded, taking a sip of his coffee. "Them firefighters up there must be hanging on by the skin of their teeth. I was listening to the scanner while I waited for you to get here. Heard that one of the crews got on the wrong side of the fire line when the flames jumped. Cut them boys off for a time and the fire caught up with them. They were able to get them out, but at least one of them must be pretty bad off. They were calling for a chopper to medivac him out."

"Someone's hurt?" Allie asked, her throat so dry she was surprised the words made it out. "I don't suppose they mentioned any names."

"No names," Bobcat confirmed. "From the chatter on the scanner, it sounded like several of them were hurt.

Only one critical, though, thank the good Lord. Could have lost them all."

Only one critical.

"It only takes one," Allie murmured, her mind racing to torment her with the worst of all possible scenarios.

This couldn't happen. Not now. Not when she was so close to finding her ever-after happiness. Except, how many times in her life had she thought that before? How many times had she been so sure that the worst couldn't happen? How many times had she been wrong?

"What did you say, girl?" her grandfather asked, cupping a hand to his ear.

"I have to get to him, Papa Flynn. Right now. You drove here, right? I need your keys."

"You need my keys?" Her grandfather pulled them out of his pocket even as his brow wrinkled in confusion. "Where do you think you're going?"

"Logan's in that canyon. He's on one of those crews. It could be him Bobcat heard them talking about. I can't stand here knowing it could be him they're calling the chopper to take out."

"You won't be able to get in there, Allie." Bobcat exchanged a glance with her grandfather. "The road's closed down. They're not letting anyone in there."

Allie deposited the coffeepot on the back counter and held out her hand for the keys. "Just so happens I know the guy running the roadblock. And if I have to, I'll get down on my knees and beg, but I can't just wait here, not knowing. I have to try."

Papa Flynn tossed the keys into her hand and she took off running, not caring in the least what any of the patrons of the coffee shop might think of her actions.

Nothing mattered except getting to Logan... before it was too late.

Counting on both Cody and his deputy manning the roadblock, Allie coaxed as much speed from the old truck as she possibly could. She remembered how after Matt got his first speeding ticket, he'd tried to convince his parents that he'd only been going fast because it was mechanically good for cars to run them hard once in a while. If that was true, her grandfather's pickup was getting the tune-up of a lifetime.

The flashing red and blue lights reflected against the backdrop of smoke, visible long before she reached the roadblock. This close to the fire, the sky itself seemed to be burning, as an eerie red glow covered the sinking sun.

Any wild thoughts she'd harbored about running the roadblock disappeared as she approached the two sheriff's department SUVs parked sideways, bumper to bumper, across the road. No way she could blow through that.

She rolled down her window as Cody approached, a clipboard in his hands and a determined scowl on his face.

"What are you doing up here, Allie?"

"Was it Logan?" she asked, going straight to the heart of her fears. "I have to know."

"Was what Logan?" he returned, his serious scowl giving way to puzzlement.

"The firefighter that was critically injured. The one they had to take out by chopper. Was it Logan?"

Cody's face blanked, any emotion hidden behind a gruff professional mask. She couldn't help but recognize how similar he and Logan actually were when he did that.

"We haven't been informed of anything like that. Are you sure it's not just some wild rumor? Where'd you hear about it?"

"Bobcat," she answered. "He heard it on his emergency scanner."

The momentary change in his expression convinced her that he believed the information coming from the newspaper man. But just as quickly, the emotionless mask was back in place.

"No. It's too dangerous up there. Besides, you wouldn't know where to find them even if I was stupid enough to let you in. Nope. No unauthorized vehicles beyond this point. Go home, Allie. I'll let you know if I hear anything."

As Cody turned to walk away, Allie shoved open her door and jumped down from the pickup. Running to catch up with him, she grabbed his sleeve and tugged at his arm.

"But that could be too late. You have to listen to me, Cody. I have to see Logan. I have to talk to him. I have to tell him… I have to tell him I was a fool. I was wrong when I said I never wanted to see him again. I'm in love with your brother, Cody. I'm in love with him and I can't let him die not knowing that."

He stared at her for the longest minute of her life before turning his gaze down the road in the direction of the raging fire.

"Goddammit," he hissed, slapping the clipboard against his thigh. "I ought to have my head checked for even considering this."

"Please, Cody. Please. Let me go to him."

"I can't let you or any other unauthorized vehicles past this point," he said. "But I guess if you happened to be sitting in my vehicle when I go down there to check in with fire command, that wouldn't technically be a violation."

* * *

Logan didn't know Rodriguez very well. Hell, he didn't even know the man's first name. But that didn't diminish the weight of the emotions he'd felt as his team had pulled the California firefighter and his crew out of that hellish inferno. Rodriguez, like all the other men out here today, was his brother. And all he could do now was pray that they'd gotten this particular brother out in time to save his life.

He was too tired to think anymore, too tired to do anything but find a small patch of earth where he could collapse and try to catch a few minutes of shuteye before he was back on the line. He pulled off his helmet and dropped it to the ground, followed by his shoulder pack, belt and gloves. He had just peeled out of his jacket when Tanner approached.

"Heads up!" his friend called, tossing a bottle of water as he spoke.

Instinctively, Logan reached out to catch the toss and popped open the lid. He hadn't realized how thirsty he was until he raised the water to his lips and began to drink.

"Bitch of a day," Tanner muttered, pulling off his helmet before dropping to sit. "I'm so beat, I'm not even hungry."

"Copy that. You hear anything about Rodriguez yet?"

"No," Tanner answered, rubbing his hands over his face, leaving long streaks in the soot blanketing his skin. "But after seeing what happened with him, I can guarandamn-tee that we're both going to double-check our fire shelters for holes before we head back out on the line."

"You got that right. First thing after I try to get some sleep."

Even dead tired, sleep had eluded him for the last two days. Every time he closed his eyes, his brain switched into overdrive, microanalyzing every moment he'd ever spent with Allie, desperately searching for some magical way he could win her back.

"You got to get your head back in the game, man," Tanner said. "Focus on the priorities. First we kick this fire's ass, then we work out your woman troubles. You don't give it one hundred percent up here, you'll go down the mountain like Rodriguez."

"I know," Logan answered. He'd been doing this too long not to recognize the dangers. "Logically, in my brain, I know."

"But it's not your brain driving you right now, is it? It's more like—" Tanner stopped in the middle of his sentence, staring over Logan's shoulder. "Well, I'll be damned. There's something you don't see out here every day."

It certainly wasn't. If Tanner hadn't said something, Logan might have been tempted to think exhaustion was finally taking its toll by giving him hallucinations.

But it was no hallucination running his direction, dodging weary firefighters and random piles of equipment.

It was Allie.

He stumbled backward when her body hit his, and only by sheer force of will was he able to remain on his feet.

"Logan?" she said breathlessly, her hands cupped on

his cheeks as she gazed into his eyes, her words tumbling out, one over the other, as if she had too much to say and not enough time in which to say it. "You're okay? Thank God you're okay. I was so afraid it was you. You are okay, aren't you?"

"I'm okay," he assured her, relishing the feel of her body pressed up against his even as his mind struggled to catch up with the reality of her in his arms. "You shouldn't be here."

She waved away his statement as if it had no importance. "I had to come. When Bobcat told me someone was hurt up here, I was so afraid it was you. I couldn't let anything happen to you without telling you how I feel."

If she'd come up here to break it off in person, this might be his only chance to tell her what had really happened. The moment she stopped for a breath, he jumped in.

"I can explain about the phone call. About what you heard when you called. It wasn't what you thought. I was—"

"I don't care," she interrupted, placing her soft fingers over his lips. "I don't care what happened with Shayla. We can work through this. I know we can. I was a fool to give up so easily. I'm going to fight for what I want." Her eyes flashed with her determination as she spoke, her voice ragged with emotion. "I love you, Logan. I've always loved you. I'm going to fight for you. I'm going to fight to make you see what you really want."

"You don't have to fight, Allie," he said, wrapping his arms around her to pull her close. "I already know what I want. I want you. I want to spend the rest of my life with you. I love you, Allie, more than I could ever have imagined possible. If you're willing to take a chance on me, I'm yours. Heart and soul."

"Yes," she whispered, tears filling her eyes as she lifted her lips to meet his. "I'll take that chance."

CHAPTER TWENTY-SIX

Odetta Flynn stood near the back wall, surveying the happy crowd milling around in her granddaughters' coffee shop. The official grand opening for Allie's bookstore appeared to have drawn almost everyone in town.

Another new business off to a good start. Things were beginning to come together nicely.

"But only just beginning," she murmured into the cup she lifted to her lips.

Her work was far from complete.

"Looks like it's going really well."

"Elizabeth!" Odie shared a hug with the young woman who'd joined her. "I'm so glad you decided to come."

"Knowing what a big day this is for the girls, I wouldn't have missed it. I should hire them to organize the grand opening for my art gallery when the time comes."

"Not a bad idea," Odie agreed. "Though, truth be

told, I doubt they'd let you hire them. I'm sure they'll want to help when their new neighbor is ready to open the doors to the public. After all, you're one of our own now."

A timid, half-smile lifted the corners of the woman's mouth and Odie resisted the urge to hug her again. Though Liz had only arrived in Chance a couple of weeks before, she and her young son were quickly becoming a part of the Flynn family. Having them living in the old garage apartment had reminded Odie of how much she enjoyed having little ones underfoot.

"I love the workmanship on the new bookshelves," Liz said, as if needing to change the subject. "They fit in as if they were part of the original decor."

"They did turn out good, didn't they?" Between the new stock the girls had ordered and the books brought in by Allie's newspaper appeal—and a little arm-twisting on Odie's part—they'd ended up having to build new shelves to hold all the books. "Which reminds me, have you found someone to renovate your building yet?"

Liz's smile vanished as she shook her head. "None that are going to work. Either their waiting list is as long as my arm or their prices for coming up the mountain are way beyond my budget. I'm beginning to think I might have made a mistake in not hiring the contractor before I finalized the purchase."

"Nonsense," Odie murmured, as a new idea began to take shape. "Have you considered hiring a local to do the work?"

Liz looked surprised. "I didn't know there was anyone local who could do the job."

"As it so happens, there is," Odie assured her. "And he's practically family, too, which makes it even better.

Hold on. He was around here somewhere just a few minutes ago. There he is! Ryan!"

Odie waved her hand in the air until Ryan headed in her direction.

"Ryan, I want you to meet Elizabeth Levesque. She's bought the old Cheevers Building next door and as it just so happens, she's in need of a talented contractor."

"Ryan O'Connor," he said, reaching out to shake Liz's hand. "I'd love to give you a bid on that project, Miss Levesque."

"Liz," she corrected quietly. "If you have some time this afternoon, perhaps we could meet to go through the building and discuss the changes I have in mind."

"That works for me," he said with a grin. "Around three okay?"

"Three it is," she agreed, pulling her hand from his.

"If you two will excuse me, I need to refill my coffee," Odie said, leaving Ryan and Liz to work out the details of their meeting.

With a fresh cup in her hand, she found herself an empty spot across the room, and studied the two people she'd just introduced. It was a good match. Ryan was just getting his business off the ground and Liz needed someone reliable.

"In more than one way," she muttered to herself. "Not bad, Odie Flynn. Not bad at all."

"What are you doing over here in the corner talking to yourself?" Dot O'Connor scooted in next to her, holding a cup of her own. "Isn't it grand? All these people in one place, it almost feels like the old days. We're making progress, Odie. Slow but sure, we're making progress."

Odie nodded, and sipped from her cup. They were

making progress, but this was no time to slack off on their efforts. "We've still got plenty of work left ahead of us."

"Well, of course we do," Dot agreed. "For one thing, we've a wedding to plan."

Yes, they did. And with her granddaughter marrying her best friend's grandson, the sky was the limit.

"Among other things," she murmured with a smile, glancing back across the room to the two people she'd left only moments before.

Yes, things were definitely beginning to come together.

* * *

"Thank you so much for coming. Please, take your time, look around, enjoy yourself!" Allie shook what felt like the millionth hand today and watched with pride as her latest customer wandered over to the bookshelves to browse through her grand opening selection.

"Can you believe this crowd?" Dulcie set a tray of freshly baked cookies on the counter next to Allie. "Everybody in town must be here. We can barely keep the coffee brewed ahead of them! Mama Odie was right on the mark with this one."

"Mama Odie?" Allie looked across the room to spot her grandmother deep in conversation with Logan's grandmother. No telling what mischief those two were cooking up. "What did she have to do with this?"

"It was all her suggestion," Dulcie answered. "She started talking up the idea of having a bookshop tucked away in the back of the Hand long before you ever decided to come home. She said it would help business. Sometimes

I almost believe that woman has the power to see into the future."

"Nope," Desi interjected as she sidled up next to her sister. "No special powers. She's just the smartest woman on the face of the planet. Remember when we were little and she would—" Desi's words cut off abruptly and her eyes rounded. "Oh. My. God. You won't believe who's coming up our sidewalk."

Allie turned to look out the window in time to see Helen Reilly headed toward the Hand, accompanied by Rio Hyatt, the chef who had captured Desi's interest.

"He called yesterday," Desi whispered excitedly. "He wanted to arrange a time to talk about the possibility of getting our baked goods into his restaurant. He doesn't know it yet, but I am so going out with that guy."

Before Allie could respond to her cousin, the door opened and the new arrivals stepped inside.

"Welcome to our bookstore's grand opening," Allie greeted. "I was hoping I'd get the opportunity to thank you in person for all the books you sent over, Mrs. Reilly." There had been hundreds, some of them looking as if they'd never been opened.

"As long as you remember our bargain, my dear, that's thanks enough for me," Helen said. "By the way, is Odetta here?"

Surprised that Helen would ask specifically for her grandmother, Allie took a moment to answer. "She is. Last time I saw her, she was over in the dining room with Dot O'Connor. If you head through that way, you can't miss her."

"In that case, I'll be back in bit, Rio," Helen said, already walking away.

Desi's elbow to Allie's side forced her attention back to her cousins and the chef. From the look on Desi's face, an introduction was clearly in order.

"Chef Hyatt, these are my cousins, the owners of The Hand of Chance Coffee Emporium."

"I'm Desi," her cousin said, moving closer to the handsome chef. "We spoke on the phone yesterday."

"Yes, we did," Rio said, lifting a cookie to his nose and sniffing before turning to Desi. "You baked these?"

"That would be Dulcie," Allie said, turning to her cousin who had moved behind the counter to stand beside her.

Dulcie lifted a hand to acknowledge the introduction.

"Plating these individually would make for a better presentation," Rio said. "Perhaps with a sprig of mint." He spoke quietly, almost as if he were busy envisioning how he thought the cookies would look best.

"It's just a tray of cookies," Dulcie said, her voice tighter than normal. "A little help-yourself, welcome munchie."

"I have an idea." Desi tucked her arm through Rio's and smiled brightly, her worried eyes connecting with Allie's for an instant. "How about you and I saunter on over to the other side and I treat you to one of our wonderful coffees?"

Rio nodded his agreement absently, still intent on sniffing the cookie in his hand, before taking a small bite. "Butter. Shortening delivers a crisper texture." He took another bite and his brow wrinkled. "What did you use to sweeten this? Too dark for granulated sugar. Honey, maybe?"

"Coffee, first," Desi said, pulling him away. "Then

we'll talk baking."

Dulcie stared after the pair, her eyes narrowing. "What a complete and total—"

"Careful," Allie interrupted, doing her best to keep any sign of a smile off her face. "Desi thinks she likes the guy. So, who knows? He could end up being your—"

"Worst nightmare?" Dulcie finished for her. "Whatever. Not my problem. And I doubt he'll be Desi's for long. I'm pretty sure it'll take more than a pair of bedroom eyes to keep her interest."

"Hey, ladies," Logan said as he approached the counter. "I hate to tell you, Dulcie, but the coffee pot's empty and you have some grumbling customers over there."

"Oh, criminey," Dulcie said, "And here I am acting like I don't have a thing in the world to do. I gotta go."

Logan came around the counter to take the spot Dulcie had just vacated. "Here's your coffee, love." He handed her a steaming cup of pure energy and leaned in to nuzzle her ear. "I probably shouldn't tell your cousin that I'm the one who emptied the pot."

"Maybe not," she agreed, smiling up at him.

"Looks like everyone in town is doing their best to make your dream come true," he said, his arm coming to rest around her shoulders to pull her close beside him.

"They're certainly working on part of it."

The bookstore was only a part of her dream. The other part, the best part, was standing right next to her, his warm breath sending ripples of excitement coursing down her body every time he dipped his head close to hers.

"Only a part?" he asked, his finger brushing over the small diamond on her left hand.

"Only a part," she confirmed, smiling up at him. "Because you already made the rest of it come true when you asked me to marry you."

The lopsided grin spreading over his face carried a special happiness with it.

"Asking you to marry me was just the beginning. We've got dreams we haven't even dreamed yet ahead of us." He kissed her then, right in front of everyone, and, with a wink and a grin, he nodded toward the spot where their grandmothers stood, heads bent together like two top-secret conspirators. "You sure you don't want to reconsider eloping? Those two are only the tip of the iceberg. There's still our mothers, your cousins, and, Lord help us, my sister."

"I'm fine with whatever they plan," she said, biting back a giggle at his skeptical expression. "I spent too many years denying how important family is to me. Now that I've reclaimed that part of my life, I'm in it for the long haul. Good, bad, and everything in between."

Over the past few months, Allie had faced her own weaknesses and learned to stand up for all that was important to her. In the process, she'd made her peace with the past. From now on, she didn't intend to run from anything, ever again. Life ahead of her was a bright, shiny fruit, ripe for the taking and, with Logan at her side, she planned on taking it all.

EPILOGUE

What were the chances that things could have turned out so very differently from what Allie had expected when she'd turned off the highway to move back home seven months ago? She couldn't even begin to calculate the odds, but she knew they had to be astronomical.

"Anyway," she said aloud, staring out the window as the snow began quietly falling again. "I hate math."

"Oh yeah?" Desi said, her head bent to study her feet. "You know what I hate? I hate these shoes. But I'm wearing them just for you. I want you to remember this. You owe me. When I get married—"

"*If* you get married," Dulcie corrected.

"*When* I get married," Desi continued, sending a grimace in her sister's direction, "you have to promise you'll go barefoot for my ceremony."

"Deal," Allie agreed. "Though I really do hope it's a summer wedding."

"Goes without saying," Desi muttered. "I am, after all, a total summer solstice kind of gal."

The door opened and Katie breezed in, a triumphant smile on her face. "I've got them right here. Your something borrowed and your something blue. See? I borrowed Nana Dot's lace hankie and this I bought just for the occasion."

Allie took the box Katie offered and slipped off the lid to reveal a blue satin and lace garter.

"It's lovely."

"I know," Katie said with a grin. "And look at the little ornament on there. Am I the perfect maid of honor or what?"

Allie turned the garter over in her hand, laughing out loud when she saw the little silver hand that had been added to the lace flower. It was an exact match to the earrings Desi had made for her something new.

Dulcie ran a finger over the little metal hand and smiled. "A fitting tribute to our wonderful business venture together."

"Do you have the pearls or do I?" Desi asked as both she and her sister scrambled to dig through their purses.

"Can I just say again how much I appreciate your asking me to be your maid of honor?" Katie said, a twinkle in her eye. "As best man, Tanner will be forced to dance at least once with me!"

"It was my pleasure," Allie assured her.

Asking Logan's sister had been the perfect solution, since there was no way she could have chosen between her cousins.

"Your something old," Dulcie announced, fixing their grandmother's pearl necklace around Allie's neck.

"Now you're all ready. And you're so beautiful!"

A quick knock at the door and Matt's voice sounded on the other side. "It's showtime, ladies."

While her bridesmaids lined up at the head of the stairs, Allie linked her arm through her brother's, waiting for her turn to march down to the parlor below.

"Nervous?" Matt asked, fidgeting with his tie as the first strains of music drifted to Allie's ears.

"No," she answered honestly. She was too happy to be nervous. After all, the man of her dreams waited one floor below.

"Well, you will be when you step off that bottom stair. I swear it looks like the whole town is in Mama Odie's parlor. How they managed to get that many chairs in there is still a mystery to me."

Allie turned a patient smile on her handsome brother and patted his hand. He didn't understand. A crowd ten times the size of the one gathered below would have no influence on her at all. When she stepped off that bottom stair, there was only one face, one set of dark brown eyes in the whole room that would hold her attention. The most handsome man in the room.

In the world, she amended as she stepped off the last stair and her eyes met Logan's. Her heart thumped in her chest like a kettle drum as Matt escorted her down the aisle, so loud she was surprised people couldn't hear it over the music.

"Who gives this woman in holy matrimony?" Pastor Gene asked.

"I do," Matt answered.

And then Logan was taking her hand, drawing her close beside him, sliding a ring on her finger and vowing to love and honor her for the rest of their days together.

With Logan by her side it didn't matter what the odds were. She'd found the happy ever after she'd spent her entire adult life searching for. Right here in her hometown, where it had been waiting for her all along.

And all she'd had to do to find it was take a chance.

Dear Reader~

Thank you so much for reading TAKE A CHANCE. I do hope you enjoyed spending time with Allie and Logan's story, and meeting some of the other characters who live in Chance, Colorado.

Next up in the series will be SECOND CHANCE AT LOVE, Liz and Ryan's story, due out Summer, 2014. If you'd like to be notified when the next books are released, you can sign up for my New Release Newsletter.

Want more info on Chance, Colorado and the people who live there? Want to talk to other readers about the series or the characters? Maybe our Chance, Colorado Facebook Group is just what you're looking for! We'd love to have you join in the discussion!

Have a comment or a question? Feel free to like my Facebook page and say hello there or contact me directly at Melissa@MelissaMayhue.com. I'd love to hear from you!

Interested in finding Dulcie's Recipe for Caramel Apple Bread? You can get it at my website:
http://MelissaMayhue.com/Dulcie's Favorite Recipes

Would you like to browse through a line of jewelry much like the pieces that Desi makes, wears, and sells at the Hand of Chance Coffee Emporium? You can see the Chance Inspired line at http://TrinketsNTidbits.com

— Melissa

ABOUT THE AUTHOR

MELISSA MAYHUE, married and the mother of three sons, lives at the foot of the Rockies in beautiful Northern Colorado with her family and two very spoiled Boston Terriers. In addition to writing the contemporary feel-good Chance, Colorado series, she's also written two paranormal historical series, The Daughters of the Glen Series and The Warriors series.

Visit her online at MelissaMayhue.com for more information about her upcoming books. She loves hearing from readers! Contact her at Melissa@MelissaMayhue.com.

If you enjoyed this book, please consider leaving a review at your favorite online retailer or at Goodreads.com to help other readers find it

.

CPSIA information can be obtained at www.ICGtesting.com
Printed in the USA
LVOW06s1715300714

396752LV00009B/1194/P